P9-DWS-732

ESCAPE THEORY

ESCAPE THEORY

margaux froley

Published in the United States in 2013 by Soho Teen
an imprint of
Soho Press, Inc.
853 Broadway
New York, NY 10003

Library of Congress Cataloging-in-Publication Data

Froley, Margaux.
Escape theory / Margaux Froley.
p cm
ISBN 978-1-61695-127-6 (alk. paper)
eISBN 978-1-61695-128-3
1. Boarding schools—Fiction. 2. Schools—Fiction. 3. Counseling—Fiction.
4. Death—Fiction. 5. Love—Fiction.] I. Title.
PZ7.F9199Es 2013
[Fic]—dc23
2012033456

Interior design by Janine Agro, Soho Press, Inc.

Printed in the United States of America

10 9 8 7 6 5 4 3 2 1

This book is dedicated to the Not-Supposed-Tos

ESCAPE THEORY: A psychological term used to explain why people may engage in self-destructive actions*

* *Handbook of Consumer Psychology* by Curtis P. Haugtvedt, Paul Herr, Frank R. Kardes

ESCAPE THEORY

Jason Reed Hutchins
1996–2012

Jason Reed Hutchins, 16, of Marin County, died Wednesday, September 5th, 2012, of an apparent suicide at The Keaton School in Santa Cruz, California.

Jason was born March 13, 1996 in San Francisco, California, the son of William Hutchins and Mitzi Barbara Hutchins. Mr. Hutchins is the founder of TerraTech, a Fortune 500 company and innovator in the field of molecular biology.

Jason is survived by his mother and father, older brother Eric, a pre-med student at Stanford University, and grandfather Reed Hutchins of Santa Cruz, California, famed biologist and owner of the Athena Estates Vineyard and Winery. Jason was predeceased by his grandmother, Athena Hutchins.

At the start of his junior year, Jason was on staff at the student newspaper, *The Keaton Hawk*, a varsity soccer player, and an avid surfer at the nearby Monte Vista Beach Cove. He will be remembered as a loving son, loyal brother, and cherished friend to many.

Services will be held Sunday, September 16th at 10 A.M. at the The Keaton School chapel. In lieu of flowers the family requests donations be sent to TerraTech Children's Hospital in Palo Alto, California. A memorial scholarship will be set up in Jason's name at The Keaton School.

PROLOGUE

Those Nutter Butters are going to need milk.

Devon glared at the package of peanut butter cookies at the foot of her bed. The bright red plastic caught the light from her desk lamp, taunting her, daring her to break into the package. Of course she wanted to devour them, but there was the problem of living in a dorm room. Milk—the milk required to have on standby when eating Nutter Butters—wasn't just out the door, down the hallway, past the living room. No: here the milk was across a grassy court-yard, past a library, two boys' dorms, and the teachers' lounge, tucked away, in the oak-paneled dining hall.

They can wait. Devon swiveled on her stiff twin bed, twisting her toes into her crisp new Ikea bedspread. It felt hotel phony, not like something that was *hers*, in her new room. She put her focus back on the smiling pair of girls she'd tacked up to her wall. In the picture her best friend, Ariel, was holding two fingers up to the camera, all-cool peace sign/Hollywood starlet, while Devon smiled but kept her eyes toward her feet. The photos always followed a pattern: Ariel confronting the camera, leading the way, Devon a willing passenger. But that was just an Instagram memory now.

Devon's eyes drifted back to the package of Nutter Butters. Her mom had snuck them into her suitcase before she left for boarding school four days ago. Devon re-read the purple Post-it: *Share with your new friends, but save one for Derek!*

The peanut butter cookies *were* a nice gesture. They were Devon's favorite after all and only because her mom had turned her on to them. The two had a ritual of demolishing a package over an episode of *Grey's Anatomy* and saving just one in case the handsome "Dr. Derek Shepherd" miraculously appeared at their door. Mom subscribed to the "ya never know who you're going to run into" philosophy. Always on the prowl for a classic Leading Man (she wore lipstick for even the quickest errands) and always leaving a cookie for a charming stranger who might appear at her doorstep.

That was before boarding school. Before Devon got a scholarship to Keaton, and before her mother told her it was an opportunity she couldn't afford to turn down. "The doors Keaton will open for you. . . ." Devon's mom had begun on more than one occasion without ever actually finishing the thought. Devon wasn't sure where those doors led, but she knew she was supposed to walk through them for one reason alone: her mom had never had the same opportunity.

That wasn't Devon's fault or problem, of course. Just because her mom's family couldn't afford some ritzy boarding school when she was a kid didn't mean Devon had to go to one now. The scholarship was nice and all, but Devon didn't ask for it. Her mom had applied and set up an interview before Devon had even heard of Keaton. To her, boarding school was full of *those people*; and nothing she'd seen so far had changed that perception. Devon still didn't want to be one of *those people* who used seasons as a verb, like "My family summers in the Hamptons" or "We winter in Aspen."

Once again, Devon felt herself getting angry. She had spent her summer break listing many cogent psychological reasons about why she *shouldn't* attend Keaton, which of course her mom chalked up to being "just an ungrateful teenager," which only infuriated Devon more. Really? Couldn't Mom come up with a more creative phrase to describe her only daughter? Sure, Devon was thirteen, and sure she was annoyed that her "mature" body hadn't quite come in yet, but mentally she felt old enough to be in control of her own life: as in perfectly justified in not wanting to live in some upscale mountain penitentiary for the absurdly rich.

Next week Ariel would be headed to public school in Piedmont. Ariel: who made Devon feel like she belonged anywhere they went simply because Ariel *acted* like they belonged everywhere they went. No awkwardness about cliques or cafeteria seating. No first day jitters. New friends, new crushes on boys, new after-school hangouts; none of that fazed her.

And here was Devon, stuck at the top of a mountain at The Keaton School.

Ariel's ease could never spill out of the photo and into her, no matter how hard Devon stared at it. She turned to the Target digital alarm clock ("Because you won't have the Mom Alarm anymore," her mom chided on a dorm room shopping trip), blinking 10:18 P.M. Twelve minutes until the bell rang and everyone had to be inside their dorms for the night. Twelve minutes until she could stop feeling bad about not socializing and reasonably crawl into bed, crossing off another day of her sentence at Keaton. Twelve minutes until roll call and Devon's dorm head would peek in. . . .

Devon Mackintosh: check.

Where else would she be? Or more importantly, as Ariel would ask, whom would she be with? Keaton was perched above the small beach town of Monte Vista. It's not like Devon could wander over to the nearest shopping mall and catch a late movie with some locals. No, Devon was physically trapped on the mountain. There was only one way up and one way down, as far as she knew. It was almost funny.

When they built these dorms Devon suspected that "durability" was the prime objective. The thin gray carpet could absorb any dirt, footprint, or stain. (And probably had. Yuck.) The cinderblock walls were painted a slick and glossy white, which made it virtually impossible to stick, pin, nail, or tape anything to the wall. But there *was* a single framed corkboard. Someone must have taken pity on the students and allowed them at least an iota of space to post mementos of their pre-Keaton lives. But apart from that teeny area of suggested self-expression, Devon's twin bed, lean closet, and rickety desk was definitely more white-collar prison than the golden door of opportunity her mom described.

"Knock, knock. Devon?" came a sing-songy voice.

The Senior RA, June Chan, poked her head inside.

Devon sighed, but mustered a smile for June. *Who actually says "knock, knock" out loud?* June was from Taiwan and spoke Taiwanese, Mandarin Chinese, and English fluently. To Devon she seemed like an over-eager cheerleader who'd been at Keaton since birth. When Devon first arrived, June was there to greet all the girls in the dorm with a neon-bright smile and a bouncy ponytail. "Hi, I'm June. Like the month!" She spoke in exclamation points. Since that first day Devon had only seen June wearing dark green The Keaton School sweatshirts and sweats, like an athlete in training. But Devon could never figure out which sport. Maybe being at Keaton was the training itself.

Behind June, doors slammed. There was a burst of high-pitched giggling, the kind she and Ariel once reserved for slumber parties. A cry echoed down the hall—"Hey, that's my bra, bee-yotch!"—followed by another round of laughter and footsteps. June smiled at the mayhem. She caught Devon's gaze and turned back. Her mouth tightened into a thin, sympathetic smile.

Even June, the month, would rather hang out with them.

"Just checking in on you," June said, sounding concerned yet upbeat all at once.

Yes, Devon was already the charity case. The girls in her dorm all seemed to have gone to volleyball camp or ski school together. Insta-Friends by the end of the first day. But somehow Devon missed her chance. Her Insta-Friend sponge pellet—the one that would turn her into a perfect friend if you just added water—turned out to be a dud.

"*Clueless* just finished," June added. "We're starting up *Bring It On* if you want to come and join us? It's the Spring House Pajama Formal. Kind of an annual tradition."

Devon reached for another photo. "Thanks, but I'm cool. Just want to get this done," she said.

"Okay, but you're welcome any time, all right, chica?" June flashed Devon another encouraging cheerleader smile.

The harder people tried, the less Devon wanted to hang out with them. Ariel *never* tried. Maybe that's why this whole orientation week sucked so much; everyone was desperate to be everyone else's friend. But, it was all too soon and would never last; couldn't they see that? She saw the way the seniors sat in the dining hall in tightly formed cliques. Surely they were all fake smiles freshman year too.

June left the door open.

Closed doors were frowned upon at Keaton. Devon had read in the rule book—in typical form, it was called *The Keaton School Companion* (as in: another fake friend)—that if a member of the opposite sex visited your room, doors had to remain open at least twelve inches. Also, "four feet" needed to be on the ground. That was Rule #4c if she remembered correctly, only to be surpassed by #5a, where having sex was an offense punishable by suspension. Basically it was against the rules to do anything with a boy in her room except stare at their dueling feet.

Maybe they were going to have to reword that rule in the future. Say if a boy might want to make out with a boy? There was apparently no rule against members of the same sex making out. The *Companion* could catch up eventually (judging from its tone, it hadn't been updated in thirty years), but for now, the gay students had a loophole they could exploit. Lucky for them. Yes, Devon did want to make out with a guy sooner than later. One fumbling, wet kiss last summer in the back booth at Peet's Coffee didn't exactly count. If Devon had one goal, it was to actually hook up in high school. Ariel agreed. Besides, Devon figured there had to be *one* benefit to coed living.

She looked at the next photo. Another one of her and Ariel: tanned, short shorts, flip-flops, and fake mustaches. Over the summer she and Ariel liked to put on fake mustaches and take pictures around town, trying to get shots of people giving them weird looks. She wished she could show Ariel *The Keaton School Companion*—now *that* would make her laugh.

The bag of Nutter Butters caught Devon's attention again.

They still needed milk.

Waiting until tomorrow seemed impossible. "So, go get some milk, loser," is what Ariel would have commanded. Devon looked at her clock. 10:21 P.M. Nine minutes. If she left right now, she could dash up to the dining hall and be back in time for curfew. She could burst into the Spring House common room with a cold pitcher of milk and cookies to share just as *Bring it On* was starting. "Look, I brought it!" she could shout. And the girls would giggle back. Boom: Insta-Friends. June would probably say something like, "Welcome to the party, chica!"

It'd be as easy as that. Right?

Or she could stay in her room eating the cookies alone without milk. But Ariel's voice would call her a loser all night long. Steeling herself, Devon stuffed the cookies into her sweatshirt pocket. She figured if a teacher asked what she was up to, it would be good to have the cookies on hand to back up her story. She shoved her feet into her sneakers and ducked out her door without even bothering to consult the mirror first. Best just to move. Best not to think.

Outside the wind had picked up. Devon pulled her sweatshirt

hood over her head to keep her hair from flying everywhere. She squinted, her eyes adjusting to the moonlight. *We're really far out here,* she thought. The night had a sharp chill to it, as if a storm was coming in off the ocean. At the bottom of the black Keaton hillside, Devon could see the straight line of faint yellow lights: Monte Vista's main drag. Beyond that the velvety black of the Pacific Ocean merged into the dark sky on the horizon. The wind whipped a strand of hair across her eyes. *Get the milk and get back to the dorm before curfew.* That's all she had to do in nine . . . no, eight minutes.

The Dining Hall stood at the peak of the hill—its façade largely floor-to-ceiling windows. A ring of classrooms encircled it, and below that, the ring of dorms. The layout meant there was a view of the valley below from every dorm room, but it also meant every meal involved walking *up* to the dining hall. While Devon's mom might find it "invigorating," Devon found it an annoying metaphor for Keaton. Everything was an uphill battle, even a pitcher of milk.

Devon hurried up and across the wet grass of Raiter Lawn and passed the cobblestone path below the senior boys' dorm, Sherman. Senior boys sat on their balconies, shirtless, comfortably nestled into crappy wicker chairs and surrounded by surfboards, stinky lacrosse gear, and passed-down hammocks. The sound of someone playing guitar drifted from behind a tapestry-covered window.

Devon kept her head down. She was short—five feet three inches and a thin frame—and she hoped she could pass by undetected. Someone whistled from the balcony above, but she didn't look up. The freshmen were warned that seniors could initiate a water balloon fight anytime during the first week. She ran quicker just in case that whistle was a precursor to getting soaked—up, up, up, her breath coming fast.

The Dining Hall doors were open. She pushed through, her heart thumping, and made her way around the polished wooden tables and benches—perfectly aligned and glistening in the moonlight—toward the drink machines. Soda, ice, lemonade, iced tea, water, and milk; they all buzzed and hummed in the silent hall.

Devon found a plastic pitcher next to the water jug and pulled the lever under the low-fat milk.

Nothing.

She tried the non-fat. Nothing again.

That's when she noticed a plastic latch above. The machine was on lockdown for the night. Water was her only option. *Great.* So much for listening to Ariel's voice. Her Nutter Butter plan was already going awry.

"Don't you know they control our diet?" a voice asked.

Devon jumped. June had warned the freshman girls about avoiding popular make-out spots around campus at night. It was considered a major faux pas to stumble upon a couple behind a bush or in an empty classroom. But this was just one voice. Sitting alone in the back of the Dining Hall. She squinted, trying to turn the outlines and shadow on a bench into someone she recognized. Long, gawky legs with knobby kneecaps. A spiky head of hair. A narrow neck that threatened to topple from the weight of a bulging Adam's apple.

Jason Hutchins.

Another freshman. Devon remembered him from orientation. He kept bumping the back of Devon's chair. After she had shot him an annoyed glare, he whispered an apology while the headmaster talked about their class schedules.

He stood up. Devon guessed he was easily six feet two inches, and only thirteen or fourteen. *No wonder he could barely fit in his seat.* He tucked something in his pocket as he walked toward her. She caught herself thinking that once he got over being gangly, he could be kind of hot. His face didn't need any help. Then again, she had to grow out of this flat-chested stage before she might be considered cute, so who was she to judge.

"Just wanted some milk. Didn't think that would be against the rules," Devon said. She tucked her hands into her jeans pockets. She had a bad habit of letting them flip and flail when she was nervous. And being alone in the dark dining hall with this boy was definitely making her nervous.

Jason leaned against the wall by the milk machine. Devon noticed he wore cargo shorts (as he would for the next three years, because he always needed pockets), and a simple belt where new holes had to be punched to account for his bony hips.

"You think they'd want us to drink milk. It's in their best interest to keep us strong." Jason clipped a pen into one of his many pockets.

"Their best interest?" Devon leaned against the counter. She remembered now that Jason was a *legacy* student. In theory it only meant that he had a sibling or parent who attended Keaton before him. But when the headmaster asked all the new legacy students to stand up during orientation, Devon understood that being a legacy put you in a special club. It meant you were a bigger piece of the school's DNA than other students. Only five kids in their class of seventy had stood.

Later, June (the month) explained that Jason was the prize legacy of the freshman class. His older brother, Eric, had graduated from Keaton last year. Apparently Eric was a perfect Keaton specimen: chemistry genius, all-star lacrosse player, but more prankster than Stepford Student. ("Keaton values individualism"—The Month's words. Uttered seriously.) Jason and Eric's very rich and very generous father, William, had also attended Keaton. June had whispered the last part conspiratorially: Rumor had it that the new science wing built three years ago existed solely because Jason's dad wanted better chemistry facilities for Eric.

Jason grabbed an apple from the fruit bowl. Threw it up in the air and caught it. "You know, for the organ donations. That's what we're here for. A big bunch of young, unsuspecting organ donors. Gotta feed the machine somehow." He took a big bite from his apple. "So, like I said, they want to keep us healthy."

Devon put herself in Ariel's shoes. The smart thing to do would be to play along.

"Silly me. Here I was thinking they were shaping us into well-rounded young adults."

"Bor-ring," Jason drew out the word as long as possible. "That's what they want us to think. Looks much better for the catalogues." He examined his apple and took another oversized bite. Some of the apple juice dribbled down his chin and onto his white V-neck shirt. Devon had to look down to hide her smile. Jason had just blown whatever cool image he was trying to create. But honestly, it was the first time she'd caught anyone doing anything remotely human all week. "You've got it all worked out then. Good thing I ran into you . . . Jason, right?"

Jason held Devon's gaze longer than was comfortable. "Yeah, good thing," he said.

Devon instinctively took a small step back. She had seen that look-into-your-soul look before. Last summer Ariel made Devon double date with these guys that worked at Amoeba Records, Luke and Spencer. Devon was supposed to date Spencer, but he wouldn't stop talking about "the importance of The Clash in music evolution." Talk about bor-ring. She remembered that he kept staring into her eyes, willing her to like him back. It was the same look Jason was giving her now. He was definitely flirting with her. Devon broke away from the stare by brushing her hair out of her eyes. She was bad at flirting. Her over-analytical brain crept in. He didn't ask her name. Clearly he knew. Now she was the lame one for asking the question. "Well, guess I'm not going to get that milk, so, see ya, Jason." Devon put her empty pitcher down next to the machine and made a beeline for the exit.

"Hutch. Jason's . . .whatever. . . . Hutch is really more my thing," Jason-turned-Hutch called after her.

Devon turned only when she reached the doors.

"Gotcha, Hutch. Well, good luck with the organs."

"Are those Nutter Butters?" Hutch asked with a smirk.

The package was sticking out of her pocket. *Great. Now it looks like I can't go anywhere without bringing cookies with me.*

"You gonna eat those all by yourself?" Hutch left his apple on the countertop and began rubbing his palms together like a cartoon villain.

"Why, you want one?" Devon asked. *Save one for Derek.* How right her mom was. She made a mental note to thank her later.

"Hells yeah." Hutch was next to her in a heartbeat, reaching for the bag. "Wait, sorry, that was rude of me. You should do the honors."

He pushed the bag back, eager for her to open it. There was nothing in Hutch's face that made Devon feel like they had just met or needed to be on their guard.

Amazing: her first Insta-Friend. Not from a sponge pellet, either. She tugged at the plastic, but stopped short of opening it.

"That brings me back to the original problem," Devon started. "You can't do Nutter Butters without milk. It's a thing."

Hutch raised his eyebrows. "Oh, it's a thing?"

"It's a thing. Like peanut butter and jelly."

"Like Simon and Garfunkel?"

"Yeah. Like Rocky and Road."

"Or like orientation week and sucking." Hutch smiled wide at his own joke.

Devon laughed.

"Let's get some milk then," Hutch said mischievously.

"The machine is locked. Think we already established that," Devon reminded him.

"This machine is. But where do you think they store the milk for the machine?"

Devon found herself smiling, again, too. What did he know that she didn't?

"Come on. If it's a thing, then we gotta go on a mission to make the thing happen." Hutch grabbed Devon's hand and pulled her through the doors. "That's just what was missing tonight. A secret mission. . . ."

Devon's thoughts were louder than Hutch's words. His long fingers clasped her hand, scrunching her knuckles together. He pulled her along the gravel path outside the dining hall, leading her around back. The ocean wind whipped at her hair again, but, Hutch's over-sized grip felt warm and protective around hers. Safe. Which was weird and definitely *not* safe, her over-analytical brain reminded her, because she'd just met him.

One solitary light jutted out from the roof in the back, illuminating stacked wooden crates and metal dumpsters. Hutch pushed on the metal handle of a lone rusted blue door. "Presto," he whispered.

Sure enough, it opened right up into the school's industrial kitchen. No locks here. Hutch led her inside, only letting go of her hand when she was past the threshold.

The door shut silently behind them.

"They don't lock the kitchen?" Devon's voice sounded ditzy in her own ears.

She tried to make sense of her surroundings while her brain tried to catch up. How did a package of cookies get her here? Five minutes ago she was alone in her dorm room, and now here she was on a "secret mission" with Hutch, the knobby-kneed prized Keaton legacy. In the dark, her heart began to thump again. Ariel would be proud. This was undeniably stupid and exciting. "A place that bases everything on an honor system leaves a lot of room for stupidity," Hutch said.

Devon reached for the light switch, but he placed his hand over hers.

"No lights. It'll give away our position."

Hutch was just inches from her now. The outside light cast a dim glow through the small window above the door. Devon tilted her face up to him and felt his warm breath on her forehead. His light brown eyes were on Devon, flitting between her nose and lips. His eyelashes were dark but barely registered compared to his wide eyebrows. And his lips had that perfect dent in the middle. Devon found herself wondering what it would be like to kiss those lips. Hutch's hand tightened over hers for an instant, but then he pushed away. The moment over. If it was a *moment* at all.

"We're not supposed to be in here," Devon whispered.

Hutch hopped on a sterile metal counter, his long legs dangling, as if he had all the time in the world. "Supposed to?

Devon, Devon, Devon," he said in a faux-mocking voice. (So he *did* know her name.) "'Supposed to' is such a loaded little phrase. Do you really want to live your life doing everything you're *supposed* to do?"

It wasn't a rhetorical question. He stopped smiling. His eyes dug into Devon, forcing an answer out of her.

"No, I guess not," Devon stammered.

"Good. Because I figure there's two kinds of people in the world. The ones who do everything that's laid out for them, the supposed-tos, and then there's the people that look above it and do what they want to do. I prefer the latter, but maybe that's just me. A not-supposed-to." Hutch shrugged and slid off the counter, tip-toeing to the industrial fridge that hummed in the corner. "Now, how about that milk?"

The school bell echoed across the dark campus.

Curfew!

Devon gasped. She clutched the cookie package to her chest. Bad idea. She was right; this *was* stupid. She was supposed to be in her dorm room right now. Why did she have to try out her Ariel-like personality so close to curfew? She *wasn't* Ariel. That was the whole freaking point.

Hutch didn't budge.

"Um, we have to go, don't we?" she hissed at him. This wasn't a rhetorical question, either. The *Companion* clearly stated that all students have to be inside their designated dorms by 10:30 P.M. Hutch pursed his lips, as if disappointed. "If you say so." He crossed to the door and pushed it—but it didn't open. "Hmm." He pressed the handle and pushed again. And again. He cracked another smile.

"What?" Devon blurted out. She could feel the panic rising up along her spine, up the back of her neck and flooding her squirming skull. No, she didn't want to be at Keaton. But that didn't mean she wanted to get kicked out before classes even started, either.

"You try then," Hutch said. He stepped aside.

Devon gripped the metal handle and pushed hard against the door. Nothing.

"What are we supposed to do?" Her voice quavered. "They're gonna wonder where we are. We have to check in. Rule #3b." Why wasn't Hutch freaking out? Did being a legacy mean you couldn't get into trouble? All she could do was imagine packing up her dorm room, taking down the pictures she'd just tacked to the corkboard, her mom's disappointed silence on the drive back home. Her mom would never forgive her—

"Supposed to. Supposed to. You keep saying that." Hutch strode back across the kitchen and opened the fridge. He leaned inside, hands on bony hips, scanning the shelves. The frost billowed around him like it was whispering dirty secrets.

"Well, yeah, sorry if I'm some annoying rule-abider, but it is boarding school," Devon muttered. She tried to fight back the bitchy tone the fear had brought on. "There are rules. And we are breaking at least one, probably more. Like, does this count as four feet on the ground? I don't know. And doors aren't supposed to be closed like this when members of the opposite sex are . . . that's 4b, I think . . . no, maybe it's 1b, no, that's plagiarism. . . ." Her voice trailed off as Hutch emerged from the fridge clutching an armload of supplies. "What are you doing?"

"Look, someone will be coming around sooner than later. We'll just flag them down, explain the cookie thing, it'll be fine. These things happen." Hutch dropped his supplies on the metal counter with a clang.

Devon started to breathe again. Maybe he was right. One of the pillars of Keaton *was* honesty, and they *were* just looking for milk. She had the cookies to prove it. "You really think someone will come by?"

"Sure, they always do. Ten minutes, tops. Your dorm head probably won't even notice if you're late. And you know what we should do in the meantime?" He was already pulling a bowl from a nearby shelf, a wooden spoon from a canister. "Finish our mission."

Devon's ears perked up at "our." She had never been an "our," "us," or "we" before with a guy. Ever. *Our mission*. Hutch poured pancake mix into the big bowl.

"Weren't we just getting milk?" Devon asked.

"Oh yeah, change of plans. We're making Nutter Butter pancakes now. Infinitely better, right?" Hutch nodded at Devon, practically agreeing for her.

She tried not to nod back. And yet she couldn't help but go along with it. With him.

"Nutter Butter pancakes? Is that even a thing?" Devon hoisted herself onto the counter next to the ingredients.

"Oh, it's a thing. You've just been too busy doing everything you're *supposed to* do to know about it. I think I'm going to have to illustrate. Commence opening Nutter Butters."

Devon broke open the plastic package. "You're lucky you found me. I was going to share these with Spring House."

"Screw Spring House. They won't appreciate your Nutter Butters like I do, Devon." Hutch reached into the package and grabbed a cookie. Devon picked one out too.

"Cheers." Hutch clinked his cookie against hers. He gave her a wink and took a bite. The two of them chewed, eyes locked. The only sound was their crunching cookies against the hum of the fridge.

"You know," Hutch began, his mouth still full of cookie. "There are two kinds of people in this world."

"The supposed-tos and the not-supposed-tos," Devon replied, trying not to spit crumbs at Hutch.

"Yeah, those too, but there are another two kinds of people in the world. Those who like peanut butter and those who don't. And we, Miss Mackintosh, are the same kind of people." Hutch pulled a measuring cup down that was hanging on the wall next to the stove. "Now be a good organ donor and crack open the Bisquick, will ya?"

"You know what I heard?" Devon poured the pancake mix into the bowl. "Nutter Butters are particularly good for the organs."

Hutch lit the gas stove.

"See, we're actually providing a service. Getting our organs nice and healthy for donating." He cracked an egg into the bowl with a flourish.

A beam of light suddenly broke through the dark kitchen.

"Duck!" he hissed.

Devon jumped off the counter and landed next to Hutch on the floor. They huddled below the table. A jerky flashlight swept past the kitchen windows.

"Isn't that our rescue party?" Devon asked. Her hands started to shake with all the adrenaline surging through her body.

Hutch wrapped both his steady hands around hers. "Except that's not a teacher. That's Tino. He'll go nuts if he catches anyone in his kitchen. Trust me." He kept his eyes glued to hers and brought one hand to his cheek. He kissed the inside of her palm and pressed her hand to his cheek again. Her heart froze. *He kissed me! Well, he kissed my hand, but still! A kiss!* She could feel his soft skin peppered with rough patches where he had started shaving. "Looks like someone's not used to breaking the rules," he whispered, smiling at her.

She pulled her hand away and looked down at the floor. "No, that's not it."

But Hutch tilted her face back up toward him. "It's okay if it is. It's kind of cute actually."

Devon smiled slightly and let Hutch's hand linger on her chin.

"I almost forgot," Hutch whispered. "Never leave evidence behind." He reached his hand up and over onto the table, and slowly, careful not to make the plastic crunch, he brought the bag of Nutter Butters down to their hiding spot.

"My hero," Devon whispered back. "How would I survive without you?"

"Without me, you and your cookies would be toast," Hutch whispered a little too loudly.

Devon pressed her lips together, holding back her laughter.

Hutch frowned. Devon bit her lip and Hutch shook his head at her. Laughing was not an option. Her chest heaved from the pent-up air trying to escape.

A key slid into the door. Hutch's eyebrows rose into two wide arcs over his eyes. Devon's right hand started shaking once more. Hutch reached for it, and kissed her palm again. He held her hand between his and nodded slightly. *Everything's gonna be all right,* he seemed to be telling her. *This place isn't as bad as it seems.*

She believed him.

And then the key turned and the lock clicked into place.

CHAPTER 1

September 5, 2012
Junior Year

Devon's eye caught the harsh glare of the setting sun. She blinked and looked down, realizing she was rubbing her right palm where Hutch had kissed her years before.

"Devon? Are you sure you can handle this?"

She looked up at Mr. Robins. The sunlight suffused the wooden blinds behind him, highlighting the chaos of his curly brown hair. He scrunched his flabby cheeks, pushing his thick, black-rimmed glasses further up his nose. A bushy eyebrow flickered. He wanted an answer.

"Devon? If it's too much—"

"No, Mr. Robins. It's fine. I can handle it," she said.

He leaned back in his chair. "Good. You're certain?"

"I'm certain," she said. Her voice tightened.

"And remember from the training guide, you don't need to have all the answers. You just need to listen. That's the most important thing you can do for them right now."

The backlighting found the details in Mr. Robins's tired face: the end-of-day stubble around his chin and upper lip, the wrinkles that were beginning to make a home at the edge of his eyes. He looked as exhausted as she felt. "Your fellow students are really going to need you."

"Whoever you think needs a session, I'm here to help," she said.

"Whomever," he corrected her.

"Sorry, whomever," she said through gritted teeth.

"You don't have to do the push-ups this time," he offered.

"Thanks," Devon seethed. Could he really be thinking about grammar right now? Mistaking 'who' and 'whom' in front of Mr. Robins actually resulted in push-ups. Sometimes the whole class would have to do them for one person's mistake. But, no, even he had no interest in these Keaton-isms today. He studied his fingernails.

"Imagine if my program had been around earlier. Maybe Jason would have sought refuge in a peer instead of turning his anger inward. . . ."

"Yeah, imagine."

"I realize we've only been through a basic amount of training over the summer, but we'll do the best we can, hmm?" He flashed Devon a tight-lipped smile. It was at once a supportive gesture combined with a hint of *I'm watching you.*

Devon nodded. *What do you mean 'we?' You're not the one being thrown into the lion's den*, she wanted to say.

"Like I said, I'm here to help. So, if we're good here. . . ." she let the words drag out, but Mr. Robins didn't get the hint. He was still pondering the mystery of his fingernails.

"You know, if you and Jason were close we can arrange—"

"Hutch. And no, not really. We talked a bit freshman year, but that was like once, ages ago . . . no, I'm fine. These things happen." Devon took a deep breath to keep her rising thoughts from spilling out. *These things happen.* Like getting locked in an off-limits kitchen with a guy after curfew. Sure, that happens all the time. Those damn Nutter Butters. That night in the kitchen. *Their* night in the kitchen.

Mr. Robins started shuffling through papers on his desk. "You should get yourself some dinner."

Devon jumped up. As she swung her worn-in backpack over a shoulder she caught a glimpse of her own haggard reflection in the window. She'd grown a few inches since freshman year. That flat chest was no longer a problem by the time she was a sophomore. She now lived in the Keaton sweats she used to loathe, and kept her hair in a messy ponytail most of the time. It was as if someone had thrown her chipper freshman RA, June, the month, into a washing machine—and Devon was what came out, her smile left behind long ago in the spin cycle.

"Thanks," she said on autopilot.

"I'll send Matt over to you first thing tomorrow," Mr. Robins replied, focusing on his desk. "Classes will be cancelled, so you can take all the time you think you need. Just remember what we talked about this summer; listen, take notes, and then we'll discuss afterward, okay?"

"Sounds good."

The next thing she knew, Devon was standing in front of the milk machine in the dining hall. It was all the same meaningless swirl: the dull whispering voices of other students eating dinner, faculty trying to keep their toddlers quiet out of respect, and the kitchen staff yelling behind the scenes. Noise in a place that should have been dark and empty. *All I wanted was some milk.*

What would she do if she could go back to that night? Would she have done it differently? She wanted to experience that newness again. She thought of that apple juice dribbling down his chin. What if he hadn't been there in the dark? She would have just gone back to her dorm without the milk. She would have shared that bag of cookies with the girls in her dorm and watched *Bring it On*. She wouldn't know him like she did. And she wouldn't be feeling this . . . whatever feeling the gnawing pit in her stomach was called. She wouldn't be feeling that.

But Hutch *was* there in the dark. And despite what had happened over the past two years, however less frequent their conversations became, however much his secret glances at her across the classroom dwindled, she did know him.

A plate clattered to the floor somewhere in the back of the dining hall. She heard applause for the klutz at fault. A few people laughed. *How is anyone laughing right now?*

Hutch was right; he'd always been right. They were just a bunch of organ donors. Drones cycling through the prep school system and getting spit out on the other end with their fancy college acceptance letters in hand. They were moving parts in the machine. Replaceable parts.

But Hutch wasn't replaceable.

Devon hated them. Hated that she was one of them. She had become a part of their machine. The same machine that Hutch had tried so hard not to be a piece of.

The words escaped her lips before she could stop herself.

" . . . bunch of organ donors."

The metal milk machine blurred in front of her, morphing into a rippling molten bubble. She reached for a glass, but her hand looked fuzzy. Only then did she realize she'd been crying.

Peer Counseling Pilot Program Training Guide
by Henry Robins, MFT

Upon completion of the Peer Counseling Pilot Program Training program, the Peer Counselor will read and sign below:

Peer Counselor Oath

I, <u>Devon Mackintosh</u>, do swear, to the best of my abilities, to uphold the standard and method of Peer Counseling as explained in the *Peer Counselor Pilot Program Training Guide* written and taught by Henry Robins, MFT.

I have completed the forty-hour Peer Counselor Pilot Program Training Course with Henry Robins, MFT.

As Peer Counselor, I will not give advice to my subjects, but will use the listening and communication skills taught to me by Henry Robins, MFT, to be an understanding and helpful counselor to my peers seeking help.

I will keep and respect the confidentiality of my subjects, and will refer any subject to a professional when warranted.

<u>Devon Mackintosh</u>   9/5/12
Peer Counselor Signature   Date

_____
Supervisor Signature   Date

Signed forms should be given to Henry Robins, MFT, before first Peer Counseling session.

Name: Matt Dolgens
Session Date: Sept. 6
Session #1
Reason for Session: Best friend to Jason Hutchins

"I DON'T KNOW WHERE he got it, if that's what this is all about."

Matt slouched in the cracked faux-leather armchair. A metal music stand lay on the floor behind him. An out-of-date amplifier collected dust in the corner. So much for peer counseling resembling actual professional therapy. Why she'd imagined a movie set—where subjects lounged on plush recliners in a cozy, neutral, book-lined room; where Devon sat safely behind and beyond their field of vision—she had no clue. She *knew* Keaton.

Nothing sat between her and Matt's angry eyes but three feet of stuffy air.

At least the two armchairs she'd secured were comfortable. Plus she'd slapped a poster of a Rorschach inkblot test onto the wall. Now she regretted it. She'd hoped it would make the room feel like a proper counseling space. But even calling this a "room" was generous. It was an eight-by-eight-foot soundproof box.

During the weeklong intensive summer training session with Mr. Robins, he'd emphasized that creating the right environment was important. "I think one of the music rooms would be ideal. Why don't you go make it yours before the school year gets going," he'd suggested. "Kids feel safe there. Believe me, I know. It's where they hook up and puff weed."

Devon remembered making a concerted effort not to cringe. Was "puff weed" ever something any Keaton student ever said, at all? Still, she'd heeded his advice. Devon could only hope that one of the music prodigies on campus (or a longstanding couple) wouldn't start a turf war. Who was Devon to stand in the way of Sue Lin's violin genius? Or to poke another hole in the soul of Keaton's resident indie guitarist, Phoenix Flowers (his real name), depriving him of the privacy to write his heartbroken love songs?

On second thought, that was probably a boon for the wh. Keaton community. How could any self-respecting female actually fall for . . . but no. She was not here to judge. She was here to be judgment-free. Besides, soundproof walls were essential for therapy too.

It was against school policy (*Companion* Rule #6c) to burn candles, but before Matt even showed, Devon had lit an oversized Scent-o-Vanilla she'd smuggled in to eradicate the musty smell. It was hot in here, though. The sun beamed through a small window, highlighting the dusty air. She should get a plant. Mr. Robins had a plant in his office, didn't he? She slid the lid off her new shiny Mont Blanc pen—a gift from her mom for completing the training course "because your notes are valuable, the pen you write them with should be to." Devon had to admit, it was the one thing right now that made her feel remotely qualified to be a peer counselor. She wrote in the corner of her notebook page reserved for Matt's sessions: Plant.

"What are you writing?" he demanded.

Devon swallowed. "Keynotes for our session," she lied. "We're here to talk about you and how you're handling Hutch's death," she added, purposefully holding his gaze. "And as far as knowing or not knowing where he got the drugs, it doesn't matter. Everything you say here is confidential." That was the truth.

His jaw twitched. He sniffed, staring down at his feet. "Good, because I found out when everyone else did in that assembly yesterday. I mean, I saw the ambulance drive up the hill. I got that 'I'm sorry' text on the night he. . . ." Matt paused. "On the night he killed himself. But I didn't put it together. *I'm sorry?* He didn't have anything to be sorry about with me, so I figured it was just a mistake, like he probably meant it for Isla. I didn't know he'd sent it to his whole address book."

"His whole address book? Like, everyone in his phone?" Devon made her first real note.

Hutch's suicide text not sent to me.

ow, the 'I'm sorry' thing. But by the time anyone
ether it was too late."

o be annoyed that she was left out? *You weren't
?, Devon. That's how close you were. So you
weren't lying to Mr. Robins when you said that Hutch was just an
acquaintance.* She looked at Matt. His shaggy blond hair was damp
and starting to curl up on the ends as it dried. From the fresh red
sunburn on his cheeks and deep tan line on his neck, Devon knew
that he'd had already gone surfing this morning. He and Hutch
were regular fixtures on the 6 A.M. van for the diehards that wanted
to catch a few waves in Monte Vista before class.

"I still can't believe he was out there all night," Matt went on.
He shook his head, like he was disagreeing with his own memory. "I
don't care what they found on him. Hutch wasn't taking Oxy. Not
him. When they do one of those toxicology things they'll know."

Devon flipped through the training guide in her mind. "So,
Hutch wouldn't take Oxy. Go on," she prodded.*

Matt crossed a bare foot over his knee and picked at a callous on
the side of his big toe. Devon blinked. He wasn't wearing shoes. She
hadn't noticed *that*, either. The bottom of his foot was calloused
and embedded with dirt. But as Devon stared at his foot she realized she hadn't seen Matt wear normal shoes since he'd started at
Keaton freshman year. He went barefoot everywhere—except when
he had to wear cleats for soccer or lacrosse, and dress shoes for
formal assemblies. His calluses were so thick they *were* shoes at
this point.

"I mean, maybe he was out there drinking a bit and he fell asleep
and the cold got him. I checked the temperatures. It dropped to freez-
ing that night. They rushed this whole suicide decision if you ask me.
It just wasn't him. I would know if he was thinking about something
like that. He would have told me. I know he would have."

---

* "If the subject is experiencing stress, the peer counselor should use a combination of
Restating the subject's words, while adding a Continuer, such as "I see," or "Mmm," or "Go
on." —*Peer Counseling Pilot Program Training Guide* by Henry Robins, MFT

Of course he would have, you two were like brothers, is what Devon wanted to say. But instead she said: "It's a shock to lose someone close." More than that, she knew it was a shock to Keaton. Even students who'd never exchanged a word to Hutch burst into tears when Headmaster Wyler made the announcement in a special all-school assembly. Rumors had already been flying. Why not? There'd been an ambulance and police cars on campus. Even *teachers* were crying. Hutch was one of those guys everyone knew and everyone couldn't help but like.

His girlfriend last year, Isla, had been at the epicenter of the largest cluster. Others had sobbed together in stairwells or hugged each other in the aisles. Devon hadn't cried then. She hadn't cried for the same reason Matt was so pissed off right now. Hutch and suicide were just two things that you would never put together.

"I know it's a hard thing to accept," she heard herself go on. Mr. Robins had told her that getting the subject to accept a situation was the key to successful therapy.*

Matt tilted his head at her. "Really? That's what you're supposed to say to me right now? 'Acceptance' crap? It's not like my dog died, Devon. This is Hutch we're talking about. I mean, no offense, but why am I talking to *you*? Big Brother trying to keep tabs on us so the suicide doesn't spread? Before it becomes the cool thing to do?"

Devon brushed her bangs away from her eyes. He kind of had a point. *Would I want to talk to me?* She tried to gather her thoughts, remember her training from the summer. It was much harder to do this with people you actually knew. This was not one of Mr. Robins's practice tests. *When in doubt say someone's name. It creates a sense of familiarity. He has to see you as someone he can confide in. Right. So even though in the outside world Matt Dolgens would NEVER confide in me, let him know he can trust you in here.*

"Matt," Devon began, "you are—"

---

* "The first stage of Egan's Skilled Helper Model: Help the helpee clarify their problem and situation." —*Peer Counseling Pilot Program Training Guide* by Henry Robins, MFT

"Required to be here," Matt finished.

Devon hesitated. "I think of it as more of an opportunity than a requirement." She cringed as the textbook answer flew from her mouth.

He sneered. "Ha! More BS."

"I know it sounds lame, but it's true. This program really is here, I'm here, to help you." Devon kept her smile even and reminded herself not to get defensive. Matt's reaction was normal. It was part of the process. It was part of what separated and distinguished Devon from Matt and Isla and everyone else at Keaton—Hutch, too, maybe. This was Devon's purpose. She was a neutral observer from the get-go. She'd made that decision when she'd met Hutch, hadn't she? Back in the days of June, the month; back when she still clung to the idea that Ariel was her true best friend (as opposed to the sporadic cheery-but-incomprehensible Facebook friend Ariel had morphed into). . . . Devon had known that she was never meant to be anything more than a fly on the wall of Keaton. "That's the only goal I have."

"Please," Matt spat back. "The only goal you have is to be a Keaton bitch. Some kid overdoses on their property so they gotta cover their asses somehow. So you narc us all out, and you get a good college rec letter? It's been done before. Must be nice to sell out like that."

Devon stiffened. "Matt, come on."

"Next question, Dev. Let's get this over with."

She was going to have to change tactics. *Hutch. Bring it back to Hutch.* She forced a gentle smile. "Remember when you and Hutch went through Buck initiation? You two showed up at like 3 A.M. at my door in Spring House in your boxers? You said you had a mission or something like that."

"A *secret* mission," Matt corrected. But his tone softened a little and a smile began forming on his lips. "Hutch loved a secret mission. The seniors made us try to get girls' underwear, but it was Hutch's idea to go to your room."

Devon nodded. A hard lump had formed in her throat. She

could see the sides of his cheeks getting red, his eyes moistening. She leaned forward in her chair.

"What are you thinking about?" she whispered.

Matt swallowed back the tears. He said in a calm voice, "Hutch was the first person to call me out on my shit, freshman year. He called me a spoiled a-hole one day when I wouldn't take out our trash. No one had ever said anything like that to me. I mean, Hutch grew up with money like I did. But I was used to being special, untouchable. He knocked me down a peg. I hated him for it. But it's the best thing anyone could have ever done for me, ya know?"

Devon leaned back in her chair. With a shaky hand, she wrote on her notepad: Hutch = reality check.

Matt cleared his throat. "More keynotes?"

She looked up to find his cold eyes boring into hers. "Right. Just notes for myself to keep track of what we talk about—"

"But those don't go anywhere, right?" Matt asked. His tears were gone.

"Well." She smiled. For some reason, she was conscious of showing her teeth. She imagined it was the kind of terrified smile chimpanzees make when they're nervous. "Don't freak out. I have to record these sessions. It's procedure."

"Are you recording this right now? You know I can lawyer up in a second?" Matt's voice escalated into a sharp bark with each word. "None of this is going anywhere without my consent. And I doubt you want to get my dad involved."

Devon blinked several times. *Right. Reality Check.* She couldn't try to be his friend. She wasn't supposed to try. In this room, in this time, a "helpee" was just that: a human being who needed help from a detached resource. And as long as she sat in this chair and did what she was supposed to, Matt would see her as the enemy. It was her purpose to win his trust, not his friendship. It was her purpose to *help* him, no matter how pissed he got at her. Still, she knew that getting his dad involved was not a bluff on his part; his family definitely had the means and most certainly kept a lawyer on retainer. Matt's family created the Dolgens Ski Company; they sponsored the U.S. Ski Team during the past Olympics. In public wasted moments, usually just before summer break, Matt had always bragged about how he'd expand the company into surfboards, how his dad would put him in charge of creating a surf team.

"Matt, I'm not a narc, okay?" Devon finally said. "Give me some credit. You know me." She stood to prop the window open.

"Do I? When was the last time you and I actually had a conversation? Freshman year? On the bus to Freshman Campout? And then Hutch ODs and all of a sudden I'm supposed to pour my heart out to you? Bring up all the sweet memories you want, I'm done talking."

Devon sat back down. "Fine, you don't have to talk. I can't make you. You just have to stay here for the whole session."

Matt lowered his eyes. "So who else are they sending to you? Me, Isla? I heard Isla's pretty wrecked. Started bawling right in the Dining Hall in front of everyone. They had to take her to the Health Center to get her to calm down; she was scaring all the freshmen. Guess it makes sense she was with Hutch all last year. They lost their. . . ." He caught himself before saying too much, drumming his fingers on his knees. "Who else are they making talk to you?"

Devon bent low to meet his gaze. "That's confidential information. That's part of this whole Peer Counseling thing. You guys have complete anonymity to talk about whatever you want." Then she leaned back and glanced out the window, as if she didn't care whether Matt spoke or not, as if she wasn't hanging on his every word. Funny: this is what it took to get a peek inside Matt Dolgens' brain. A guy that most girls (who hadn't already) would give anything to hook up with. Most girls but her.

"Isn't that redundant?" Matt muttered. "Isn't anonymity by definition complete?"

"It's not redundant if it's emphatic," Devon pushed back.

"Touché." He finally glanced up.

Devon wasn't supposed to give advice. That would ruin the whole counselor/peer dynamic. Nor was she supposed to accuse a subject of anything. But something was off with Matt. It all came down to *how* she found out. This could take a wrong turn very easily, but all her instincts told her this was the conversation she should be having. So what if she told a *slight* lie to get to the point.* Screw it. She'd already lied. She'd blown it already.

"Since the Oxy Hutch took wasn't registered with the Health Center, I'm supposed to double check if there's anything you're taking that Nurse Reilly should know about. What did you have a prescription for again? Adderall? Anything else?" Devon kept her voice light and curious, careful to avoid sounding like she was accusing him of anything.

Matt sighed loudly. "Gee, *doc*, let me think. Of course the Oxy wasn't registered. It wasn't his. He didn't take the stuff."

"Okay, well, what about you? Anything potentially dangerous?"

Matt leveled his dark green eyes at her, his sun-bleached eyebrows narrowed together. "This is total Amateur Hour, Devon. You're not my shrink and you're definitely not a doctor. You're a sixteen-year-old that took a class or two this summer and you wanna talk about Adderall? You're in over your head."

It was too late to retreat now. "Matt, come on, everyone knows you live on the stuff. And with the way Hutch—"

"It's got nothing to do with Hutch," Matt interrupted, his voice thick. "It's got nothing to do with Hutch, okay? Trust me. It doesn't matter how he. . . . Isla's the one with the problem, not Hutch. Why do you think they broke up? Hutch had like some awakening this summer. The guy freakin' started meditating every morning. Suicide was not on his radar, I'm telling you." For the first time since he'd sat down, his expression pleaded with her to believe him. "It doesn't make sense. I saw him right before. . . ." He buried his head in his hands.

Devon leaned forward but stopped herself. She wanted to hold

---

* "Section IV: Personal Ethics: Although it might be tempting, never lie to your helpee." —*Peer Counseling Pilot Program Training Guide* by Henry Robins, MFT

his hand, hug him, anything to comfort him, but that wasn't appropriate. Matt Dolgens, a guy she'd known for two years, was crying over his best friend in front of her—and all she was allowed to do was ask questions and take notes.

"When was the last time you saw him?" she managed. "It might help to get that off your chest if you tell me."

Matt exhaled long and slow. "Tuesday night. He was in my room. We were checking the surf report for Wednesday and he got a call. It pissed him off, I don't know why, but he said he had to deal with it. Then a 'good night' and that was it. I heard him talking on his cell in his room and then he put on some music. He must have snuck out to the Palace after curfew, but I didn't hear it. And then I saw that text the next morning, but it was too late." He drummed his fingers on his knees again.

"I'm listening." Devon whispered.

"We were supposed to be friends from here on out, ya know?" Matt stared at the window. "We had plans. Boulder for college, live in San Francisco after. Surf Maverick's on weekends. I always thought he'd be there. That's the whole Keaton promise, isn't it? Make friends for life. Well, I did that, and he reneged. It just doesn't make sense."

"You're right, it doesn't make sense," she agreed.

"And the mess he left me with." Matt shook his head and rubbed his wet cheeks with the back of his palm. "Like I said, you're in over your head, Devon."

"How am I in over your head? I'm here to help you, Matt. Whatever you need to tell me, please tell me. I can help you solve it. What was Hutch in to?"

He stood. "I can tell you this," he offered in a hoarse voice. "Hutch was going to ask you to prom next year. He said, no matter what happened, or who either of you were with, you two were going to prom together senior year." Matt looked back at her, gauging her reaction. There was the slightest hint of a crooked smile on his lips, as if he knew he was pushing one of her buttons. "Random, right?"

Devon brushed her bangs out of her eyes again. She wouldn't cry in front of Matt. No way. "Yeah, random," she replied.

The alarm on her cell phone chimed. *Thank God.*

"Our time is up," she said.

Matt nodded. He hesitated for a second. "Well. Guess it's a good thing I was already on my way out."

She kept her eyes glued to her notebook.

The door slammed behind him. She forced another trembling scrawl.

Hutch = It doesn't make sense.

As QUIETLY AS SHE could, Devon shut herself in her dorm room. The Bay House doors were heavy and tended to slam. Everyone always jumped at the chance to pin the loud bang on something deliberate and PMS-y. Devon didn't need to draw any attention to herself right now. What she needed was a little quiet time.

Bay House, one of the oldest dorms on campus, was far less prison-like than Spring House. Here she had cream-colored plaster walls with dark wood trim. A sliding door still opened to the outside view of the Monte Vista hills below. Her windows faced west, giving her the best views of the sunsets over the Pacific.

After two years in the jail cells of Spring House, she'd earned those views—right?

Outside, junior and senior girls were spilled across the lawn, soaking in the September sun in bikinis. Soon enough everyone would be stuck inside studying, but this was the last remnant of summer. Classes had been cancelled today; still, everyone was already bombarded with homework. The girls' beach towels were covered with suntan lotion bottles, biology books, dog-eared *Hamlet* editions and portable translators for the international students.

Someone dies and they break out the bikinis. Amazing.

On the other hand, what the hell else did she expect? Black shrouds?

Devon slumped in her favorite chair, warmed by the sunlight through her doors. The wooden armrests were chipped, but worn smooth. The cushions were just cozy enough she could pull her legs up and let her head drop onto the oversized headrest. She absent-mindedly wove her brown hair into a braid. In training she'd learned some techniques to keep the emotions in therapy from going home with her. But this wasn't training anymore. And she couldn't get the image of Matt crying out of her head.

She tried to make sense of all the puzzle pieces. Hutch was found at the Palace by a faculty dog. Probably the English teacher, Mrs. Freeman: she loved walking her Golden Retrievers, Franny and Zooey, at ridiculously early hours. Even though the Palace wasn't technically Keaton property, it was on the no-man's land hillside leading down to town—a hillside that belonged to Keaton in all but name. It wasn't hard to imagine Hutch at the Palace: an old rundown military bunker carved into the mountainside. Built to spot incoming enemies during World War II, it offered a perfect defensive view of the mountains and Pacific Ocean below school.

Of course, Keaton students had converted the cement shelter into a hub for illicit activities. *Brokedown Palace* was painted on a wall, in honor of an ancient Grateful Dead song, and signed by *Class of '74*. Even though the paint was chipped and weather-beaten, a certain breed of Keaton students considered it their sacred duty to repaint the name and song lyrics every year . . . year after year after year. Every class added their signature, as well as piles of cigarette butts, bottles of booze, and creatively engineered bongs—the most renowned being a ceramic "four-puller" in the shape of Mount Rushmore.

Sucking smoke from Lincoln's head had never really appealed to Devon. She had only been to the Palace once as a freshman, and only because her friend, Presley, had forced her to check it out. ("Some of the stoner guys are hot," Presley had promised.) But when they arrived, it was deserted. The noises in the dark woods below freaked them out and they ended up running back to their dorm rooms. Devon hadn't had a reason to go back since.

Hutch had probably snuck a drink down there as an underclassman or brought Isla down there last year for some privacy. But what was he doing out there on the second day of the school year? And wasn't it true that people who committed suicide wanted to be found? The Palace was so remote. And why go out there to take pills? Was he trying to send some kind of message about Keaton? The thought of his body lying among the dirt and broken bottles made her eyes sting. He was better than that.

Devon closed her lids, remembering the last time she'd seen him. Just three days ago, in a world *with* Hutch, as opposed to this new world *without*. He was pulling an army-style duffle bag out of a dirt-covered, black Range Rover. He looked tan, relaxed, his hair curly and wild; and as usual, he wore his white V-Neck and faded cargo shorts—which finally fit. She was walking across Raiter Lawn to get an early lunch in the Dining Hall.

Hutch yelled across the parking lot, "Mackintosh!" and she yelled back, "Hutchins!" He pulled off his sunglasses. "Whatdya say to some pancakes?" He punctuated the question with a smile she could see from a hundred yards away. Devon laughed a little and shouted, "Maybe later!" And that was it.

Sitting here now, by herself, it struck Devon that she and Hutch had never talked about *that night*. Not out loud. It was an inside joke so fragile that even mentioning it would shatter it beyond repair. But no . . . it was more than an inside joke. Wasn't it? Wasn't that what Matt had hinted at in his session, that she and Hutch shared a secret bond nobody but the two of them understood? And suddenly, two years later, he brought it up like no time had passed. Why didn't she stop and talk to him? Ask him how his summer was, or which APs he was taking that year?

She knew why. It seemed like the trivial BS Hutch hated. They didn't share small talk; they were deeper than that. That's what she'd been telling herself anyways. That's what she'd been telling herself since that night, basically. So she'd kept walking. But what if he'd wanted to tell her something?

There was a knock at the glass door.

Devon flinched, and broke into a shaky smile at the sight of Grant Kerrington, his signature white Keaton LAX hat pulled low over his eyes. She exhaled. She didn't want solitude at all, she realized. She wanted some good old-fashioned fun, Southern-style. She wanted to be a regular junior, seeing an old friend.

"What's going on, Miss Mackintosh?" Grant asked in his slight Georgia twang. "You need to get out of that room and come hang out with me."

Before she could protest, he pulled her outside. The warm brick patio felt good under her bare feet. She breathed in the salty air.

"How you holding up?" he asked.

She shook her head.

He wrapped an arm around her shoulder and pulled her close. She leaned into his chest and closed her eyes. Funny how soothing the menthol-y smell of men's deodorant could be. "That well, huh?" he murmured.

Devon pulled back. "I am in serious need of a distraction."

Grant smiled down at her with that toothpaste-commercial-perfect smile of his.

Wait. Had he changed over the summer? He'd always been soft and round—easy to hug—but now there was the slightest ripple of a bicep muscle. *Was Grant hot now?* The thought left Devon's mind as quickly as it had come. This was Grant. Always there for a laugh and a piggy backride. On the other hand. . . .

Without warning, Grant grabbed her and swung her by her armpits, swinging her in a circle on the narrow balcony. "Woo-hoo!" he hollered. "How's this for distraction, sugar?"

Devon giggled, part shock, part release.

She squeezed her eyes shut.

Let Matt go. Let the session go.

Peer counseling was supposed to be a mechanism, a service.

That was all. Her feelings should never make a difference. A few books, a few days of in-person training, a couple hours a week during the year talking with homesick freshmen, or stoner sophomores . . . and she'd be right on her way for applying for a psychology major at Stanford.

But with Hutch those assumptions had flown out the window. She wished she had someone other than Mr. Robins to talk to about all this. The only other Peer Counselor, Tamsin Stitch, had dropped out of the program over the summer to go to soccer camp instead. And with this being a pilot program, Devon was determined not to let Mr. Robins down by quitting too.

Right then and there, dizzy in Grant's arms, Devon made a deal with herself.

If she was going to be polite, helpful, by-the-book, and still take the abuse from anyone she tried to help (natural under the tragic circumstances), it was okay to take a small break and let Grant distract her. It would only help her keep her overly analytical thoughts from winning out, and would make her a better therapist to her subjects. And if it was all in the spirit of helping others, why not?

"Fell House thought we'd play a pick-up game of flag football, you know, get people smiling again," he said, setting her down. "And your services are needed. Whatdya say?"

"You mean my totally unskilled-at-flag-football services?" she gasped, her head still spinning.

"You're the element of surprise. Small, quick, no one will see you coming. Come on, there's a big dare on the table for the losers. I've already volunteered you, so unless you want to sing 'Dick in a Box' at assembly tomorrow, you're coming with me."

Devon laughed, leading him back into her room. "I'll never sing 'Dick in a Box.'" She turned to close the sliding door—and froze.

A girl with stringy blonde hair had appeared before them, her eyes puffy with tears. Her skinny arms hung limp against her frayed cut-offs. She clutched an orange prescription bottle in one shaky hand.

Devon didn't even recognize her at first. "Isla?" she whispered.

It was the hair that threw her. Isla had always been a perfect blonde, as if she'd just stepped out of a shampoo commercial. Now it looked as if she'd stepped out of an airplane crash.

"Devon, I need your help."

CHAPTER 2

Name: Isla Martin
Session Date: Sept. 7
Referred by: Mr. Robins
Reason for Session: Hutch's girlfriend

"You're such a sweetheart," Isla said in a soft, high-pitched voice. She was lying on her side in bed, one arm tucked under her head. Her other arm was extended, fingers wagging like jazz hands that had lost most of their jazz. She beckoned Devon to her with a limp flick of her wrist. "Lemme see," she whispered.

Devon placed the green sweatpants and sweatshirt on the edge of Isla's bed in a neat pile. "I just grabbed the first stuff I saw, hope it's okay."

That wasn't exactly true. When Nurse Reilly sent Devon to grab overnight clothes for Isla in the Health Center, Devon found most of them in a massive pile on Isla's floor. Funny: it had reminded Devon of the piles of leaves her mom would pay her to rake up in their yard every fall. Five dollars for the whole yard. She'd always have to fight the urge to leap and belly-flop onto the middle of the pile. It was worth an extra half hour of raking for one chance to fly into the air and land in the soft cushion of leaves, sending them flying up around her in a *whoosh!*, as if the pile was exhaling an excited burst of leaf breath. She would slowly sink closer to the ground as the leaves crunched beneath her.

Isla's laundry pile was limp and sad in comparison: a miserable support group for lost and found items. If Devon tried to belly-flop on the clothes, they would probably just sag and give in to her weight, a frail moan in response. She had found the sweats and sweatshirt by picking the first two colors that seemed to match. She also made a mental note to return to the room later, to fold and put away the rest of Isla's clothes. That way when Isla left the Health Center she could return to a clean room.

Not like Isla would ever do the same for Devon, but that was the power of Isla. She was always getting people to do nice things for her. Devon was used to being an audience member of The Isla Martin Show. Isla's flowing skirts, wavy-blonde hair and glittering blue eyes swept everyone under her spell—and the only acceptable responses would be, "of course," "here you go," and "do you need anything else?" And when she and Hutch were together it seemed that the combination of their beauty and charm could power the entire school.

Now she seemed . . . small.

"These are great. I just want to be cozy, you know." Isla sat up in bed and stretched her arms to the ceiling in a long, luxurious yawn. If she hadn't been such a mess, the gesture might have been sexy: a lean cat just waking up from a nap. But all Devon could think was: *This girl is way too skinny. And she needs a shower.*

The afternoon had been a blur, mostly a fight to get Isla to the Health Center, in spite of her shaking and sweating and incoherent mumbling. The prescription bottle was for OxyContin. There were still a few pills inside. Devon's peer counselor mode took over. Her first priority had been to get Isla to the Health Center to make sure she was physically okay. Devon deliberately avoided explaining the Oxy to Nurse Reilly when they got there. It would have escalated the situation from "distraught girl" to "drug addict," which could have brought with it a whole army of unwanted faculty.

Devon needed a chance to figure out how to approach this one first. Isla was more than a bereaved girlfriend: she could be suicidal, or she could have been Hutch's pill supplier, or both. Being in possession of the pills alone could get her expelled. But there was too much Devon still wanted to know about Hutch's death; she couldn't turn Isla over to the faculty just yet. It wasn't selfish, Devon reasoned, as a peer counselor she was looking out for Isla's best interests, and maybe there'd be helpful insight into Hutch. They'd discuss it in session together and Devon could ascertain if Isla really was a suicide risk.* She'd get Mr. Robins involved if she needed to, but only in a worst-case scenario. That's what a good counselor would do, right?

Isla rubbed her eyes and glanced around. She wrinkled her brow, as if confused by the fact that she wasn't in her dorm room. She blinked at the rows of neatly made-up twin beds and fluorescent lights. A faded quilt was folded at the end of each bed: a flimsy effort at making the Center feel more homey. Of course, most Keatonites who used this part of the Health Center were freshman going through a bout of homesickness. A quilt that reminded them of Grandma—and a cup of hot chocolate with Nurse Reilly, whose wrinkled face and gray-haired bob would look equally at home in a nurse's uniform as it would on a box of cookies . . . the standard and most effective cure on campus.

Devon knew. She'd been here herself.

With marshmallows floating in the mug of cocoa, Nurse Reilly had let four-week freshman Devon babble on and on about everything she missed at home. When she'd finally wrung herself out, Nurse Reilly took Devon's hand in her own—silky soft and

* "Is Your Subject Suicidal?: A Checklist." —*Peer Counseling Pilot Program Training Guide* by Henry Robins, MFT

gnarled—and promised that before she knew it, Devon would have all of those things and more at Keaton.

For better or worse, Nurse Reilly was right. Going home over the summers the past two years felt like a limited stay in a vaguely familiar hotel. Devon often wondered if the boarding school experience was an extended case of Stockholm Syndrome: where the prisoners started to identify and even bond with their captors. Did being a peer counselor mean she had gone to the other side? Was she the prisoner that betrayed her fellow prisoners for a bigger slice of bread: in her case a recommendation to Stanford?

No. She was here to help. She *wanted* to help, bigger slice of bread or not.

Isla crawled out of bed and pulled her black tank top over her head. Her purple padded bra looked wrong, almost too bright and happy on the sad shape her body was in. Devon could see her ribs jutting out over her flatter-than-flat stomach. Hip bones popped out of the top of her jeans. Faded red scratches ran up and down her arms. Devon turned her back while Isla unzipped her jeans.

"Please, like we've never seen each other naked before," Isla said with a short laugh.

That was true. But Devon had never seen Isla in this state before, either. Even though they had lived in the same dorms for the last two years, shared the same communal showers, and brushed teeth in their pajamas next to each other countless times, Isla's inner light always burned brighter than everyone else's. Her perfection made the guidelines of beauty clear to the rest of the girls: Isla on top, Keaton mortals below. It was one less thing to think about. But now, Isla looked broken, like a phoned-in version of her former self. Devon didn't want to accept it. If Isla's standard of beauty could be cracked, what did that mean for the rest of them?

Of course, if Devon were to *work* with Isla, she would have to start seeing beyond the glorified image of *the* Isla Martin. She would have to accept the dark rings under Isla's eyes and the way she couldn't hold eye contact. In session, Isla wasn't superhuman. She was just another sixteen-year-old who needed help.

"You slept through the afternoon. Probably needed it," Devon said, pulling a nearby rocking chair next to Isla's bed. "Nurse Reilly said your pulse was racing. Like you were having a panic attack or something."

Isla pulled her long blonde hair out from underneath her sweatshirt and tied it into a knot on the top of her head. Frayed split ends poked out like a warped halo. She pulled the covers over her lap.

"I didn't need a trip to the Health Center, you know," she said after a minute.

"Sorry about that." Devon turned away, and instantly regretted it. Bad form. She was losing her footing in this conversation before they got started.

"Whatever, it's pretty chill in here," Isla added. "It's easier than being out there. Everyone giving me their pity faces, the forced frowns. I'm so over it."

"Well, I promise not to give you a forced frown if that helps." Devon smiled, but Isla rolled her eyes and studied her fingernails. "Mr. Robins said he spoke to you about seeing me."

"Yeah, I'm, like, supposed to talk with you about my issues and stuff."

"It's just for a few sessions." Devon pulled her notebook from her bag and dropped it unopened into her lap, then leaned back. She hoped the gesture was non-threatening.* It felt good to have something to write in, something that made her feel removed from their existing relationship, however thin that was.

Isla smirked at the pad of paper. "So, what? Are you going to peer into my soul, Devon? Show me the error of my ways?"

"How about we start with the Oxy. Why'd you give me those pills?"

Isla chewed a nail.

---

* "Egan's Model of Effective Listening: S.O.L.A.R.," **R**: Be a **Relaxed** Helper —*Peer Counseling Pilot Program Training Guide* by Henry Robins, MFT

Devon smoothed out the empty page of her notebook, shiny Mont Blanc pen poised. But her heart had started to pound again. "Isla?"

"I didn't give them to you. I just wanted you to hold onto them for a bit. There's a difference."

"Fair enough. Why did you want me to hold onto them?"

"I just did, okay? With Hutch and everything. . . ." Her voice trailed off and she studied her fidgeting hands in her lap. *Therapy is what happens when you let the subject fill the silences*, Devon reminded herself. Isla's eyes brimmed with tears. "Maybe I didn't want to end up like him," she said in a hoarse voice. "Is that the answer you're looking for?"

"Why do you think you would? Are you planning on taking those pills?"

She stared back down at her hands. "I wasn't there for him. And now he's not here. I just worried about, like, what if I got into a bad place like Hutch did and had those pills around. . . . I just didn't want them in my room anymore, okay? I thought I was making a good decision." Her tone hardened. "Why are you grilling me for it?"

"No one is grilling you. You're right; it was a good decision." Devon made sure that her tone was warm, inviting Isla to open up. "I'm glad you asked me to hold onto them for you. Do you think Jenny Martin will miss them, though?"

Isla's head snapped up to meet Devon's gaze. "What?"

"The pills. I noticed the prescription is made out to Jenny Martin in Portland. Is that someone in your family. Maybe your grandmother?"

Isla scratched at her arm and stared at the yellow daisies on her quilt. Her pupils flickered. Devon had struck the vital nerve.

"How about an alias for Isla Martin?" she pressed, even though she knew she was reaching. "Is Jenny Martin a name you use to get prescriptions filled in Portland?"

"Shut up!" Isla snapped. "You don't know what the fuck you're talking about. Why am I even talking to you? Just give them back."

Her voice was no longer raspy or choked. She held out her trembling hand, palm up to Devon. "Give them back, NOW."

Jackpot, Devon thought. But having her suspicions confirmed gave her no pleasure. "I'm sorry, but I can't. I'll hold onto them for you though, okay?"

"You're not going to rat me out?"

Devon shook her head and gazed into Isla's bloodshot eyes. "Part of the deal here is that nothing we talk about gets shared with anyone else. So, as long as we keep talking, and I feel like you're not a danger to yourself or others, no. I won't rat you out. That's the truth."

Isla folded her arms. "That's still a pretty lame reason for not giving back what's mine."

Devon held her hands up in a mock surrender. "Hey, you gave them to me in the first place. I'm just doing what you wanted."

"Touché." Isla leaned against the cold cinderblock wall.

"You and Hutch have been together since last year. Did you talk to him at all that night? Did he give you any indication of what he might be thinking of doing?"

"I didn't see him that night, okay?" Isla said.

"Okay. Was that for any specific reason or just circumstance?"

Isla laughed in a hollow breath. "We broke up over the summer. Clearly you didn't get the memo."

Devon swallowed. "Oh, I'm sorry, I didn't know." Her mind raced to process. They weren't together anymore? Hutch was single again? When he asked to have pancakes with her again he was single? His smile, his question all had new meaning. She shoved the swirl of thoughts away. "Do you want to tell me about that?"

Isla sighed. "You don't have a cigarette on you, do you?"

Devon laughed. "What we say in counseling is confidential, but that's the only rule I can slightly bend. Smoking in the Health Center is definitely not going to fly."

Isla had to laugh, too. "Figured it was worth a shot. If regular rules are suspended in these little sessions, ya never know."

"I've got gum." Devon offered her a piece of Winterfresh from the pack in her pocket. "Might be stale, but it's better than nothing."

Isla took the gum and started chewing, opening her mouth wide. Devon tried not to stare at the gum being violently tossed back and forth between her teeth. *She really is a wreck.* Isla twisted the wrapper into a long wormlike strand and rolled it between her fingers.

"It was the first week of summer. We were supposed to go on some boat trip with his parents, but we were arguing all the time. Hutch said he wasn't happy anymore. I thought he meant he wasn't happy with us. But now maybe he meant. . . . He wouldn't have done it if I was there for him. He should have let me be there for him." Her voice caught.

"Isla, what happened to Hutch is nobody's fault, okay? This isn't your fault." Devon leaned forward, forcing eye contact. It was important that Isla knew this. If she took the blame, then she was at risk. The girl was using an alias to feed an addiction; she was more than capable of hurting herself. She already *had* hurt herself.

"How do you know?" Isla sounded as if she were talking more to herself than Devon. "You didn't know him like I did. I mean, we kind of pissed each other off from time to time, but there was a while there we were really in *love*. Like, I didn't think it was possible to love someone that much, kind of love. It sounds like a stupid movie when I say it out loud but it's true. And he all of a sudden says he didn't want to see me? Thought we'd grown apart. It was so cliché, but it was my life." She laughed bitterly. "That sounds like a stupid movie, too."

"How did you grow apart? What happened?" Devon wasn't sure this was actually relevant to counseling Isla, but she couldn't help herself.* Their coupledom had turned them into Isla-And-Hutch, a unit, a *thing*; how could that relationship fall apart?

Isla shrugged. "I don't know. He wanted me to lay off the pills,

---

* Whenever possible, keep the subject focused on the topic at hand. —*Peer Counseling Pilot Program Training Guide* by Henry Robins, MFT

and I thought he was being controlling. I refused to change for him. I thought I was proving to him that I could be strong. And once I was home in Portland it was easy to get whatever I wanted. So I didn't have to change. I think I kept using just because he didn't want me to. But, I don't know. The way he did it, looking down on me, he was so fucking smug about it. It pissed me off."

"What about now? Do you still think it was him, being controlling and smug?" The words just popped out of her mouth. Devon gritted her teeth. She was starting to sound like her mom. *Don't judge; be supportive.* On the other hand, the non-counselor voice in her head couldn't believe that Isla had essentially chosen pills over Hutch. Epic mistake. Any girlfriend would have talked Isla out of it, gotten her to kick the pills—whatever it took to stay with someone like Hutch. But maybe Isla with all her magic spells couldn't conjure up any real friends to step in before her addiction took hold.

Can I? Devon wondered. That's what she'd signed up for with this peer counseling stuff. She had to try, to finish what Hutch would have wanted for Isla. She could help Isla see the error in her ways, without being pushy of course, and Isla could stop blaming herself for Hutch's suicide—

"I saw him earlier that day, you know?" Isla began, almost as if reading Devon's thoughts. "The day he . . . his last day. He was making a sandwich in the Dining Hall before going into Monte Vista. And you know what he did? Typical Hutch. He wouldn't talk to me. He said I hadn't changed at all. He knew I was still using. Condescending prick." Isla twisted a handful of quilt into her clenched fist.

"And then he committed suicide that night with pills," Devon murmured.

Isla snorted in disgust. "Hypocrite. Typical Hutch working his magic: Look at my right hand, so you don't see what my left hand is doing. And I fell for it. We all did."

Devon nodded but her head was spinning. "Was Hutch always

against the Oxy? He never took it with you?" If Isla was using a drug like that, he had to know. Maybe that's why Hutch had inexplicably reached out to Devon again a few days ago, across the parking lot and all that time. Her chest squeezed tighter. He'd wanted to get pancakes. Like that night, *their* night. Like he'd been in an Isla haze, and had finally emerged to see that Devon was there the whole time.

"At first, maybe a few times," Isla said. "But then he wouldn't touch the stuff. Talked about not wanting to pollute his body and other crap like that." She chewed another nail and spat it onto the floor. She squinted at Devon. "You really didn't get the memo, did you?"

"About what?"

"Look, I can say this because he's gone. Otherwise I wouldn't be telling you shit. But, Hutch was supplying pills to like half the school. Nothing like Oxy, he wouldn't go that far, but Adderall, Ritalin, Wellbutrin, Xanax, Prozac, Valium. If you wanted to go up, down, or sideways, Hutch was your guy." Isla's mouth curled into a half-smile.

Devon adjusted her notebook in her lap, anything to hide her face. "Yeah, I heard something like that," she managed as nonchalantly as she could.

"It wasn't a big deal or anything. Just a little Adderall to help kids study or Valium to help them take the edge off the Adderall. Whatever they needed. But Hutch made sure they actually needed it. He knew how much everyone was taking, kept the doses low." Isla shrugged. "I guess he was still kind of looking out for people, in his own twisted way."

Devon's chest constricted again. Images of Hutch—smiling at Devon, leaning against that dirt-covered car . . . toasting her with a Nutter Butter . . . they popped and were gone. Her mouth was dry and she had to lick her lips to speak. "So why'd he do it all? If he wasn't taking anything himself?"

"I guess because he could. He had access. Most of the campus is taking this stuff anyways, so might as well bring a little quality control to the situation. He said it's like that in Europe. At the bigger raves out there they have people who will test your ecstasy to see what it's cut with. At least someone could make sure they're taking stuff that doesn't kill 'em. Ironic, huh?"

"Yeah. Definitely." Devon picked at a loose piece of rubber on her flip-flops. Her head was swimming in a million questions, new shades of Hutch rising to the surface like bubbles.

"But at the end of last year he quit it all," Isla continued. "Stopped dealing. Even stopped drinking coffee. Didn't want to be controlled by it anymore. That's why he wanted me to stop using too."

Devon couldn't think of an appropriate response. This version of Hutch wasn't new to Isla. But to Devon he'd always been a faraway buoy in the choppy ocean of Keaton. Now, in death, the closer she swam to him, the further away he seemed.

"I don't know what he got into this summer. But something changed. If we were still together this wouldn't have happened. It just wouldn't." Isla sighed heavily. "What are we supposed to do now? How come he gets to check out and leave the rest of us to pick up the pieces? It just doesn't seem fair. What about me? How could he do this to me?"

"I don't know," Devon said. *I really don't know. But I have to keep swimming.*

DEVON WAS WRITING ABOUT Isla's deteriorating physical condition. It would be good to keep track of if she got better or worse: The red scratches, the low weight—

Her door flew open.

She straightened her back against the wall. Sitting cross-legged on her bed was always a more comfortable place to study, as long as she remembered to stand up every now and then.

"Yo, bitch, did you steal my Origins mask again?" Presley demanded, barging into the room. She started rooting through the bottles of lotions on the bedside table. "It's made of volcanic ash and you know that doesn't come cheap."

Devon tucked the session notes under her pillow. "So the 'Quiet, studying' note on the door wasn't clear enough, I see. Good to know."

"Please, you know that doesn't apply to me," Presley was already opening and smelling different bottles. "Whore-ella Deville, cough it up, where's my volcanic ash?"

"Bitch, please, I have my own volcanic ash. Why would I need yours?" Devon smiled. As much as she loved quiet privacy, Presley's reliable interruptions insured that Devon would laugh her ass off every once in a while, like a normal human being.

Presley rubbed a glob of lotion into her palms. "You don't have any like Pepto or something do you? My stomach's been kicking my ass. I totally barfed up dinner."

"Eww. That might have just ruined taco night for me."

Presley threw the hand lotion bottle at Devon. "If the mystery meat hasn't ruined taco night for you yet, then I just did you a favor."

"Good point." Devon sighed. "But, I don't have anything for your stomach."

Presley checked herself out in Devon's mirror. She was wearing her typical dorm uniform, flannel pajama pants and a sweatshirt, and her curly blonde hair in a loose knot on the top of her head. "I hope I'm not like *sick,* sick. That would totally blow. Oh, speaking of blowing, b-t-dubs, what's up with you and Gaa-raant! Roar. Someone worked out over the suuuh-mmer." Presley liked to sing words for emphasis. She reveled in her terrible voice, an invisible karaoke mic on at all times.

Devon stretched out on her bed. "Pres, this whole Hutch thing. . . ."

"What?"

"I just—I don't know. I don't want to gossip about how hot Grant is."

Presley turned to her. Her blue eyes softened for a second. "Sweetie, the Hutch situation totally sucks. But that doesn't mean you're not allowed to have a little fun." Presley smelled her hands. "Mmmm, lemon. I like that one. You should get more of that."

Devon had to laugh again. "How are you not more, like, in shock about all this? You and Hutch were on the newspaper together."

"Look, I'm not like some heartless jerk. I get it." Presley applied some of Devon's mascara as she spoke, her mouth curled into an 'O' as she forced her eyes open. "But listen: The whole school moping around isn't going to change the fact that Hutch is dead and gone, and that it was his decision. I mean, I feel bad for his family and all, but writing poems in my journal or contemplating life over tacos isn't going to change anything. Hutch was clearly in a shitty place. I just hope he's happier now. You need more mascara."

Devon blinked. She felt like *she* was being counseled now. Hearing these cliché condolences wasn't helpful; it was just annoying— even coming from Presley, whom Devon loved precisely because she never, ever engaged in bullshit. But the fact remained: Devon didn't believe Hutch really meant to kill himself. Now she understood Isla's irritation at everyone's fake frowns and false hugs. They all felt like futile attempts to remedy something that could never be fixed. No matter what anyone said, Hutch was gone. The emptiness left behind sucked up each stupid platitude ("He will be missed.") like a vacuum, leaving behind what you started with. Nothing.

"Oh come on, is this counseling thing going to make you a downer all year? Cause, if I gotta find a new best friend who actually likes to have fun, tell me now." Presley had a goofy grin on her face. She waited for Devon to pick up the cue.

"So . . . Grant." Devon said, without much enthusiasm.

"Grant," Presley said back. She plunked down in Devon's chair.

"He did come to visit me, and not during visiting hours. You think. . . ."

"I totally think. If he dropped by unannounced during the first week, you know what that means. He was thinking about you this summer." Presley drew out the last sentence as if she'd just cracked the Da Vinci Code.

"Ya think?" Devon doubted it. Guys didn't exactly seek her out. Presley usually acted as Devon's hook-up guru, pushing her together with whatever wingman was attached with Presley's current boyfriend. Their system had yielded precisely 2.5 hook-ups for Devon in the last two years. The half was when Presley was hooking up with a local surfer in Monte Vista. Presley and her surfer made out on the beach while Devon and the surfer's friend, Whateverhisnamewas, huddled in his crappy van for warmth. He smoked joint after joint until just before passing out he said to Devon, "You're totally bang-able. You can go down on me, if you want." A true charmer. The ever optimistic Presley had insisted that if Whateverhisnamewas hadn't passed out, he would obviously have hooked up with Devon—thus the half point.

"Yeah, I think. Someone's gonna get la-aaaa-id." Presley sang again.

"I don't know." Devon flopped onto her back. The glossy white ceiling reflected her room in rippling waves, Presley's blurry head of yellow hair and blue pants, and Devon, a wavy white form on her colorful bed. "Hey, did you know Hutch was dealing pharmaceuticals last year?" Devon asked the ceiling.

Presley plucked a lip gloss from Devon's table and tried it on. "Yeah, I scored some Adderall off him last year for finals. Way to change the subject, President Ho-bama."

Devon rolled over. "Whatever, Former Vice President Al Whore." Her smile faded. "Jesus, am I the only one that didn't know what Hutch was doing?"

"Probably," Presley said.

"Do people think it's weird that Hutch OD'd on the one kind of pill he didn't sell?" Devon was beginning to feel like the only one at Keaton who was left out of the Hutch party. First she doesn't make the list for his suicide text. Now she discovers that everyone *but* her knew he was running a pharm ring at school. Yes, it was petty, but why *not* her? Not that she was waiting around to buy pills from him, but it felt unfair that Hutch kept a huge piece of himself hidden. Weren't they closer than that?

"I wouldn't say weird." Presley's voice broke into her thoughts. "More like, 'not totally surprised.' But you're right: Hutch never had Oxy. It was like a rule of his. Wouldn't give out the hard stuff. Strictly performance enhancers. He said it was something about messing with the system. Fighting the Man, all that. Like, I heard he even hooked up Jin Soo with prescription strength Rogaine because Jin was freaking out about losing his hair early."

"Jin is losing his hair?"

"Not anymore." Presley flashed a smile. "Look, dork, it's almost nine thirty P.M. Pete's coming over and we're getting the language lab before anyone else. Seriously, who told these freshman all the hook-up spots? It's not cool. Not cool at all."

Devon mustered a smile in return and sat up in bed. "Wait, I'm seriously behind on the intel. I thought you and Pete broke up?"

"We did. He apologized yesterday. Bought me flowers, and this necklace. See?" Presley leaned over to Devon. She could smell the lemon hand cream. "It's a compass. He said I'm his True North. Isn't that cute?"

"I wonder if Hutch and Isla—"

"Dev?" Presley interrupted. "You're going to have to ease up on the Hutch talk, okay? You're kind of obsessing."

"Humor me. The *Hawk* met already this year, didn't you guys? Did Hutch go? Did you notice anything weird about him?"

"I don't know. Hutch was going to do the arts roundup. Profile rising art stars at Keaton and all that." Presley burped and grinned at Devon in the mirror. "Damn, excuse me. That was gross."

Devon rolled her eyes. "Look, I'm not the expert, but do people who are going to kill themselves the next day plan on writing articles that month? It doesn't add up. . . ." She suddenly noticed sweat glistening on Presley's forehead. "Are you okay?"

"Fine, whatever. And no, it doesn't add up. But. . . ." Presley burped again. She steadied herself against the wall. "It never adds up. That's the thing about suicide. You can't. . . ." Another burp. Her moist skin suddenly went white. "Shit, not again." Presley grabbed Devon's trash can and vomited.

"Jesus, Pres." Devon jumped off the bed and pulled Presley's hair back while Presley caught her breath. "What's wrong?"

"Ah, man. This is beyond mystery meat. I think I'm sick." Presley held onto the school-issued rubber can. She blinked apologetically at Devon, wiping her mouth. Her lips trembled. "I'll clean this up for you."

The school bell rang: 9:30 PM. Study hours were over. One hour of free roaming around campus before everyone had to be in their rooms.

Presley grabbed the garbage can. "Damn. Pete will be here in a second. Tell him to hold on if I'm not back. I gotta brush my teeth." She hurried out of Devon's room, can in tow.

Devon opened her sliding door to welcome in some fresh air before the vomit stench could set in. The rest of Presley's evening was Presley's business.

She pulled her notebook from under her pillow. She had just finished describing Isla's decaying body, the scratches, her skeletal frame. Should she write about Isla using an alias for her prescription? Mr. Robins had promised Devon that students couldn't get in trouble for whatever they discussed in their sessions. In turn, Devon had promised to share her session notes with him to better help him oversee her. It seemed like a good plan, but that was before Devon started counseling. Her notes wouldn't reveal a small infraction like vodka stored in water bottles or a new hideout on campus for smokers; most of the school was either using or complicit in an illegal drug ring. If Mr. Robins read them he would have no choice but to show Headmaster Wyler. Given the climate at Keaton post-Hutch, the school would go into lockdown. Rooms would be searched. Weekends would be restricted. And no doubt, Devon would be scapegoated. Isla and Matt were too smart; they'd figure out who'd ratted out Hutch, in spite of Devon's promises to them. No, there was no way Mr. Robins could see these. For now they were for Devon's eyes only. She would write down everything she could if it meant she was helping her subjects. She'd deal with Mr. Robins later.

Someone banged on the window next to Devon's room. "Pres! You in there?"

Devon sighed and put the notes away again. She poked her head outside. Pete stood with a quilt draped over his shoulder.

His dark hair was cut short, an effort to control his 'Jew Fro' as he called it. He wore a short sleeve shirt and even in the dim outside lights Devon could see the black hairs blanketing his arms. "Presley's coming. She's been kinda sick."

"Thanks. That sucks." He checked his watch and pulled the quilt off his shoulders with a big sigh. It hung in his hand, limp.

"Yeah, you probably won't be needing that," Devon said. Quilts, blankets, even sheets at this hour were for one thing only. On the grass behind a dorm, on the carpet of a music room, even between the bleachers in the basketball court, carrying a blanket at this time of night was a badge of honor. No doubt Pete made a point for his dormmates to see. "Congrats, by the way, on you two getting back together. I didn't think she'd take you back after . . . well, you don't need me to tell you what you did."

Pete's wide forehead wrinkled. "No, but you like reminding me."

"That's probably your guilt reminding you, actually. Me? I'm just looking out for Presley." Devon crossed her arms and leaned against her open door.

"Hiiiiiii, baby!" Presley sang as she stepped out of her room.

Pete leaned in for a kiss.

"Better not, I'm sick," Presley croaked.

Devon watched as they disappeared into the dark behind the dorm. She envied Presley's ability to neatly compartmentalize. Presley had been on the newspaper staff with Hutch the past two years. They'd been friends. She was within her right to be publically upset about Hutch. But Devon? No one, not even Presley knew about her night with Hutch. Devon had just been locked in a kitchen with him for one night. One night, two years ago. Maybe she didn't have a public claim on being his friend, to being more upset than anyone else, but she couldn't shake the voice in her head, *You were more than friends.*

She pushed the thought away. Instead, she headed down the deserted hallway—back to Isla's empty room and her lonely pile of clothes.

A WIND CHIME MADE of seashells clinked when Devon walked in. She flicked on the light to avoid feeling like she was sneaking around in Isla's room. Bright lights equaled purpose. She reached for the top of Isla's clothing pile and started folding.

A white V-neck. Folded. Plaid long-sleeve shirt. Folded. Devon glanced around as she worked. Aside from a large purple and brown tapestry with swirls of elephants and 'ohm' symbols, there were no pictures on Isla's wall. Her iPod dock was stickered with *Vegetarians Taste Better*. On her bedside table lay a piece of driftwood with jewelry draped across it. Devon moved onto a pair of black sweatpants. One leg flicked the driftwood, sending an earring into the open top drawer. When Devon reached inside to retrieve it, another pill bottle rolled out.

Adderall, 10 mg. The prescription was for 'Isla Mayfair.' The bottle was pretty full. Devon dumped what looked like twenty blue pills into the palm of her hand. Instinctively she made sure Isla's door was closed. This would be a hard one to explain to a teacher passing by. Isla must have thought these pills weren't that big a deal if she hadn't mentioned them. But Devon knew if she took the bottle Isla would notice. She poured half the pills back in the bottle and tucked the remaining pills in her pocket. At least she could limit how much Isla was taking.

The bottle rolled to the back of the drawer and Devon spotted a familiar head of brown hair: a photograph of Hutch and Isla on the beach. Isla was smiling at the camera, her cheeks fuller and brighter, her smile wide and real. Hutch was kissing her cheek, his eyes closed. Under the picture was an index card wrapped with a hemp necklace. Two nickel-sized shells were threaded through the hemp. On the back of the card was handwritten, "Love, H."

Even though it was wrong, even though this wasn't hers, Devon unwrapped the necklace. She stood in front of Isla's mirror and hung it around her neck. The iridescent white and pink of the shells caught the light, as if they were showing off.

"Love, H," Devon said to herself.

But this wasn't hers to take. Hutch and Isla had created this. Devon wrapped the necklace back around the card, her hands shaking. She shoved it behind the photo. Devon hadn't even been in Hutch's phone to receive his suicide text. Isla—the Keaton Prize Girlfriend for whom Hutch had made a necklace, for whom Hutch had texted "I'm sorry"—must have had other Hutch pictures around. Devon tucked the photo in her back pocket. She deserved some little memento, didn't she?

Devon felt her cheeks getting hot. This was bad. She couldn't hate them: Isla, Matt . . . even Presley, any of them. She was just as guilty of turning away from Hutch. They needed her help. She had to help them. It's what Hutch would have done.

Before leaving, Devon shook out the clothes she had folded and tossed them back on Isla's pile.

CHAPTER 3

Name: Cleo Lambert
Session Date: Sept. 10
Referred by: Headmaster Wyler
Reason for Session: Caught shoplifting at
Monte Vista Pharmacy

"This is my punishment? *Trés magnifique*," Cleo tucked her black bob behind her ears. Her bright-yellow-painted nails tapped on the wooden armrest.

"Does that mean good or bad?" Devon asked. She opened her notebook to a new page and took the lid off her pen. "Maybe, for the sake of clarity, let's stick to English."

"*C'est bien*. It's better than getting kicked out, right?" Cleo let out a hollow laugh.

Devon smiled back. "Good point. So, do you want to start with what happened in Monte Vista?" Devon made a point to keep her face blank, eager to hear Cleo's answer. *

---

* "At the beginning of sessions, it's important that the Counselor has a look of expectancy, inviting the subject to talk." —*Peer Counseling Pilot Program Training Guide* by Henry Robins, MFT

Cleo checked her watch, even though she'd arrived right on time. Rose gold, chunky, men's watch. Devon couldn't see the brand but the diamonds on each number made a clear statement: *You can't afford this.* Cleo's uniform of black biker boots, skinny jeans, oversized black sweater, thick black eyeliner—it was straight out of a fashion spread in *Vogue. Black is the new black!* Her eyes wandered around the room, deliberately bored. "I'm tired of the Monte Vista story. Wouldn't it be easier for you if I sat here and cried about Hutch being gone and contemplated the meaning of suicide or something to that effect?"

She bit her bottom lip and eyed Devon up and down, no doubt noticing the grass stain on Devon's jeans. Devon crossed her legs again in a feeble attempt to hide it. Maybe she would try to wear a better choice of clothes for Cleo's next session. Anything that Cleo couldn't mentally rip to shreds.

"This isn't about making anything easier on me. This is about you and whatever happened in Monte Vista." Devon quickly added, "But, we could talk about Hutch if you want, if you have something you want to talk about, about Hutch. . . ."

"I saw him in Monte Vista. On his last day, you know, alive." Cleo let her sentence hang in the air. She clearly enjoyed the suspense it created.

"Okay. What happened?"

"It's not like I couldn't pay for the nail polish, you know. It was just so easy to take it. So I did. Tucked it up my sleeve. But the trick is not to leave right away; that's too obvious. You gotta walk around, like you're still shopping. Look like you haven't found what you're looking for. *D'accord?* So I go into the tampon products. Always a safe place; no one wants to talk to a girl surrounded by pads and plugs. And there he is, the man of the hour. Jason Hutchins. In the tampon aisle. He doesn't see me see him, but he grabbed a pregnancy test. One of those Early Response things. Shoved it in a pocket in his cargos. You know the ones he always wore. The Hutch uniform of sorts. You okay?"

"Huh? Oh. . . ." Devon realized her mouth was hanging open. "Of course." She exhaled and sat up straighter in her chair. "So, you were saying Hutch bought a pregnancy test?"

"Stole. Hutch stole a pregnancy test. Aren't you listening? Anyways, he puts the box in his pants just as he turns and sees me. He knows I know. And classic Hutch, he winks at me and walks right out of the store." Cleo tucked her hair behind her ears again. She leaned back in her chair and looked at Devon like she was waiting for a prize.

"He walked right out? He didn't get busted?"

Cleo laughed. "Oh no, the alarm went off. The store manager grabbed him the second he tried to walk out. And then the manager, *connard*, grabbed my arm too. Walked me and Hutch to his little back office. You know, it's sad. A man his age with an office that size. Kinda pathetic he has to get off busting teenagers. But *c'est la vie*, right?"

Devon stared back down at her notebook. Cleo's French-isms were crossing the wires in her head. Did Cleo always talk like this? Maybe they'd never had that long of a conversation before. How could she without pulling her hair out or craving a croissant? "Wait, sorry, I'm confused. Hutch also got caught shoplifting? Why didn't the school know about it?"

Cleo leaned forward and her voice dropped to just above a whisper. "Dig this. So Hutch and I are sitting there in this guy's office. I'm sweating it a little. I mean, if the store complains to Keaton I could get expelled, and that involves dealing with my parents, *non merci,* if you know what I mean. But, Hutch, he's whistling. Literally whistling in his chair. Not a care in the world. It's almost infectious, you know Hutch. So I try to joke with him about that pregnancy test because, come on, I want to know who it's for considering he and Isla broke up over the summer."

"You knew about that?" Devon realized how petty that sounded. She put the lid back on her pen. Taking notes at this point would just slow the story down.

"Of course. I make a point to know these things."

"So, who is it for? Was it for, I mean? Did you find out?"

Cleo's ruby lips curled in a smirk. "Wait, it gets better. God I love that kid. Loved, past tense, sorry. So Hutch leans over to me and whispers, 'Don't tell anyone. But I'm late.' And winks at me again. And then, here's where it gets interesting. That kid that works in the pharmacy, Bodhi, comes in."

Devon blinked. She wanted to grab Cleo by that stupid black sweater and yell in her face, *Who did he steal the damn pregnancy test for? TELL ME!*

"You know, Bodhi Elliot?" Cleo said, reveling in milking the suspense. "He graduated Keaton a few years ago. His little sister is a freshman day student this year. Raven. She follows in the family tradition of having a rat's nest for hair. Hippies. *Le gauche.* You know, Bodhi would be semi-hot if he cut those rancid dreads off his head. Apparently he was some big science genius, but dropped out of MIT after the first year. No one knows why. He's been slumming it back in Monte Vista at the pharmacy. Anyway, Bodhi comes in and asks for Hutch to come with him. Hutch says to me, 'Here's my Get Out Of Jail Free card. Good luck.' And he walks out with Bodhi and never comes back. Untouched. God, that kid was untouchable. Until he wasn't, I guess. *C'est triste.*"

Devon released her crushing grip on her notebook. "So you never found out who the test was for?"*

Cleo took a deep breath and leaned back. "Is this session about me or Hutch?"

"About you, of course," Devon said, trying to recover from her misstep. "I just want to understand why you're the only one that got in trouble. How did they know you were shoplifting?"

Cleo shrugged. "Manager claims he saw me in the overhead mirror. We had a little chat in his office and he let me off with a

---

* Section V: Self-Awareness. "The Peer Counselor should always strive to keep his/her own emotions and motivations at bay during a session."—*Peer Counseling Pilot Program Training Guide* by Henry Robins, MFT

warning. Said he wouldn't press charges but was going to tell the school. I told him I was troubled, bullied, unsure of my sexuality . . . you know the type of caring adult. Anything to help the troubled youth. So then Wyler sent me to you. Required therapy. And *voilà*, here I am."

Devon folded her hands in her lap.

Cleo tugged at her Burberry boots. "You'd think for $500 bucks these things could at least guarantee no blisters, huh?" She didn't seem to be interested whether Devon answered her or not. She was killing time here because she had to. Devon was background music to her; the piano player in a mall you might walk past, but would never consider an actual musician.

"Do you think you're troubled? I mean, if you said that to the pharmacy manager, do you think there's an element of truth to it?" Devon asked.

Cleo lifted her gaze from her boots. "How much training have you actually had?" Devon hated this question. Mainly because her own answer made her cringe. *Not very much.* "Does it matter?" she finally asked.

"Yes, because, we're not exactly BFF, *n'est-ce pas*? I started here last year, we've never been roommates, never taken a weekend away together, never laughed over a crush on a hot guy, so, remind me . . . why the hell would I tell *you* anything?"

"You don't have to tell me anything. You're just required to be here for five sessions. What we talk about is up to you," Devon said.

Cleo shrugged. Her face softened the slightest bit. "*Tres bien.*"

Devon placed her notebook and pen on the floor. Maybe that would be less threatening. Just keep Cleo talking; that was the bare minimum she could accomplish. "So, what do you want to talk about?

"I wanna know who that pregnancy test was for," Cleo responded immediately. "Hutch and Isla broke up this summer. Maybe that changed and they hooked up again. If not, there's a mystery lady we don't know about. A black widow so to speak. A *femme fatale* who will do anything to protect her secret. All I know is: Some girl who's too scared to get her own test is walking around wondering if she's pregnant with a dead guy's baby. Don't you want to know who that could be? I'd kill to know who it is." Cleo was leaning forward now, drawing Devon into her gossip circle once again—eyes wide enough so that Devon could see the smoky blue color behind the layer of black eyeliner.

Devon could only nod. Her heart raced. A secret pregnant girl on campus? Not Isla. Hutch had written her off. Did Matt know? No, because if he did know Hutch was sleeping with someone else, why would he mention Hutch's plan to take Devon to prom? And then there was Hutch himself. When Devon saw him that first day of school he hadn't acted like someone who was hiding a terrible secret or hanging out with a girl on the side. She hadn't even gotten the "memo" about Isla. But, Devon had to admit, he also didn't act like someone who was about to commit suicide the next day either. Happy, flirty, planning ahead. Devon couldn't shake the thought: *A black widow.* Hutch may be gone, but this girl was still out there, if what Cleo was saying were true.

"Come on, where's your imagination?" Cleo demanded. "Golden Boy kills himself out of the blue. Something drove him to it. And maybe our mystery lady knows. Or maybe she's the reason he did it. Think about it. Hutch knocked somebody up. That's gotta weigh pretty heavy on the conscious don't you think? A good guy like Hutch?" She raised an eyebrow at Devon.

"Why'd you call him a Golden Boy?" Devon wondered out loud, forgetting the peer counseling setting. The question had nothing to do with her shoplifting, or helping Cleo become a better person.

"Hey, I'm just the messenger. Hutch was born like that. Lap of luxury. Never had to work at anything, except making sure his smile was as perfect as it could be. Our parents belong to the same golf club in San Fran. All of this drama kind of just goes with the territory."

"What do you mean: the territory? Was there a suicide before in Hutch's family?"

"No. Nothing as scandalous as all that. It's just rich people, you know. Embezzlement, drug problems, alcoholism, secret children. . . . It tends to happen in the higher tax brackets because they think the world revolves around them. Ponzi schemes? Those have nothing to do with investing; it's all an ego trip. A massive pissing contest between a few über-wealthy guys with other people's money. And suicide? It's pretty much the most selfish thing a person can do. Hey, everyone pay attention to me, I'm dead. Only, joke's on them because they're still dead whether anyone cares or not."

Devon swallowed. "Wow, I guess I never thought of it that way. Then again, that's not my tax bracket, so to speak."

"That's just the world as I've seen it thus far. Who knows? I could change my mind about it all tomorrow. Not likely. But, I could."

"So, if suicide is selfish, are you saying that Hutch was selfish too? Wasn't he just buying a pregnancy test for someone? That doesn't seem like the act of a selfish person."

"Oh, I'm sorry." Clew frowned. "Did I crush your vision of the Golden Boy?"

"No, it's not . . . I didn't have some vision of Golden. . . ." Devon stammered.

"Wow, Devon, you little minx. Here I was thinking you were the Good Grade Girl, but you got a chocolaty chewy center, don't you?" Cleo's eyes lit up.

"What? I don't have a chocolaty chewy anything," Devon fought back.

"Puh-lease. You have a hard-on for Hutch, don't you?" Cleo turned her voice into a small whine and pretended to be Devon. "'He's not selfish. He was doing a good thing up until he accidentally took too many Oxy pills.'" She folded her arms and sat back in her chair. Her voice dropped back to normal. "Do you want to think this through a little bit more before you come down on the side of the defense?"

"I don't have a hard-on for Hutch," Devon began.

"You totally do! You've got a serious case of *amour fou*. Shit, why am I the one in the hot seat?"

"Seriously, I don't . . . wait, what's *amour* . . . forget it." Devon took a deep breath. She couldn't lose control of the session like this. "Whatever Hutch was going through, and clearly none of us really knew, it was something painful. And even in death, I think he deserves our compassion and respect. Is that so difficult to imagine, or does that make me self-centered too?" Devon stared Cleo down, hoping Cleo wouldn't notice that she was walking an uncertain tightrope of authority.

Cleo turned to the window. The slightest blush appeared on her porcelain cheeks. Her hair fell to her face from behind her ears, but she didn't put it back in its place. Finally she sighed.

"Whatever. Just make sure you're looking at what's really there, not what you want to see. Otherwise you'll be disappointed."

"Noted. Thanks. I think our time is up for the day, so for next week—"

"Save it. See you next week, *counselor*." Cleo said the word with disdain dripping from her tongue. She pushed her way out of the room and slammed the door.*

Devon exhaled deeply. It wasn't personal; she knew that. Cleo just didn't like being required to be here. Who would? Devon reached for her notebook and pen on the ground, but only found the notebook. She got on all fours on the thin carpet and looked under Cleo's chair. The pen hadn't rolled under there.

All at once, she smiled. First lesson of doing sessions with a kleptomaniac: Expect something to be stolen. It's not like Cleo could go far; they were all stuck on the same mountain. She'd calmly and politely ask for her pen back at their next session, even though she kind of wanted to sneak into Cleo's room and steal it back. But starting a stealing war with a klepto probably wasn't a good move. Klepto lesson number two.

---

* "Try to end every session with a positive affirmation of the work you've done together."
—*Peer Counseling Pilot Program Training Guide* by Henry Robins, MFT

As Devon tucked her notebook into her backpack, she couldn't shake the thought: *Hutch got someone pregnant.* And Cleo was right. Sure, Devon could run to his defense. But who she defending, exactly?

DINNER WAS WRAPPING UP. Plates and glasses clanged from the back of kitchen. A tray of limp Sloppy Joes and mushy peas waited at the end of the serving line for the last stragglers of the evening. Devon grabbed a Sloppy Joe but left the peas alone. A Keaton rule: If something looked bad, it tasted worse. After all, Presley had just been reminded of that the tough way.

As Devon moved to the salad bar, she spotted Mr. Robins at a table chatting away with Ms. Ascher, the French teacher and girls soccer coach. Devon kept her head down. Hopefully Mr. Robins wouldn't feel the need to chat. Jicama. Cherry tomatoes. Romaine lettuce from the student vegetable garden. That always made her smile. Leave it to California boarding schools to not only have students willingly eat their vegetables, but grow them too.

"Devon?" Mr. Robins called.

Shit. "Oh, Mr. Robins, hey. Didn't see you there." Devon poured dressing on her salad. He stood and strode toward her. *Keep moving.*

"How are the sessions going?" he asked. Funny: For the first time, Devon noticed that he wasn't actually as tall as she had thought. He probably wasn't taller than five feet nine inches. She wondered if he had a girlfriend somewhere or if he was just a thirty something single guy stuck on this hill with a group of hormonal teenagers. What adult would choose that lifestyle?

"Um, great. We're still meeting tomorrow to discuss everything, right?" Devon looked around. Most of the tables nearby were empty, but still, she didn't want to talk about this stuff in such a public place.

"Right, right. Tomorrow's still on. Just wanted to see how you were holding up."

"It's great. I'm great. I'll fill you in at our meeting."

With that, Devon made a beeline for the back of the Dining Hall. No quicker way to get flagged as a narc than to talk about this therapy stuff in the middle of freaking dinner. She put her tray down at an unoccupied table two tables away from the Corner Table—the preferred home base of freshman troublemakers. The kids who sat here were out of the teacher's sightline so they could throw food, make towers with cups, or spit balls to stick to the ceiling. True to form, a few freshman boys were shooting sunflower seeds at each other through their straws. Two girls sat with them, clearly bored.

Devon almost smiled to herself. She remembered those days when tentative friendships were formed—not with roommates or classmates, but accidentally, during the in-between times on campus. After dinners, lounging on lawns before study hours, late nights in the kitchen. . . .

"No, I'm telling you. That stuff is totally easy to OD on," a freshman boy with spiky blond hair was telling his friends. "My uncle lived in the building next to Heath Ledger's place. He said accidental overdoses happen more often than you would think."

"Whatever," one of the girls with a fishtail braid said back. "I heard he was taking Oxy like every day. Total addict." Devon's ears perked up.

"I heard he wrote a suicide note in blood," another boy said.

"That's totally not true. I heard he made a YouTube video right before," said Fishtail.

Nice: a game of one-upsmanship about how Hutch killed himself. But not surprising. Every freshman aspired to be a Keaton expert.

"Makes you miss a home-cooked meal, huh?" a voice said behind Devon.

Maya. She dropped her tray at Devon's table. Maya was a fellow junior: half Vietnamese and with her almond shaped eyes and petite frame Devon always thought she looked like a really pretty doll. Devon could easily imagine her in a pink tutu, spinning to music in a little girl's jewelry box.

"I'm sure there are jails with more edible food." Devon scooped up her Sloppy Joe; most of it plopped back down onto her plate as she took her first bite. Maya had a big glass of iced tea, jammed with ice, and a plate with a few cucumber slices and carrot sticks.

"Not hungry?" Devon asked.

"I had a big lunch." Maya took a polite sip of her drink. Her jet-black hair was twisted and clipped on the top of her head, every hair in place. "I heard you were talking to folks about Hutch. Like grief counseling or something?"

"Yeah, just helping out where I can," Devon replied, trying not to stare at the pink powder dusting across Maya's cheekbones. Devon had never seen Maya without full make-up, even during sports. The rumor was that Maya woke up at 5 A.M. every day so she would have enough time to get it all together before 8 A.M. classes. She apparently had her own airbrush machine to keep her foundation perfectly applied. Devon wouldn't know where to start with and airbrush.

"That's cool of you. Hutch was one of the good guys. It's. . . ." Maya picked up a cucumber slice and put it back on her plate. She bit her lip. "It just sucks, what happened."

"How much does dinner blow?" Presley slammed her tray on the table next to Devon. "What'd I miss?"

Maya blinked several times. "I was just leaving. I've got a pack of Ramen in my room that is way better than this." She pulled a lipstick tube out of her pocket and expertly applied a bright coral color to her lips, then blotted on her paper napkin and tossed it on top of her plate—sealing her scant meal with a kiss. "Later."

Devon had always noticed that Maya didn't so much walk as she sashayed—even when dumping her dinner tray. *She dresses like she's going to a board meeting.* Button down shirts, knee-length skirts, ballet flats; Maya was the queen of Grace and Proper. She looked like a foreigner in the country of Lazy and Comfy, a sea of sweats, flip-flops and ripped jeans. But maybe that was envy talking. Lipstick blotting and sashaying were not things that came either easily or gracefully to Devon.

"What a bitch, right?" Presley took a monster bite of her Sloppy Joe.

"I don't know if bitch is the right word, but she's something," Devon said.

"You're right. What I meant was, stuck-up bitch. I mean, who wears lipstick around here? What, are we going to the opera?"

Devon grinned in spite of herself. "I'll bet her mom is wired like that. My mom would love it if I cared more about looking good, but I can't say I'm wired that way."

"Of course her mom is wired to be a little sex kitten. She married Eddie Dover. Gotta look good to be a millionaire's wife. And we know the Queen of Big Pharma can't go around looking, heaven forbid, less than perfect." Presley wiped her mouth with the back of her hand.

Maya's mother, C. C. Tran, had married Eddie Dover—owner of the pharmaceutical giant Dover Discovery—in a highly publicized marriage that still made the gossip pages, and of course was always news around Keaton. C. C. was painted as the ultimate gold digger, a Vietnamese immigrant sinking her claws into a wealthy American businessman. Not that Devon particularly cared. After all, nobody gossiped about *her* mother.

"You seem better, Pres." Devon took a bite of her Sloppy Joe. She felt too much like a cow eating in front of Maya and her cucumber slices. "You feeling better?"

"Man, I had to hit up the health center this morning I was so freakin' sick but I think it passed. Some twenty-four-hour thing, I guess."

"Lucky you. Just in time"

"No kidding. Lacrosse starts tomorrow, too. I'm gonna be sucking wind. Five bucks says I'll be barfing again by the end of practice. Speak of the devil, the drillmaster herself." Presley nodded across the dining hall.

Sasha Harris, captain of Varsity Girl's Lacrosse—with her perfectly creamy black skin, too-short running shorts and sports bra to highlight her six-pack abs—strolled across the dining hall, grabbing an apple from the community fruit bowl.

"Little Miss Harvard," Presley said with her mouth full. "I'm already dreading graduation next year when she's valedictorian and my dad wonders why I wasn't better friends with her."

"Please, she doesn't have friends, just people she hasn't conquered yet," Devon heard herself say. She felt a twinge of regret. If she knew Sasha better she would probably find a way to sympathize for her and her perfectionist ways.

"Too right, Drew Barry-whore," Presley said.

Devon laughed. "Good one. What about, All Quiet on the Western Slut?"

Presley smiled and almost choked on her Sloppy Joe. Devon stiffened, glimpsing Matt as he entered the dining hall. He went straight to the soda machine and poured himself a Coke. Maybe he had an idea of girls that Hutch was hanging out with.

Devon stood up and grabbed her tray. "I gotta go. See ya back in Bay."

"What?" Presley frowned. "You're gonna leave me with the Freshman 15 over here? Whatever, I'll catch you later, Moby Slut."

"That one sucked," Devon said over her shoulder.

"Oh, there's more where that came from, John Malko-bitch." Presley yelled across the dining hall.

"Jennifer Ho-Pez!" Devon dumped her tray through the window to the dishwashing station and dodged the steam escaping from the industrial sink. She hurried past the teacher's table toward Matt, but she stopped in her tracks when she saw Sasha sidle up next to Matt at the soda machine. Sasha also poured herself a Coke. *Seems like a lot of sugar for an abs-obsessed star athlete*, Devon thought. She pretended to analyze the fruit bowl instead as she eavesdropped. "Hey, Matt. How's your class load?" Sasha asked.

"Maybe you wanna help me with that AP Bio test next week?" Matt said back.

Devon glanced at them, and caught a glimpse of Sasha slipping a folded piece of green paper in the pocket of Matt's hoodie.

"Let's meet up after study hours. I should have my questions ready for you by then," Matt said. He turned and walked away, sipping his Coke. Sasha dumped her soda in the nearby drain and walked out the side door to the dining hall.

Devon suddenly realized that someone was staring at *her*. Right on the other side of the fruit bowl. Deep green eyes on a tanned, freckled face. A girl with black hair in a nest of braids and knots. Could it be the rat's nest Cleo had mentioned? Raven, the pharmacist's sister? She was practically glaring at Devon. Devon opened her mouth to say, "Can I help you?" when—

"You know what they say, an apple a day. . . ." Two hands reached around and squeezed Devon's waist. She jumped and spun around.

"Oh hey."

Grant smiled at her, his eyes twinkling.

"I haven't seen you all day. Where you been? I'll walk you back to Bay. Come on." He held out an elbow and Devon took it. She turned back, but the girl was already gone.

It was still light out, but a peachy-pink shade filled the air as the sun set over the Pacific. They walked across Raiter Lawn in silence, Devon's head falling against Grant's shoulder. It wasn't as pillowy as it was last year, but was that a bad thing? It still comforted. Anyone else would have filled the silence with small talk. Grant knew better.

"There's still a bit of visiting hours left. Want to come up?" Devon asked.

"I thought you'd never ask." Grant winked as he led the way inside.

Was that a loaded question? It hadn't been until now; she'd asked Grant the exact same thing dozens of times. She could almost hear Presley beside her, egging her on. As Grant signed his name in the dorm ledger of visitors, Devon snuck a peek at his tanned neck, the perfect line of bicep poking below his sleeve. *Maybe I should just go for it.*

Devon opened the door to her room. Weird: The light was already on. Then she froze. An old man was lying on her bed. She tried to process what she saw. Phrases like 'Who are you,' 'What are you doing?' and 'Get off my bed' rattled through her brain. Instead Devon just cowered against Grant and let out a scream that devolved into "Ahhhhwhatmyroom?"

The old man sat up and slowly pushed himself off the bed. He held a cowboy hat in his hands and extended a wrinkled hand out toward Devon.

Grant immediately sequestered Devon behind him. "Go call someone, Dev. I got this."

"Wait!" The old man barked.

His brown eyes were milky, his skin weathered behind a gray scruffy beard. A homeless man who wandered up the hillside and randomly into Devon's room? Except that Devon had never known homeless people to tuck in their shirts and wear cowboy boots. He had a large silver belt buckle: three trees. Somewhere deep in Devon's memory, that logo looked familiar, but she couldn't be sure.

"You can't be here," Grant stated. "This is private property. I'll count to three for you to get out of here or I'm forcing you, okay?"

Devon whirled and ran off to find any teacher. Anyone.

"Devon!" the old man croaked. "I'm here for you."

How did he know her name? He must have seen something in her room with her name on it. Devon ran down the stairs and found her dorm head, Mrs. Sosa, already running toward the screams.

"There's a stranger—strange man. . . ." Devon stammered.

Mrs. Sosa ran to Devon's room with Devon close behind. The sliding door was open and Grant was on the patio. The man was already gone.

"Where'd he go?" Devon asked.

"Took off down the hill. He looked like he was about to pass out at the end there. Must have wandered up here off some back roads." Grant squinted toward the trees at the edge of the school property.

Mrs. Sosa gently placed a maternal arm around Devon. "You okay?" she asked, with the trace of a Spanish accent. Her long black hair was tied into a braid down her back, and she wore jeans and a flowing peasant blouse. She was in her early thirties, teaching at Keaton this year through a teacher's exchange program.

"I think so," Devon said automatically.

"I'll tell security and we'll keep the doors locked tonight, mmm?" Mrs. Sosa asked.

Devon nodded in agreement. The bell rang for the end of visiting hours. Mrs. Sosa nodded at Grant but left the two alone to say their goodbyes. Devon leaned against her door.

Grant put a hand on both shoulders. "You're going to be okay. That was just a totally freakish random thing."

"If you weren't here. What do you think. . . ?" Devon didn't want to think about it. What was the old man capable of? He said he came here for her. To kill her? To rape her? To help with her calculus homework? Did he really know who she was?

"Hey, I can see the wheels turning in there." Grant ran a finger down her jawline, stopping at her chin. Suddenly his lips were on hers. The thoughts in Devon's head stopped in their tracks and redirected everything to her lips. What was happening? She was kissing Grant. His lips were soft and strong at the same time. His hands moved down her back and pulled her closer to him. His chest heaved into hers, and she felt herself breathing in rhythm with him so as his chest swelled, hers condensed.

"Who's got AP bio?" someone shouted down the hallway, bringing her back.

She pulled away.

"You have to go." At least that's what she hoped she said. What she was thinking was, *Don't go.*

"I'll come by after study hours, okay?" Grant brushed Devon's bangs to the side. His eyes moved, taking in every inch of Devon's face. A smile twitched on his lips.

"Okay," she whispered.

He squeezed her hand, then hurried out the door. No doubt he would have to explain his tardiness to his dorm head, but his excuse would be campus-wide news in minutes over texts and emails. Strangers wandering onto their hill? In three years at Keaton, a few random townspeople had heckled students, but always outside the gates.

She went to the door, just to make sure Grant was safe on his way home. Her eyes fell to the guest sign-in ledger. Grant's name was at the top, but below it a large swirling signature she hadn't seen before. And Devon's name was written next to the signature. She stepped closer. The old man had signed into her room. How did he know to do that? The name made the blood drain from her cheeks, *Reed Hutchins*.

NIGHT HAD LONG SINCE fallen, but Devon was still wide awake. She lay in bed, staring at the shadowy ceiling. *Reed Hutchins*. Somehow the old man was related to Hutch. His grandfather maybe? The name was definitely familiar; she'd heard it around campus. She closed her eyes, trying to calm the out-of-tune orchestra playing in her head. Her thoughts wandered to Grant's kiss. What did this mean now? Was he officially out of the Friend Zone? And then Cleo's story about Hutch and the pregnancy test surged back to the forefront of her mind.

Her eyes flew open. The shelf above her bed, like every other shelf at Keaton, was carved with etchings from the past: "Misha was here" and "Class of 2002 rulz," dug into the wood. A newer carving stuck out, darker than the rest, even in the shadows. Devon ran her fingers over the scratched words, "We're half-awake in a fake empire. —K. Bell."

Devon remembered a senior had this room last year. Kaylyn Bell. Not a stand-out student. No awards as a senior, not a sports or academic star, and she got into some middle grade university. Something good, but not flashy; nothing her parents were probably bragging about. But Kaylyn had left her mark regardless. Everyone left a mark.

Devon drifted back to her session with Cleo. Hutch had left much more than a song quote behind; he'd left a girl pregnant. A piece of Hutch was still out there. Maybe Devon could help this girl. That's what Hutch was attempting to do by stealing the pregnancy test, wasn't it? *Make sure you're looking at what's really there, not what you want to see.* At this point Hutch was a drug-dealing, girl-knocker-upper, whether she wanted to see it or not. But underneath the secrets he kept, Devon was still certain that she knew who he was. The drugs, this pregnancy, his suicide, they wouldn't be his legacy. Couldn't be. Hutch was more than his mistakes.

Devon grabbed a pen out of her bedside table and wrote the words above her, digging them into the soft wooden shelf. Tracing and re-tracing each letter.

Hutch was here.

CHAPTER 4

Name: Devon Mackintosh
Session Date: Sept. 15
Referred by: Mr. Robins
Reason for Session: Peer Counselor Review

"We just want to make sure this doesn't escalate from here," Mr. Robins said. He used his teeth to rip off the top of a disposable lens wipe packet. The silver wrapping crinkled, and the alcohol-soaked paper instantly assaulted Devon's nose. She squeezed her nose to stifle the rising sneeze. "Suicide clusters tend to happen in smaller communities. And when you add a personality like Jason's, well, we just want to make sure no one follows in his footsteps."

Devon nodded.

Mr. Robins took off his glasses and wiped them down. In four precise moves his glasses were clean and back on his face. "So? How do you think we're doing?" He looked up at her.

"Um. . . ." Devon couldn't get past "suicide clusters." Really? That's what was worrying Mr. Robins? The huge amount of prescription pill abuse, rampant under the faculty's nose, was maybe a better place to start. But Devon couldn't tell him that. *Suicide*

Clusters? It sounded so serious, so blown out of proportion. And when things were blown out of proportion that meant one thing at Keaton: parents. Of course. The parents must have been calling in droves, panicked that whatever had happened to Hutch could happen to their kid.

"I think we're doing well," she finally said. "Matt and Isla were the closest to Hutch, and I don't think suicide is in their immediate plans." Devon wiped her sweaty palms on her jeans. What if she was wrong? Could she be sure Isla wasn't going to take a handful of pills? *I hope not.* Was that really enough to rely on right now? "I'm not seeing any red flag behavior."*

"How is Isla doing? She was quite visibly upset the other day."

"Isla's okay. She's sad, of course, but I'm checking in with her a lot. She had a bit of an anxiety attack before our first session, but I, um. . . ." Devon's thoughts drowned out her voice. Isla had all those pills. The alias to get more pills. Devon could turn her over to Mr. Robins right now and let him worry about her. But she knew that Isla trusted her.

"But you?" He opened his notebook and scribbled something Devon couldn't see.

"Huh? Oh, but, she and Hutch already broke up over the summer so she wasn't technically his girlfriend when he died. Just in case that mattered for your notes." Devon took a deep breath and opened her own notebook. "I was wondering, do you have any suggestions for what to say when anyone asks about how much training I've had? That one's been a little tough to answer."

"Well, that's part of this experiment. You're their peer, you're not meant to be a professional. They can come to me if they want a professional. That's why I have the MFT after my name, see?" He pulled a business card from his blazer to prove the obvious point. Again, Devon contained the urge to roll her eyes. "When they ask I would say it's fair to tell them that you are a concerned

---

* "Drug use, sudden weight loss, and fluctuating emotions are all potential red flag behaviors."
—*Peer Counseling Pilot Program Training Guide* by Henry Robins, MFT

peer. You've been taught everything required to give them adequate support."

"Thanks, I'll try that." *Yeah, like that will work when Cleo Lambert is staring me down.* It was like Mr. Robins didn't speak Human properly. Or maybe he just failed in Teenager.

"Sounds good so far," he said. "We'll keep a close eye on Miss Martin, make sure she works through the grief process properly. And I'll review your notes before your next session with Matt." Mr. Robins wrote a few more things in his notebook. Devon couldn't read upside down, his writing was messy and loose across the page. She did see her and Isla's names written a few times.

"My notes?" Devon played dumb.

"Well, yes, your records are our records. This is a trial program, remember." Mr. Robins scrunched his nose to adjust his glasses. He leveled his eyes at her to drive home the point.

"Right, yeah, of course. Except, the thing is, my notes are really sloppy right now. You know how it is when you're writing fast. Let me just type them up for you so it's easier to read."

"All right. I'll expect them next week." He turned the page in his notebook and kept writing. "I hope you're keeping your clinical distance, Devon."

"Of course. I know that's important. Being impartial helps me see their overall picture better."*

"Good, I glad you remembered that. That's good for today, unless there's anything else you want to discuss?" He leaned back in his chair, arms crossed. She chewed her lip. Mr. Robins was acting as a mentor, so maybe he would come through for her now. She had to find out more than the student rumor mill knew.

"I guess I can't stop thinking about it. Hutch. Are they really sure it was suicide? I was researching OxyContin and the possibility for an accidental overdose is pretty high. And Hutch didn't fit the profile. He wasn't depressed, he wasn't an outcast. . . . I guess I'm

---

* "Working with Feelings" —*Peer Counseling Pilot Program Training Guide* by Henry Robins, MFT

still having a hard time accepting it. I know that's just another stage in the grief process, but I'm not sure this should pass. Shouldn't we find out more? Isn't someone looking into it? They should be, you know."

Mr. Robins cleared his throat. "I know this isn't easy. One of the hardest things about becoming an adult is accepting that we can't change the past. All we can do is focus on what's in front of us, having learned what we should learn. The grief will pass, I promise."*

"Yeah, but—"

"Jason Hutchins had his own troubles," he interrupted in a clipped voice. "We all have to accept that."

"I'm not in denial, if that's what you're thinking. I want to know more, that's all. It's a little tough calming people down when I don't have any information to back up my position. Isn't there something more you can tell me? Was there an autopsy?"

He sighed. "Devon, this isn't a crime show or case that needs to be solved. Especially not by a student. It's done. Now, tomorrow the Hutchins family will be on campus for Jason's memorial service. I expect you to continue to counsel your fellow students, be respectful of what this family is going through, and to drop any theories you might have. Am I understood?" Mr. Robins pushed his glasses up his nose again and leveled his eyes at Devon.

"Understood."

"I think that's good for today." Mr. Robins stood up and Devon followed suit. "I know Stanford is going to love seeing all your success with this program on your application next year. Keep up the good work." He gave Devon a thin-lipped smile.

"Thanks," Devon said, smiling tightly in return. She understood completely.

BROWN OXFORDS STUCK OUT from underneath the stall door—the only one closed, at the end of the row. Devon noticed that they

---

* "List of Don'ts: Don't make promises based on a subject's emotions."—*Peer Counseling Pilot Program Training Guide* by Henry Robins, MFT

were attached to small feet and tan legs. The gagging sound was quickly followed by the contents of someone's stomach filling the toilet.

Devon finished drying her wet hands.

After a few seconds, a flush; a minute after that, Maya emerged. She looked like she'd just been washed up ashore after a shipwreck. Her face was pale, sweaty, and strands of her hair stuck to her cheeks and forehead.

"Presley had the same thing," Devon said as gently as she could. She pretended to look at herself in the mirror. "I'm going into town. Want me to get you anything? Ginger ale? Saltines? Nyquil?"

Maya leaned over the sink next to Devon. She smoothed her hair into a slick ponytail and fished a tube of lipstick from the pocket of her purse. She drew the coral red onto her lips. Devon realized she was staring at Maya's reflection.

"Thanks. I was going to go later." Maya spoke to Devon's reflection with a tired smile. She turned on the faucet and used some water to tame her flyaway hairs. Devon took another look at her own hair. It was still in the braid she slept in. Behind her, Maya burped, loudly and very unladylike. She steadied herself over the sink while the wave of nausea passed.

"You sure?" Devon asked. "It's really no problem."

Maya nodded, squeezing her eyes shut. "A six-pack of Sprite or something would be cool if you see it. Just until my stomach calms down."

"Sure, I'll grab it. And don't worry. Presley said it was just a twenty-four-hour thing."

THE KEATON VAN DROPPED students off in Monte Vista every hour on the weekends. It was only a ten-minute drive up or down the hill. With a deli, a pharmacy, and outdated video store, Monte Vista wasn't much of a town to brag about. But for Keaton students it was the perfect escape from their overscheduled lives. The local beaches were what put Monte Vista on the map and brought

a constant flow of surfers. Surfing defined the town; surfboard wax
was sold next to packs of gum at every cash register.

Devon crossed the street to the Monte Vista pharmacy. As she
cut across the parking lot, a rusted red Volvo with two surfboards
on a roof rack peeled around the corner and nearly took off Devon's toes. The car parked and the driver popped out: a girl a little
younger than Devon wearing a red bikini. Devon noticed her black
hair in a thick pile on the top of her head.

Raven. Here she was, right in front of Devon, again. Devon
thought she had seen that Volvo in the student parking lot before.
Yes, it must be Raven.

She shot a brief blank stare at Devon before walking away.

SHAMPOO AND CONDITIONER (COMBINED for better time effi-
ciency): check. Deodorant: check. Sprite for Maya: check. Devon
crossed item after item off her shopping list until she drifted past
the shelves of pregnancy tests. She stopped to take a closer look.
Early Response. Accu-Test. Positive Plus. Paternity test kits. Who
was Hutch stealing the test for? And why not just buy it?

She glanced up at the angled mirrors leering over the aisles. The
dirty linoleum floor and shelves full of dizzying colors reflected back
from the ceiling. And at the other end of the store, the pharmacy
counter glowed white. Devon spotted a guy in a white lab coat with
blond dreadlocks tied at the nape of his neck, organizing bottles on
the shelves. *Bodhi*, she realized: the former Keaton student Cleo
mentioned. He looked familiar. Of course, she must have seen him
around Monte Vista. In her memory he blurred into all the other
surfers around town, but that was before he had a name.

Cleo had mentioned that Bodhi was Hutch's Get Out Of Jail
Free card that day. Devon watched in the mirrors as Bodhi passed
a tray of filled prescription bottles across the counter. So, he was
a pharmacist: a convenient partner for the school's prescription
pill supplier. Hutch probably helped Bodhi make a fair amount
of money off Keaton students who wouldn't bat an eyelash at

paying $20 for a dose of Vicodin to liven up (or deaden) a Saturday night stuck on campus.

She thought about approaching him, when Bodhi suddenly took off his white lab coat and ducked out a side door. Maybe he was just taking a break? Devon left her basket in front of the pregnancy tests and hurried out to the parking lot.

THE TOWN OF MONTE Vista was full of secrets that only Keaton students found valuable. The Monte Vista Deli would sell cigarettes without carding for one. The grocery store always carded, but the gas station would sell liquor to the fakest of IDs. Presley had once used her gym membership card from home to buy vodka, and the clerk never questioned it. They knew that as long as the cameras caught them showing *something* to the clerk, no one would get in trouble. Devon figured it was because Keaton students lived by so many rules on campus, rules in real life were just another set of boundaries to be pushed and worked around. Working around rules was the true cornerstone of the Keaton education, the one no one ever discussed.

The three dumpsters behind Monte Vista Pharmacy hid another secret: They formed a half circle that shielded any illicit activities from the outside world. Students bought pot from local Monte Vista surfers, shoulder-tapped older locals to buy booze, and even sometimes went dumpster-diving for rejected pharmacy items.

Knowing all that, Devon was still shocked when she spotted Bodhi giving Matt a bro hug within the dumpsters' safe confines. She crouched low and peered through a crack between two of them. She could see Matt and Bodhi clearly, passing a joint back and forth and talking quietly about something. Hutch probably, but who knew what else these two had in common? Matt reached into his jeans pocket. Devon only saw the flash of green before it hit her: The same green paper Sasha Harris had passed Matt in the dining hall. Now he was passing it to Bodhi. She sat on the hot asphalt to absorb this new information. It was all quite clear. Matt was getting his pharmaceuticals from Bodhi. Which also confirmed that Hutch and Bodhi had been doing the same thing before Hutch overdosed.

Devon still couldn't picture Hutch as a drug dealer. But clearly she was the only one who couldn't. Why would he get himself tangled in this world?

We can't change the past. All we can do is focus on what's in front of us. Mr. Robins's words floated to the front of Devon's mind.

She peeked between the dumpsters again. Matt was giving Bodhi another half-hug/half-handshake. Then he walked away, disappearing around the far corner of the building. Devon stood up and wiped the dirt off her jeans. Somehow she had to get Bodhi to talk to her.

Summoning her courage, she rounded the dumpsters. "Hey. You're Bodhi, right?"

He turned and shoved his hands in his pocket of his low-hanging plaid shorts. His black-and-white-checkered Vans bore the telltale scuffs of a skater. Without the white coat he'd worn inside, Bodhi looked like just another local surf bum.

"Who's asking?" His eyes flickered behind her, as if he expected a handful of cops to appear.

"I'm Devon. Devon Mackintosh. I go to Keaton."

Bodhi laughed. "No shit."

"That obvious, huh?" She smiled and kept a safe distance. It was just like counseling: Make him comfortable, don't be threatening.

"I've seen you in town before. What's up? I don't have anything, you know. Somebody gave you old information." Bodhi checked his frayed, Velcro watch.

"Do you have a minute to talk about Hutch?"

"Jason? Yeah, I read about it. Shame, right? That kid seemed to have everything going on." Bodhi looked past Devon again. He shifted from one foot to the other.

"Yeah, shame," Devon said.

Bodhi turned to go. "I didn't really know the kid, so I don't—"

"Was it yours?" Devon interrupted.

He whirled to face her. The sunlight picked up blond whiskers sprouting on his chin. He was only a few inches taller than Devon, but his broad shoulders made him seem bigger, more powerful than most of the scrawny guys at Keaton. Hutch had shoulders like that. So did Matt. Devon had to admit, surfing came with an automatic sex appeal.

"What are you talking about?" Bodhi's hands went back in his pockets.

"The Oxy that Hutch took. Did it come from you?" Devon could hear her voice; it sounded much sharper and more stable than she felt. She knew she had no right to talk to a stranger this way.

Bodhi cleared his throat and spat on the ground next to him. "Look, I heard it was an overdose too, but that doesn't mean shit. He could have gotten that from anywhere. Hutch was resourceful like that." Bodhi stared hard back at Devon. "And I don't appreciate the accusation. You should watch yourself. No need for a girl like you to get into trouble."

"I don't think it was suicide," Devon blurted out.

"That doesn't change the fact that he's still dead."

She moved closer to him. "I know he was here that day. He stole something and you helped him."

He shook his head. "That didn't happen," he said. She was now close enough she could see where the tan line started at the base of his throat.

"Was he here with anyone that day?" she pressed.

"Why are you digging all this up?" Bodhi demanded.

She held his steely gaze. "Hutch is going to be remembered as the boy who killed himself. The troubled teen that OD'd. And I don't think he did it. Don't you think we owe it to him to dig a little deeper? He'd do it for you."

Bodhi looked at his watch again and drummed his hands against his thighs. "I can tell you this; he didn't get it from me. That's a controlled substance; I wouldn't be handing it out. And besides,

Hutch hated that shit. Wouldn't even take cough medicine any-more because he didn't trust it. If he really wanted to kill himself, it wouldn't have been with pills, let alone Oxy. But judging from the look on your face, you've figured that out already. Now I gotta go." Bodhi started for the back door, then hesitated. "You know, the coroner is in town from Santa Cruz. He surfs. Maybe I'll see him on the water."

Devon smiled. "And maybe you'll let me know if you find any-thing out?"

"Maybe," Bodhi said back. "Yeah. Maybe I will."

BY THE TIME DEVON finished her shopping, the Keaton Van was pulling out of the pharmacy parking lot. She waved after it, but the van didn't stop. *Great, I've got an hour to kill.* She let her can-vas shopping bags slip onto the ground. Maya's Sprite cans clinked against each other.

Spotting a shady corner across the parking lot, she set up camp. She pulled a copy of *Chekhov: The Essential Plays* out of one of her bags. At least she could catch up on some homework while she waited. She'd only read a few lines when a car honked.

"Get in," a hoarse voice commanded.

Devon looked up to see the beat-up red Volvo from earlier. The black-haired girl was smoking a rolled cigarette, her hand dangling out the window. She was still wearing her red bikini.

"You're Raven, right?" Devon asked.

"Yeah, duh. Get in. My brother said I should give you a ride back up the hill. Saw you miss the van." The girl started scrolling through an iPod.

Better than sitting on this curb for the next hour, Devon thought. "Cool, thanks. A ride would be great." She stuffed herself and the bags into the passenger seat.

"Nice to meet you officially," the girl said. She held out a hand for Devon to shake. A thick row of hemp bracelets dangled from her wrist.

"You, too. I'm Devon."

"I wasn't stalking you, I swear. Or was I?" Raven gave Devon a wide-eyed crazy look and then laughed. "I'm just screwing with you. Bodhi said you were a little uptight." She plugged the iPod into a mini set of speakers precariously perched on either side of the dashboard. There seemed to be a thin layer of sand over everything in the car. Devon saw a pile of beach towels in the back seat. "You got the right one."

"The right what?"

Raven pressed on the gas. The right speaker slid forward. Devon caught it just before it fell into her lap. She wedged it back in place onto a sticky spot on the dashboard. *Ah, the right one.*

She suddenly noticed Raven's iPod sitting in a homemade-looking dock, with a tangle of wires attached to an outdated tape deck.

"You, ah, make your own iPod adapter thing?" Devon asked, amazed.

"Yeah, it's easier than you think. Pretty basic wiring." Raven kept driving.

Yeah, basic wiring for you, Devon thought. The most sophisticated wiring Devon had accomplished was a second-grade science experiment involving a battery and an anemic light bulb.

Raven turned onto Via Montana Road. Devon counted the bracelets on Raven's right arm. One, two, three, four, five . . . hand-woven, wet, with frayed edges. One of them had a small shell looped through the string. It reminded Devon of the necklace Hutch had made for Isla. Guess hemp was the cool thing these days. She must have missed the memo, as Isla would have said. Raven's hair was still wet, but the sticky smell of saltwater was inescapable.

"Bodhi said you wanted to know about Hutch," Raven said. She kept her eyes on the road ahead.

"So, Bodhi's your brother? Sorry, I didn't see the family resemblance." Devon tried to avert her eyes from the rat nest of hair. She saw that Raven was driving barefoot. At least she was wearing jean shorts.

"The black hair did it? Yeah, the whole family is scarily blond, had to rebel somehow, ya know." She shrugged. But she did have the same piercing green eyes as Bodhi, and a batch of freckles dusted her cheeks and nose. "So, what'd you talk about?"

"I was asking if Bodhi had seen Hutch before he died. Sorry, this all must be a lot of boring talk about someone you didn't even know. Crappy way to start your freshman year I'll bet. . . ." Devon's voice trailed off.

Raven was crying. A tear dripped from her lashes

"We don't have to talk about this if you don't want to," Devon said gently.

Raven kept her eyes on the road. Her lips pressed tightly together. The surfboards rattling in their rack overhead. Neighborhood streets were getting farther and farther apart the closer they got to the mountain, replaced with pine trees and boulders. The carved wooden The Keaton School sign loomed ahead. Devon glanced at Raven again, but she seemed oblivious to the approaching turn.

"You can drop me at the bottom of the hill if that's easier?" Devon tried. Raven didn't acknowledge her or the sign. The Volvo sped right past where Devon needed to go. Raven used her bracelet-laden hand to wipe the tears off her cheeks.

"Or, if you want to take me back to Monte Vista? I can wait for the next bus." Devon realized she didn't know this girl at all. Really, Raven could be anyone: a crazy girl scooping up stray Keaton students and taking them on joyrides. Bodhi could have turned this lunatic onto Devon out of spite. Had she pissed him off enough to deserve this? "Raven?"

"Hang on," Raven said.

She turned a quick left onto a dirt road. Once again, Devon caught her speaker as it slid across the dashboard. Once that was back in place she gripped the sides of her seat. The Volvo kicked up a cloud of dust and the decade-old shocks lurched at every bump as they climbed up the gravely hillside. The dense trees gave way to grapevines tied to stakes. Row after row, the grapevines stood tall in perfect precision. Devon felt the cans of Sprite jostle around her feet; she'd have to remember to tell Maya not to open those immediately. If she ever got them to Maya. Where the hell were they going?

Out the window the vines seemed endless, stitched across the hillside. To her left a row of pines seemed to demarcate the property line. Devon caught a glimpse of the Keaton flag waving proud at the top of the hill in the distance; they were on the mountainside behind school. The car took a right turn and suddenly Devon was sitting in a circular driveway in front of a small craftsman house. They lurched to a stop.

Raven killed the engine.

"This property belongs to Reed Hutchins, Hutch's grandfather. This is the Athena Vineyard, named after Reed's wife. Reed hired Bodhi and me to work here over the summer. Hutch came down in July and lived here in the guest house."

Reed Hutchins. The name rattled in her head. He'd gone to Devon's dorm room and now here she was on his property. What was the connection?

Raven nodded toward the battered wooden door. She turned to Devon, fresh tears brimming from her eyes. "Every day Hutch. . . ." She exhaled slowly, collecting herself. "Every day he brought me lunch. No matter where I was on the property, he made sure I didn't work through lunch. It was just a stupid peanut butter and jelly sandwich, but he never missed a day." Raven looked out the window toward the vines.

She's looking for him, Devon thought. She recognized that look, that searching, like Hutch could still be hanging out where you last left him.

"You know, he said there were two kinds of people in this world." Raven said.

"Those that like peanut butter and those that don't," Devon responded without thinking. She could almost see Hutch in the vineyard, walking through the dirt in his hiking boots, bringing

Raven a sandwich on the vineyard. He probably made a game out of it.

Raven's mouth fell open.

"I heard him say that once, too," Devon said. "He was a peanut butter person."

"Yeah, he was." Raven smiled, but her chin quivered. She leaned across Devon and flipped open the glove compartment. She pulled out a small pouch of tobacco and rolled herself a cigarette. "Want one?"

"Um, no thanks. I don't smoke."

"Of course you don't." Raven licked her cigarette and lit it. After a long smoky exhale, "It wasn't suicide, Devon."

"You and I are the only ones that seem to think so," Devon said. She found herself heaving a shaky sigh of relief. Raven was no psychopath. Raven was a girl in pain, just like she was. True: No matter what she thought, Hutch was still gone. But here was Raven, fighting just as hard as Devon to keep her memories of Hutch fresh. Devon wasn't alone in her beliefs anymore. "Maybe, it's up to us to prove it."

CHAPTER 5

September 10, 2010
Freshman Year

The lock clicked into place. Devon flinched at the sound. Hutch
grinned like a little boy about to open his Christmas presents.

"That was exciting, wasn't it?" he said. Hutch crawled out from
underneath the table and extended a hand toward Devon, but she
stayed on the ground.

"We're officially screwed, aren't we?" she asked.

"I wouldn't say 'officially.'" Hutch used both hands to pull
Devon to her feet. "More like a temporary forced relocation."

"You make us sound like refugees," Devon said.

"Aren't we? I mean out there," Hutch pointed to the door.
"Out there is kind of like war. Every day we gotta fight to keep up
appearances, grades, athletic ability, but in here . . . in here it's just
you and me and Nutter Butter pancakes." Hutch cracked an egg
into the mixing bowl of batter. "Come on, you gotta crumble up the
cookies."

Devon pulled a cookie from the container and crunched it in her hand. Her over-analytical brain was working overtime on other matters. *Were they stuck in here for the night? Had Hutch known this would happen?* She thought he seemed disturbingly not disturbed by their situation. As far as she could track it, this night had gone from boring → exciting → romantic → nerve-racking, all in a matter of fifteen minutes. Devon stayed frozen with her hand clenched above the bowl. Hutch tossed an eggshell into the trash at the end of the counter and noticed Devon's pensive stare.

"Hey, we're fine, you know. This night will end at some point; it's just that how it ends remains to be seen. All we can do is enjoy the time we have now." Hutch wrapped a hand around Devon's wrist and slowly pulled her fingers back, letting the cookie fall into the bowl below.

Devon looked up at him. That spiky hair, his eyes brown or hazel, she couldn't tell in this light, but they were deep, melted chocolate, standing out in contrast to his bushy eyebrows. And the way he looked at her—calm, unflinching, solid—made her relax.

"How are you so . . . so . . . you?" Devon asked. As soon as she heard the question out loud she knew it sounded as stupid as she thought. But she didn't know how else to ask. How did this guy, this guy who theoretically had been alive for the same amount of time as she had, come to have such a different attitude? Hutch seemed to have the kind of calm people meditated for years to find. Here he was, fourteen and already a Zen master.

Hutch laughed and reached for another cookie. "How am I me?" He used two hands to crush a cookie into the batter. "Kind of an existential question, dontcha think?"

"No, come on, you know what I mean." Devon crumbled a cookie now too. It felt better to be doing something with her hands, a reminder that she was still breathing. Like the stories she heard about people getting stuck on desert islands; it wasn't the elements that could kill you, it was the boredom. Or was it the solitude?

Either way, staying busy was the best way to avoid going stir-crazy, she was sure of it. "It's like nothing fazes you."

Hutch chuckled. "That's my brother, Eric. Everything fazes him. He got the burden of being older and worried about what everyone thinks of him, especially our dad. That's just not me. I don't care what anyone thinks. I refuse to bend over backward for everyone else until I'm broken like he is. I'm broken in my own way, I guess."

Devon noticed that as he stared into the batter bowl, the top of his jaw twitched just in front of his ears. He had an over-analytical brain, too. "Aren't we all?" Devon said back. She sounded more cynical than she'd planned. She didn't want to. She wanted to make Hutch comfortable, like he had for her.

"Oh yeah? How are you broken?" Hutch stopped crushing the cookies and gave Devon his full attention.

"I don't know." Devon thought back to a therapy session her mom made her attend over the summer: a preemptive strike against any teenage rebellion that might have been brewing. "Well, I was a sperm bank baby, so I really don't know anything about my dad, which means I probably have daddy issues. And I'm on scholarship, which means I probably have a complex about money." Devon stopped. Why was she telling Hutch all this? *The cookies might have brought him in, but psycho-babble would definitely send him running out the nearest door.*

"Impressive," Hutch said as he poured the batter onto the hot frying pan. The *hiss* pulled Devon out of her inner monologue. "Sounds like someone spent a little time in therapy. What's with the sperm bank thing? You have two moms?"

"No, just the one."

Hutch nodded and scanned the shelves for something above them, but Devon wondered if he was avoiding eye contact.

The pancake blobs simmered in the pan. The smell of peanut butter made Devon's mouth water. She grabbed a spatula on the shelf behind her and went to work flipping the pancakes over. Hutch stepped back, letting her slip in between him and the stove.

She could feel his eyes on the back of her head. And then his hand was on the back of her neck, gently smoothing stray strands of hair into place. Maybe she hadn't scared him away. Maybe he was pitying her now. Maybe there was something else going on.

Stop thinking, she thought. Devon turned around to face him.

Hutch's lips curled into a slight smile. He stroked her hair away from her face and brought her hand to his lips and kissed her palm again. Devon's heart thudded. He reached for her chin and pulled her face toward his and kissed her. It wasn't the usual teenage boy tongue-groping kiss she expected. He pressed his lips against hers and lingered softly. Devon closed her eyes. The electricity in her body relaxed into a warm glow.

He pulled away and Devon realized she was standing on her tiptoes. She slowly lowered her heels to the ground and opened her eyes to Hutch. He was watching her, smiling, waiting.

Devon smiled back. Hutch exhaled.

"I've wanted to do that all week." Hutch reached around Devon and turned off the burner.

"All week?" The red glow pulsed through her body again.

"Since our first day assembly. You sat in front of me. Red shirt with the corner of your shoulder poking out."

"So you've been planning this mission since then?" Devon laughed. The fears she had before, the tension in the air, all of it vanished. This adventure was theirs now, as if they'd planned it together all along.

"Yeah, that's it. I willed you to arrive in the Dining Hall with cookies tonight."

"Well, I willed you to make Nutter Butter pancakes. I guess we're even." Devon raised an eyebrow at Hutch. Up until now, Ariel was the one who raised her eyebrow whenever she flirted with guys. It was Ariel's way of acknowledging she may be crossing a line, but happily crossing it anyway. Ariel reveled in kicking up trouble, the kid that can't help splash in a rain puddle. Now it was Devon who'd splashed.

Hutch grabbed a plate from a nearby shelf, and Devon slid the pancakes from the pan onto the plate. "And the most important part of this nutritious meal. . . ." He wandered back into the walk-in fridge. Devon hoisted herself onto the counter. "Jackpot!" Hutch reemerged from the fridge carrying two glasses of milk. "The culprit that started this whole mess."

Devon felt herself grinning stupidly. She handed him a fork.

Hutch shoved an oversized bite of pancake in his mouth. "Dude, that is amazing. Just wait."

Devon took her first bite. She wasn't even thinking about pancakes, but the crunchy peanut butter cookie bits melted into the pancake flavor perfectly. "Wow, Nutter Butter pancakes. Officially a thing now."

"See, I told you. Hold up. I think we gotta go next level." Hutch pried open the tin of chocolate syrup and dipped a spoon into the goo, drizzling it over the plate. "NOW it's a thing. Just needed the chocolate to call out the peanut butter, you know."

"You think we could get the kitchen to make these again?" Devon asked.

"I'm sure if you smile that smile of yours, my guess is you could get the kitchen to do just about anything you want," Hutch said as he stuffed an oversized bite in his mouth.

It never occurred to Devon before that she was a girl that could get guys to do things for her. What was it like to wield that kind of power? She'd seen Ariel use her feminine ways to get free coffee at coffee shops, free rides on the BART, and even free clothes. But what would happen after this? Would she and Hutch become a couple? Would Hutch be the guy she married years from now and they could say they were high-school sweethearts? What did it really mean to be someone's "sweetheart?" *Don't jump too far ahead—you're still locked in a kitchen,* her over-analytical brain reminded her.

"I didn't mean anything before, about the two moms stuff. It's totally not my business. And no biggie if you went to therapy. My parents made me go a lot. They were obsessed with finding the right medication for me when I was younger and 'out of control.' Turns out I was just a ten-year-old boy, and that's kind of what happens." Hutch leaned back on his elbows and kicked his shoes off.

"Well, you know what they say about an unexamined life not being worth living. I kinda always liked the idea of that." Devon finished the last bite of pancake and dropped her fork next to Hutch's on the plate.

"Mine's a tie," Hutch said.

"A tie?" Devon leaned back onto her elbows beside him.

"My philosophy. It's a Robert Frost tie. Between 'The Road Not Taken' and 'Snowy Evening.'"

"Oh, is that about choosing the road less traveled? I think I remember that one."

Hutch looked up at the ceiling and recited, "'Somewhere ages and ages hence: Two roads diverged in a wood, and I, I took the one less traveled by, and that has made all the difference.'"

He finished and looked to Devon with that crooked smile of his. She now understood that this is the face Hutch made when he was proud of himself.

"That makes sense. The not-supposed to part of you, it's the road less traveled."

"I just like the idea of looking back at my life and feeling like I made different choices than everyone else, you know? Most people are inherently boring if you really dig deep. They don't want much, they don't veer from their chosen path, and they're generally scared of change. I don't know, at least that's how my grandfather tells it. I don't want to be like fifty and realize that I was one of those people who didn't bother to think outside the box. That's why the other poem is tied."

"What's the other one about?" Devon asked, rapt.

"I won't do the whole thing, although, I could, it's one of my hidden talents, reciting poetry. But the part I love the most is, 'The woods are lovely, dark and deep, But I have promises to keep, and miles to go before I sleep, and miles to go before I sleep.'" Hutch closed his eyes. A small, contented smile was fixed on his lips. Devon wanted to kiss those lips again, but it seemed better to let the poem have some space. She let the last line hang in the air a moment longer.

"I really like that one," she said. "I'm not sure I totally get it, but it's cool."

Hutch rolled to his side and looked at Devon, his head resting in his hand. "There's always something else to do. Like it'd be easy to stop or be lulled into something, but there's miles to go before I can stop doing any of it. I don't know, that probably sounds really lame."

"No, I get it. I think we all need that thing, whatever it is, God, family, pancakes, that keep us going even on those days when you just don't want to get out of bed. You've got miles to go, and I've got Nutter Butters." Devon leaned down now, level with Hutch.

Hutch's face grew serious. His fingers intertwined with hers. "You should always have Nutter Butters," he said, his eyes locking with hers. "Always." Devon waited. The way Hutch bit his lip, she knew there was more to come. "This kid at my school last year. I didn't know him. I mean, I'd seen him around, but . . . he committed suicide. They did this all-school memorial and the principal read some lame poem that no one listened to and then the band played that Sarah McLachlan song, 'I Will Remember You.' I remember thinking that this kid, wherever he was, must be laughing his ass off or hating this stupid ceremony, or both. The whole thing was royally wrong. Like you're here one day and the next they're playing Sarah McLachlan in your honor, and no one knew the kid well enough to play a song he would have actually liked. How could no one know what song he would have wanted?"

Devon squeezed his hand. "Okay, so what song would you want played at your stupid memorial service?"

Hutch sat back up. "First off, my memorial service wouldn't be stupid. I expect people to laugh at my funeral, have fun. I don't get why funerals have to always be so sad. And 'Kodachrome,' for sure. That's what I want playing at my funeral."

"Never heard of it."

"Paul Simon. He's kind of awesome. My grandfather got me into it. I'll burn it for you."

"If we ever get out of here," Devon said.

Hutch leaned over her, blocking out her view of the stucco ceiling.

"I've never told anyone that. Only you and my grandfather know I'm a secret Paul Simon fan. Can you handle that kind of secret?"

"I don't know. Sounds like a lot of pressure." Devon said back with a smirk.

Hutch reached out and stroked the side of her cheek. "As far as I can tell, you handle pressure well."

Present Day, September 16

DEVON'S EYES SNAPPED OPEN. The sunlight pierced the curtains. She found herself blinking at, Kaylyn's carved words in the bookshelf: *We're half-awake in a fake empire.* She rolled to her side and curled into a ball. Her clock blinked 9:30 A.M. Thirty minutes until she had to be there. Forty minutes until reality would invade. She closed her eyes again, hoping for another glimpse of Hutch. *You handle pressure well.* His words clanged around in her head. *Kodachrome.* She still hadn't heard the song that Hutch wanted played at his funeral. Should she have told someone that it's what Hutch would have wanted? Was it too late? Would anyone have believed her anyway?

Devon forced herself out of bed.

She ripped the tags off her black Banana Republic dress. So ironic! It was perfectly plain and boring, but her mom insisted she have a formal interview outfit on hand for her college trips this fall break. College trips that Hutch would never take. Her fingers paused on the buttons over her stomach. There were lots of things Hutch would never do again. Make pancakes. Surf. Graduate from Keaton. Kiss a girl.

She left her dress hanging open and snapped her laptop open, searching Paul Simon. There among a list of his songs was 'Koda-chrome.' Devon pressed play and sat back on her bed. It sounded old, a relic, but the upbeat guitar made her smile. Only Hutch would want a happy cheerful song at his funeral; this was no Sarah McLachlan anthem.

The first lyrics came out, "*When I think back on all the crap I learned in high school, it's a wonder I can think at all.*" Devon laughed out loud. This was exactly Hutch's sense of humor. "*Koda-chrome, it give us the nice bright colors, it give us the greens of summers, makes you think all the world's a sunny day. . . .*" Her cheeks were wet. She was smiling, but couldn't stop crying at the same time. It was so simple. It was Instagram, but real. A song about old camera film that made everything look better; that's just what Hutch did. He could make everything brighter, memories better, jokes funnier. Or maybe that was just her experience of him.

Tap, tap, tap!

Someone was knocking on her glass door. Devon wiped her cheeks and quickly finished buttoning her dress. She pulled the curtain aside, and there was Matt. Black slacks, a white button-down with a red striped tie draped open around his neck. He held his black blazer squished in one hand while his other hand shielded his eyes as he peered through Devon's glass door. She slid the door open.

"Matt? Are you okay?"

"Hey, I'm glad you're here." Matt walked right into Devon's room. 9:45 A.M. on a Sunday morning was definitely not part of visiting hours, according to the *Keaton Companion*. But rules would probably be lax today.

"I need your help." Matt said. He parked his feet in front of Devon. He stood up straight, eyes toward her ceiling, and chest puffed out. His hands tapped against his thighs. From the sweat glistening down the side of his face and his pulse throbbing along a vein in his neck, Devon figured he was on some kind of upper. More Adderall probably.

"Matt. . . ."

"Go ahead, I'm ready." He said still looking up.

"Matt! What do you need help with? You need to tell me that part."

He sighed and shook his head. The tapping stopped for a moment. "Sorry, I'm a mess. My tie. I don't know how to tie it. I mean, I know how, but not today. I've been trying all morning and it's like my hands just forgot. So, could you?" He looked back up at the ceiling and puffed his chest out again, waiting.

Devon sighed. "Don't take this the wrong way, but you live with at least twenty other guys. Wouldn't asking any one of them make more sense?"

Matt gave her a weak smile. "Today doesn't exactly make sense."

Devon smiled back. He didn't need to say anything else. "Lemme just look it up, I've never done this before." She flipped her laptop open again and pulled up an instructional video. "Okay, I just grab here. . . ." She pulled at the tie ends. "Wait, this is backward. Here, you gotta sit." Devon guided Matt to sit on her bed. She knelt behind him, hands draped over his shoulders as she tried to follow the video.

Matt's foot tapped on the floor. Devon could smell his cologne. She had never been this close to Matt before. It struck her: Any freshman girl would trade places with Devon in a second. This was Matt Dolgens, gorgeous, cool, beyond connected, beyond rich, beyond everything and everyone. Except that now he couldn't tie his own tie. She finished the last loop and gave him a final pat on the chest.

"There. That should do the trick," she said.

"Wait." Matt grabbed her hands and wrapped them across his chest. Devon knew he didn't want her to let go. She felt the same. She just wanted someone to hold her close, make her feel like this Hutch darkness wouldn't trap her alone forever. She leaned forward, resting her chin on Matt shoulder and shut her eyes tightly. He squeezed her back.

For what seemed like a very long time, they sat together on her bed in a silent embrace, breathing in the same rhythm. Devon looked at the clock. 9:55 A.M. Gently she pulled away. "It's time to go," she whispered. She leaned back, sitting back on her heels. Matt leaned forward and adjusted his shoes, shiny black oxfords; he'd probably never worn them before.

There was a spot of green paper poking out of his pants pocket. Devon swallowed. It would be wrong to take it; Matt would hate her and they'd just shared a moment—something real and profound. Matt wasn't faking. He was in pain. But . . . Hutch. They were on the way to his funeral. If a stolen scrap of green paper did anything to explain why Hutch was being buried today, it would be worth it.

Devon rubbed Matt's back while he was still leaning over. With her right hand she slipped two fingers into his pocket and pulled out the green scrap. Matt turned around to face her. She quickly smiled at him and palmed the paper. "You know, Hutch was right about you," he said with a genuine smile. He stood up and held out a hand. She froze. Had he seen what she'd done? *Play dumb. That usually works.* She offered her left hand and Matt helped her up from the bed.

"Thanks for the help with the tie and all," he said.

Devon nodded. She took Matt's hand and led him through the glass doors, tucking the crinkled green paper into her pocket.

"Let's make him proud," she whispered.

THE CROWD OUTSIDE THE Keaton Chapel was even bigger than Devon had expected. Seniors, juniors, most of the sophomores, and even a few freshmen lingered on the grass outside, still wet from the morning dew. Mr. Robins chatted with a circle of students, his red tie sticking out in an ocean of black. Devon quickly dropped her hand from Matt's before he spotted her.

"I gotta say hi to the family," Matt said to Devon. "See ya in there."

He wandered to the chapel entrance where Hutch's parents stood side by side with Hutch's older brother, Eric. At Family Weekend events over the past two years Devon remembered seeing Hutch's mom, Mitzi, always at the side of his father, Bill. Mitzi wore a black pencil skirt with matching black blazer, probably Chanel. Everything was fitted to highlight her small frame, Pilates-sized within an ounce of perfection. Her hair was a deep walnut color, too deep and dark to be natural for a woman in her fifties. Devon fought to push the judgmental thoughts out of her head. Mitzi was at her son's funeral. She wondered what it must have been like for Mitzi to get dressed for this morning. Bill, too, for that matter. Mitzi gripped her husband's arm while Headmaster Wyler approached to console them.

"You're doing morning sessions now?" a voice called.

Devon whirled around to see Grant running to catch up with her. His blond hair was wet and slicked back. For once, he wasn't wearing his signature white hat. But he still looked sporty and casual: a gray suit and white shirt with no tie. For some reason the lack of tie bugged Devon, like it was rude of him not to dress more formally.

"Morning sessions?" she asked.

"You and Matt seemed awfully . . . intimate." He said the last word with a bite to it.

Devon stopped walking. She wanted to be mad. But she felt the paper in her pocket, poking against her thigh and knew she wasn't riding high on morality at the moment either. She sighed, changing her tone. "Today's pretty difficult for everyone. I was just helping, okay?"

Grant reached out and took her hands in his. "Sorry. I saw you two holding hands." He pulled her into his chest for a long hug. He swayed a little from side to side. Devon closed her eyes, letting herself be lulled into him. "Let's just get through this," he whispered with his cheek pressed to her head. Then he leaned back and faced her. His blue eyes caught the sunlight. "I want to see you later. Think we both need a little distraction? What do you say?"

Devon took his hand and turned toward the organ music emanating from the chapel. "Like you said, let's just get through this first."

Inside the chapel doors, Eric Hutchins was the first to greet the mourners. This was a Keaton legend, right in front of her. So many rumors and stories. The best: Headmaster Wyler had lost a bet to Eric, and had to run a lap around campus in nothing but his running shoes and underwear. But here now, Eric was just someone who'd lost his brother. He was tall like Hutch, with long brown hair that was gelled back and tucked behind his ears. His eyes had the puffy, swollen look of someone who has been crying. Still, he was classically good-looking, like Hutch would have been. Devon noticed his cheek twitching at the top of his jaw, clenching like Hutch's used to. What could he possibly be feeling right now? She resisted the urge to hug him.

Grant gave Eric a one-armed hug. "I'm so sorry, bro," he murmured.

"Thanks, man. Hey listen, will you be a pallbearer? My knee's still busted and can't take the weight." He plucked the white rose from his lapel and tucked it into Grant's. "Thanks."

"Of course. Anything you need. Oh, this is Devon." Grant said.

Devon stepped forward and shook hands with Eric. "It's nice to meet you. I'm so sorry. Hutch, I mean, Jason, was. . . ." She stammered looking for the right word.

"Don't worry. I know. Hutch was Hutch." Eric gave Devon a reassuring pat on her shoulder and turned to the next guest in the receiving line.

Devon snuck a glance over her shoulder, then another. It was Maya, looking stunning in a black cocktail dress.

"I wasn't sure. . . ." Eric started.

"I wouldn't miss it," Maya cut in before Eric could finish. She continued inside without shaking Mr. and Mrs. Hutchins' hands.

Eric stared at Maya as she slid into a pew. Devon tried to stop staring, herself, but couldn't. Was Eric really checking Maya out? At
his brother's funeral?

The Keaton chapel was small, built for no more than two hundred people, packed tightly into narrow wooden pews—and far
beyond full capacity today. The entire wall at the front was made
up of windows facing the North, so the sun was always bright but
never direct. Normally, the effect was uplifting and almost other-
worldly—but with the glossy closed coffin up front near the altar,
Devon found herself wanting to turn away. The coffin was strewn
with white roses and draped with the green Keaton flag. Next to it
sat an easel with a blown-up picture of Hutch in a boat: smiling,
tan, happy.

Devon forced back tears. She clenched her jaw. Who decided to
put the Keaton flag on his coffin? It almost made sense. The venue
usually reserved for chorus recitals, poetry readings, and holiday
services was now a funeral home. But it would have bugged Hutch.
He refused to wear clothes with visible labels. The flag was like an
overbearing corporate sponsor: *Hutch's Funeral, brought to you by
The Keaton School! Keeping track of your kids, dead or alive!*

But it all came down to money. No doubt Headmaster Wyler
was making a big showing about Hutch since there weren't any
future Hutchins kids coming up the pipeline to fill his ranks and
keep the donations coming in. Wyler was an expert at reminding
the parents that the school was basically raising their kids and turning them into productive adults. Or trying.

Whispering thinned into silence as Headmaster Wyler stepped up
to the podium. After he welcomed the Hutchins family and Keaton
community, he turned the floor over to seniors Thomas Anders and
Becca Linden for a musical interlude. Naturally: Thomas and Becca
were stars of the music program. (Even though, of course, they'd
probably spent less time with Hutch than Devon had.) Thomas was
considered a piano genius; Becca, a shoo-in for Julliard or *American Idol* or both with her angelic voice. And Devon had to admit,

when Becca took to the front of the room, her backlit blonde braid almost looked like a halo.

Thomas sat down at the piano and started playing. Devon wasn't sure if she wanted to laugh or barf. "In the Arms of an Angel," by Sarah McLachlan. This was Hutch's nightmare, come true. He wasn't here to defend it, to wake up from the bad dream, or have anyone in his family protest. Devon remembered hearing somewhere once: "Funerals aren't for the dead, they are for the living." That made perfect sense now. This display was all about Hutch's parents. They had to hold their heads up high.

Devon looked around the chapel. Two pews in front and to her left Presley sat with Pete, their heads were lowered, but Devon could see they were passing notes on the program back and forth. Sasha Harris was a few rows in front of Devon, trembling slightly. Maya sat near the front with her head bowed. She used a tissue to dab at her eyes every few minutes. Devon spotted Cleo standing in the back, looking bored. But where was Isla?

Matt sat in the front row next to Eric. The song came to a close (mercifully!) and Devon noticed Eric pass a few white index cards to Matt, who then stepped up to the dais. Devon sat up a little straighter, nervous for Matt, and congratulating herself for a good job on his tie. Grant patted her thigh, and she slipped her hand under his. It probably caught him off guard to see her holding hands with Matt, especially considering she and Matt weren't friends publicly. She shouldn't have been annoyed. Besides, it wasn't as if she could ever tell Grant that Matt was in Peer Counseling with her, even though it was easy enough to assume.

Matt cleared his throat and read his index cards. The audience shuffled in their seats, blew noses, and dried their eyes. "The Hutchins family asked me to say a few words about Jason, Hutch to those of us who knew him best." Matt projected his voice nicely to the back of the room, made good eye contact with the audience, but the cards shook in his hands. Devon held her breath for him to be able to finish this speech without breaking down. Matt exhaled slowly before continuing. Everywhere he went, Hutch made it his mission to make people happy."

OUTSIDE THE CHAPEL, DEVON watched as the pallbearers loaded Hutch's coffin into the waiting black hearse. The crowd started to dwindle. Students slowly walked uphill to the dining hall to get a late breakfast . . . when Devon heard something. Was it singing? A man's voice . . . a thumping, like hooves . . . and that's when she saw him: An old man in a cowboy hat, galloping downhill on horseback, singing out loud.

Reed Hutchins.

Devon blinked. She wasn't hallucinating. This was really happening. She looked for Hutch's parents. They stood by the limos near the hearse, mouths agape. That's when Devon heard the words clearly, "Kodachrome. You give us those nice bright colors. You give us the greens of summers. Makes you think all the world's a sunny day, oh yeah!"

Devon's throat tightened. She almost laughed. At least someone was representing Hutch as he would have wanted. Reed slowed to a stop by Hutch's father, Bill: his son. Devon couldn't hear what Bill said, but she saw taut lips and the bulge of a pounding jaw. Reed simply shook his head and smiled. "Kodachrome," he hollered, then started coughing. Bill stepped forward and grabbed the horse's reins. He pointed sharply down the hill, but Reed kept singing in a raspy voice. "Mama don't you take my Kodachrome away!"

Bill let go and stalked into the nearest limo. Eric and Mitzy followed. The old man on his horse followed the somber procession, singing the whole way as they drew closer to Devon, following the road that would take them off campus. "I got my Nikon camera. I love to take a photograph. So Mama, don't take my Kodachrome away. . . ."

"That's Grandpa Reed," a girl said.

Devon turned. She hadn't even noticed, but Raven and Bodhi were standing next to her. Bodhi looked almost comical in a dark suit with his blond dreads in a knot at the top of his head, like a toddler forced to dress up for a grown-up occasion. Raven wore a long black flowing dress, which complemented the black hair in clumps around her shoulders. Devon turned back to Reed. He was fewer than twenty feet away now, plodding along behind the blackened faceless cars.

The old man saluted with two fingers from the top of his hat to Raven and Bodhi as he passed, still singing. Bodhi and Raven saluted him back. He nodded at Devon. Reflexively, she saluted, as well. It seemed like the polite thing to do. She wanted him to know that she knew he wasn't a scary homeless guy. Crazy, yes: clearly. Although what was crazier, taking a nap in her bed or arriving late—in full cowboy regalia, singing and on horseback, no less—to his grandson's funeral? And why *was* he in her room? She still had no idea.

The hearse and limos continued down the dirt road. Grandpa Reed followed on his horse. Raven sobbed next to Devon and Bodhi put a comforting arm around her, letting her cry into his chest.

"That guy loved Hutch more than anyone," Bodhi said to no one in particular. "Bill and Mitzi think Reed has gone off his rocker. They've practically disowned the guy. But if you ask me he is the only sane one in the bunch. Hutch thought so too."

"They disowned him because he's crazy?" Devon asked.

"Because they're a bunch of money-grubbing a-holes," Raven said between sobs.

"Hutch's parents," Bodhi said to Devon over Raven's head. "They're going up to Reed's land right now. Athena is buried up there too. At least Hutch will be with his grandmother on the vineyard." He hugged his sister tightly.

"Saw the coroner this morning," he added, still looking across the hillside.

"And?" Devon asked.

"He confirmed it was Oxy in Hutch's system. A lot of it. But he said the weird thing was, usually with overdoses you find a few pills undigested in the stomach. Not with Hutch. The Oxy must have been crushed up before he took it. The only reason someone does that is if they plan on never waking up."

Raven sniffed and stopped crying. She glanced up at her brother.

"Or, if they don't know they were taking it," Devon said.

CHAPTER 6

Name: Matt Dolgens
Session Date: Sept. 17
Session #2

"You did a nice job with the eulogy," Devon started. Matt sat across from her in the leather chair, studying his fingernails. Another morning session and Matt had wet hair, fresh off the surf van again. He shrugged.

"I guess. The whole thing is kind of a blur," he said, eyes still on his fingers. He zeroed in on a particularly long cuticle and picked at it.

"A blur because it was Hutch's funeral or because it wasn't your speech?"

Matt looked up at her finally. "What's your point?"

"No point, really. I just noticed that Eric had your speech prepared."

"So what? The whole suicide thing looks really bad for the family. The least I could do is say a few words to help them out."

"Of course, there's absolutely nothing wrong with helping the family out during a difficult time. I just want to know where you come into all of this. How do you feel about it? In your words, not Eric's." *

Matt turned his head at Devon, eyeing her up and down. "Look, I appreciate you helping me with my tie yesterday and all, but feelings? Really?" He drummed his fingers on his thigh, filling the silence in the room with his tapping.

Devon put her notebook down. Time to change tactics. "Fine, no feelings. We're just here to talk. So, anything you want to talk about. Anything."

"Nah, I'm good." Matt bobbed his head to the beat of his finger drumming. He blinked at the walls, avoiding her eyes. He was revved up.

"You know, after Hutch, Robins really stressed that I report anyone abusing drugs, pharmaceuticals included."

Matt stopped drumming his fingers. "There are so many things wrong with that sentence I don't know where to begin. Let's see, first, you're a narc. Second, you're a narc. And third—oh, right, I covered that. I'm not staying here to be lectured by you." He stood up.

"Just tell me I'm wrong. Tell me you've got a prescription and you get it from Nurse Reilly every morning like you're supposed to." Devon pressed on. "Or, what if I wanted some Adderall? Just a few pills to get me through the Chem homework this week. All I need is a piece of green paper, right?"

Matt's eyes darkened. "You're an asshole, Dev." He reached for the door.

"If I figured it out that easily, don't you think someone else will too?" Devon called after him. Her words stopped him at the door. "Matt, I really don't want you to get in trouble. I just want to help."

Matt pushed his wet hair behind his ears. "Yeah? How are you going to help me?"

---

* "Giving the subject the opportunity to connect with his/her own feelings is crucial." — *Peer Counseling Pilot Program Training Guide* by Henry Robins, MFT

"Will you sit down?"

"Fine." He plopped back down in the leather cushion. His lips twisted into an uncomfortable smirk. "You haven't told anyone?"

"No, and I'm not going to tell anyone. Not even Robins. Okay?"

"Okay." Matt chewed on his cuticle again.

"I know you give the orders to Bodhi in Monte Vista," Devon continued. Matt stopped chewing. She had is full attention now. "Can you tell me how the whole thing started?"*

"I. . . ." His fingers started drumming again.

"Matt? Please. I think it's an important piece of what happened to Hutch."

Matt sighed and folded his arms. He wouldn't look at Devon, but at least he started talking. "Bodhi used to have a friend that worked at the Monte Vista Pharmacy, like years ago. I don't even know his name. At the time, Eric was at Keaton taking all sorts of stuff for depression, anxiety, ADD, so he had all the prescriptions anyone at school could have wanted. The guy at the pharmacy would slip Eric a few extra pills here and there and Eric hooked up other students from time to time. That's kind of why he was so good at chemistry. It wasn't a class; it was like a way of life for him. But then Eric graduated, went all pre-med, and went off the pharmaceuticals."

"So when Bodhi got the job at the pharmacy, he and Hutch started it up again?"

Matt shrugged. "Bodhi's guy left the pharmacy, and Bodhi and Eric went to college. But Bodhi dropped out of MIT and came back to live in Monte Vista because of his dad. Since he was back, he got the gig at the pharmacy, so he called Eric. Eric introduced him to Hutch sophomore year, and the whole thing started up again. PharmClub Version 2.0."

"But why would they sell the pills? Hutch and Eric didn't need the money. You don't either, right?"

"It's not about the money. I don't know why Bodhi and Eric

* "A Peer Counselor should never encourage the subject to discuss a tangential topic."—*Peer Counseling Pilot Program Training Guide* by Henry Robins, MFT

started in the first place, probably just to see if they could get away with it. That's kind of Eric's thing, pushing against the rules to see how far he can bend them before they snap. Bodhi, I don't get. He's pretty chill. I guess when he started up again with Hutch he wanted to stick it to the Keaton powers that be, make a little extra cash, something like that."

"Okay, but what about you? Hutch is gone, why not just end it?"

"It's not that easy. Do you know how many people depend on me?" Matt finally stopped twitching and looked at Devon.

The thought hadn't even occurred to her. It was amazing to think how different their worlds were, even though they lived in the same community with the same 300 people. Matt was talking like most of the school bought from him. Did they? Was she really that much out of the loop? Keaton didn't have easy-to-define cliques, of course; the whole vibe was more free-flowing; computer nerds could be jocks; cheerleaders could be drama geeks; they were often the same people, just flexing different talents. But a few kids did rule, just like at every school. Hutch had been one of them. And Matt still was. And The PharmClub, if that's what it was called, seemed to cover everyone. The only requirement was people that were willing to do or take anything to be better than the rest. Or maybe it was another example of Keaton students in the habit of bending rules in their favor. Either way, Devon still felt the sting of being left out—yet again.

"Don't you think this is bigger than your social standing at Keaton?" She took a deep breath. "I'm sorry. I'm not judging—"

"Yes, you are."

"Okay, sorry. I'm judging a little. But, do you know what would happen if you got caught doing this?"

"Yeah, yeah. I'd get kicked out, easy. Whatever. I'm sure Boulder will still take me next year."

"Kicked out is the least of it. You could end up in jail."

Matt laughed shortly. "Doubtful. I just want to enjoy the

moment. People need me right now, and that's kind of cool. Like you, you must get off on this therapy stuff a little bit."

"I don't know that 'get off' is how I'd describe it. But, yeah, okay, I get it. It does feel good to be needed."

"See? We're speaking the same language." Matt smiled at her and smoothed back his hair. Devon flipped the page in her notebook to buy herself a moment to think. *Did I somehow just condone the fact that he's selling drugs?* * Mr. Robins would make her do push-ups until she graduated if he found out. Or worse.

"Before you got involved, Hutch was doing this with Bodhi on his own?"

"Yeah, this summer he called and wanted me to take over this year. He wanted out."

"You don't think anyone would have wanted to hurt Hutch because of this? Maybe they were mad he stopped, or he was going to rat someone out?"

"Rat someone out? Did you watch *The Sopranos* over the summer? Seriously."

"I know it sounds a little weird, but you were kind of saying the same thing the other day. Hutch overdosed on Oxy, yet he apparently never took the stuff. Maybe someone wanted him out of the picture. Like, Bodhi? They *were* partners. Maybe Bodhi felt betrayed."

"As cute as this little detective act you've got going on is, I've already played it from every angle. Trust me. Hutch had no enemies; he was a good guy to a sickening degree. I think he just had more demons than any of us knew."

"Is that how you really feel? You think Hutch chose to end his life?"

"Devon, seriously. Don't become that obsessed chick. He's gone. None of this changes anything."

She swallowed. First Presley, now Matt, telling her to back off

---

* "As convincing as your subject may be, do not take sides with or against your subject."
—*Peer Counseling Pilot Program Training Guide* by Henry Robins, MFT

for the same reason. Was she obsessing? "But it does change every-thing. If someone . . . someone. . . ."

"Murder? You're going to say that someone murdered Hutch? Come on, Devon. Stick to your counseling and straight As. You're not Nancy Drew. Just. . . ." His voice softened again. "Just keep all this between us, will you?"

"Of course." Devon slumped deeper into her chair.

"Our time's up," Matt said, standing. "See ya next week, Doc." He walked out the door, leaving Devon staring at his empty chair.

Murder. It sounded much more dramatic when Matt said it. But Matt was right. As long as Devon and Raven refused to believe that Hutch took those pills on purpose, or that he accidentally took too much of a drug he apparently never touched, they were looking for a murderer. With all the drugs circulating around campus, there was one obvious place to start.

THE LIGHTS WERE STILL on in the Health Center when Devon stopped in. A knitted strand of bells hanging from the door announced her arrival.

"In here," Nurse Reilly called from her cramped office. Devon moved toward the voice. Nurse Reilly was just putting her Sudoku book down on her desk next to a steaming cup of tea. Mint, like always. With tight white curls in her hair, her round face with rosy, wrinkled cheeks and her small half-moon glasses, the Keaton joke was that Nurse Reilly missed her calling as the mascot for a cookie company. Devon remembered when she had strep throat last year and Nurse Reilly had taught her how to knit to pass the time. Even though Devon had more than enough homework to keep her busy, knitting with Nurse Reilly was probably the closest she'd ever come to hanging out with a grandmother. A grandmother who always wore brightly-colored scrubs and matching Crocs, but a grand-mother nonetheless.

And here was Devon, working up a lie to tell her. It was wrong. It actually *did* make her feel sick.

"Devon? Are you alright, sweetheart? What can I help you with?"

"Yeah, I'm fine. It's just that . . . um . . . cramps. They've been really bad this month and I'm out of Aleve. Do you have anything I could take?" It sounded pitiful, but what else was she going to say? *Hi, Nurse Reilly. I really need to see the medical files of my subjects, and while we're invading people's privacy, could I see a list of the entire school's prescriptions?*

"Sure, I can help you with that. Give me a sec."

Nurse Reilly pushed herself out of her chair with an *oomph!* and walked past Devon to the exam room. Her orange Crocs squeaked on the checkered linoleum floor. Devon's eyes flitted over the "When Mama Ain't Happy, Ain't Nobody Happy" needlepoint framed on the wall behind her desk. Next to it, a thin curtain covered the one window in the room. Other than this window and the front door, these were Devon's only ways into the Health Center later. Devon quickly darted across the small office and unlatched the lock on the window. Breaking in was her only option, wasn't it? Nurse Reilly would never let her look at the files or prescriptions. Devon would have to come back tonight when Nurse Reilly was tucked away in her apartment. Hopefully that mint tea would lull her into a deep sleep.

"Here you go," Nurse Reilly chimed as she returned. A small paper cup held two blue pills.

"Thanks so much. I'm sure these will help."

"You okay otherwise? I haven't seen you since you were in here with Isla a few weeks ago. I heard you've been an exemplary Peer Counselor."

"You heard that? Thanks. I'm trying. It's more work than I thought." Devon smiled weakly. (*Like unexpected late night breakins.*) "But I like it. Feels good to help."

"Well, that's the most important thing. Now, you should be getting back to your dorm. It's almost curfew. Nurse Reilly clicked off her desk lamp and grabbed her mug of tea, walking Devon toward the door. "I'm headed off to bed myself."

∞

AS DEVON TRUDGED UPHILL to her dorm, she saw a few guys with lacrosse sticks playing catch on Raiter Lawn. A white baseball hat glowed in the faint moonlight. *Grant.* She had ducked out to the Health Center the second study hours were over at 9:30 P.M. to try to avoid him and now she had to cross the lawn to get to Bay House.

She hung back for a moment on the dimly lit path. To her left a silver BMW idled in the day student parking lot. The interior lights were on, highlighting a figure in the driver's seat with a phone pressed to his ear. Devon didn't remember any day students driving BMWs. Someone's father must be picking them up after study hours. How nice that would be, if someone showed up to whisk her away to a cozy home somewhere, just for one night.

It's not that she was really avoiding Grant. But she had other things on her mind than making out in the bushes with him. And at 9:30 P.M., she knew that's what he probably wanted to do. She watched him toss the ball, his back still turned. There were other places to play a game of catch; she wondered if Grant parked his game here on purpose. The dirty yellow ball came whizzing toward her, and Grant ran for it. His lacrosse stick reached out and swooped up the ball into its net before it could reach Devon.

"Bam!" He grinned and twirled the ball in the net. "Where you been, Miss Mackintosh?"

"Chatting with Nurse Reilly." The curfew bell would ring any minute. She squinted across the lawn at the guy with the waiting lacrosse stick: Raj Kahn. Grant lobbed the ball back to him. Devon barely knew Raj, other than that he was a junior with Indian parents who'd moved to Dallas, and had one of the more confusing accents at Keaton. She wondered if *he* were part of PharmClub 2.0. Chances were more likely than not.

"We missed you, Devon," Raj teased across the lawn. "I mean, Grant missed you." He cackled.

"Hey Raj, aren't you missing a date with your right hand?" Grant said, rolling his eyes. Raj waved his middle finger back, and made his way toward his dorm for the night.

"But I did miss you," Grant murmured. He pulled Devon's hair off her shoulder and kissed her neck. "I thought we were gonna hang." Devon's eyes fluttered. For a second she wondered why chatting with the school nurse was more pressing than sneaking off with Grant. She looked up at him and ran her fingers across the brim of his hat. He just wanted to be with her. So why did that make her so nervous?

The curfew bell rang.

"Tomorrow, we'll hang," she promised. She gave him one quick kiss and hurried off to Bay House.

"YO, LINDSAY WHORE-HAN," PRESLEY yelled as soon as Devon entered Bay House. She stood at Devon's door, wearing oversized purple pajama pants and a flowered pink bra, drawing a very explicit graphic representation of the male anatomy on the dry erase board. "Where you been? And more importantly, were you there with Graaaaant?"

Devon ran her hand across Presley's drawing, wiping it out. She immediately took off her shoes and started clearing books off her bed.

"What's up, Whore-den Caulfield?" Presley hung in her doorway, waiting. "Seriously, cough it up."

Devon collapsed face-down on the covers. Presley took this as an invitation to settle in for a chat and plopped in the armchair. Devon couldn't help but smile. "I saw him," she started, "But, I don't know, I just don't want it to be like we have to hang out every night. Is that weird?"

Presley threw her legs over the arm of the chair. "I don't get how you two are not like bunnies right now. He's hot, you're hot, these all equate to good sex whenever you want it. Kind of a no-brainer if you ask me. Do we have to have the birds and the bees talk?"

"No, I got that covered, thank-you-very-much."

Presley frowned. "But, you've still got your V card? I thought you took care of that last year. Last summer at least."

"Yeah, well, I didn't." Devon rolled over in bed. "Nothing ever really seemed right, like, would I want to think about this person for the rest of my life as the person I gave my V card to? No one really fit the bill."

"Until Graaaaant."

Devon laughed. "Yeah, maybe."

"Well, if it matters, from what I've heard, he won't disappoint." Presley stood up.

"Wait, what do you mean?"

But Presley was already running down the hallway, laughing.

"Slut!" Devon yelled after her.

There was a tap on her shoulder. Devon whirled around.

"I assume you did not mean me," Mrs. Sosa said with a smile.

"Sorry, no, that was for Presley." Devon slunk back into bed. Mrs. Sosa hung in the doorway a minute longer.

"Maybe instead of me punishing you for using that language, you two come up with more, *Como se dice*, appropriate nicknames?"

"We can do that," Devon replied. "Night."

"*Buenas noches*," Mrs. Sosa said and closed Devon's door.

ONE HOUR AND THREE chapters of *The Birth of America* for her AP History homework later, Devon pulled open her sliding glass door. The campus was dark. The fog had rolled in, which meant the stars and moon couldn't help light the way. Devon grabbed a small flashlight from her desk drawer.

Just as she stepped onto her outside patio, the payphone in the hallway rang.

Devon froze. Late night calls were rare, especially since the students weren't allowed to be out of their rooms past curfew. Only family emergencies or secret boyfriends could justify the risk of getting caught on the phone in the dorm hallway. Plus, if it was a secret late night call, why not just call on a cell? Maybe it was a wrong number. Devon waited, listening for footsteps. The phone rang again. And again. Hurrying back through her room, she poked her head into the hallway. Maya, in a bathrobe and towel wrapped in a turban on her head opened the door to the phone booth. She said a few words that Devon couldn't hear, then slammed the phone down and went back to her room in a huff.

The phone started ringing again.

Let Maya handle it. I've got a break-in to attend to.

GETTING THROUGH THE WINDOW was no problem.

As she hoisted herself up, a red light glowed in the distance. The day student parking lot again. Brake lights. The fog made everything blur together. Could it be the same BMW from before? The engine kicked into gear with a deep hum and peeled out, gravel churning.

Would the car wake up Nurse Reilly? If the light went on, Devon would have to abandon her mission. She sat there, halfway through the window, the word *mission* hanging in her brain. Only when Hutch was involved did she find herself taking on secret missions.

Ten seconds passed. Then another ten.

The night settled back into a constant cricket chirping. Nurse Reilly hadn't stirred from her apartment.

Devon's tennis shoes whispered softly as hopped down and padded to the filing cabinets. Nurse Reilly refused to update the school system to a computer database: "Cards have served this school since its founding." The result was a room full of putty-colored metal file cabinets with the medical history of every student that had ever attended Keaton.

Devon used her flashlight to locate the file drawer marked C–D. *Dolgens, Matt.* A note about a broken finger his freshman year. Devon remembered him sitting on the lacrosse bench that season with a cast on his arm and a grumpy look glued to his face. The flu freshman year. Chlamydia sophomore year. Ha! Being that good-looking and constantly hooking up with girls did have its downside. Nothing whatsoever about prescriptions for anything, which meant that any pharmaceutical Matt took, he was taking illegally. Abusing a substance is how the *Keaton Companion* would look at it. Rule #2a.

Devon's head swam with how many other students could possibly be in the same boat as Matt. Did Hutch get his Oxy illegally? Despite almost everyone's insistence that he wouldn't take the stuff, what if he had a prescription for some unknown reason? Her fingers walked to the G–H drawer. She put her hand on the metal handle, but stopped and closed her eyes. What if she opened this drawer and found out that Hutch did have a prescription for Oxy? What if his file mentioned bouts of depression, or bi-polar disorder? She promised herself: If any of that were in his file she would drop this whole murder theory and begin to accept that Hutch did indeed commit suicide. But she needed proof.

She opened the drawer and scanned the files. *Harris, Sasha. Harrington, Joel. Heyman, Alexa. Hoth, David. Hutchins, Eric. Hyde, Grace. . . .*

No 'Hutchins, Jason'? She ran through the drawer once more. No. She pulled Eric's file, maybe something in there would help. Stomach flu, sophomore year. Torn ACL junior year. And that was it.

Devon closed the drawer as quietly as she could. Why would Hutch's file be missing? Would the police or coroner have needed it? Nurse Reilly would have made copies for them rather than let any of her files out of this office. There had to be a reasonable explanation, except that the gnawing pit in her stomach was acting up again, telling her there was nothing reasonable about any of this.

What about Isla? Matt had said Isla was the one with the problem, not to mention, Isla had actually given Devon Oxy to hold on to. What secrets was her file keeping?

Martin, Isla.

Wow: a regular in the Health Center. Freshman year; the flu and panic attacks that followed with a prescription for Xanax. A chest infection, sore throat, and severe cramps. Sophomore year: a cold, severe cough, sinus infection, prescription for Z-Pak. Then she had a bruised tailbone, for which a small dose of Vicodin was prescribed. Complaints of depression, followed by a prescription for Paxil. As of junior year she started the year with a prescription for Xanax, 10 mg. No Oxy or Adderall. But the line between abusing pharmaceuticals and using pharmaceuticals was starting to seem pretty thin.

Devon's eye caught the flash of *Mackintosh, Devon*, as she started to close the drawer. Well, she had already broken into the Health Center. One little peek at her own file wouldn't hurt. Mackintosh, Devon. Freshman year, height, weight. Sophomore year, *jeez, they weren't kidding about the Freshman 15*.

> Blood type: AB.
> Mother's Blood Type: B
> Father's Blood Type: A (10/11)

That's weird. Why would her father's blood type be listed? Was that a date next to it? As far as Devon knew, her father was a sperm donor. Did her mom even know the blood type of the donor? Maybe the school had asked for it and her mom had to go back to the sperm bank to find out? *Wait, why did this matter now? My blood type is not why I broke into the Health Center in the middle of the night. Stick to the game plan, Devon.*

She had to think about Hutch's death scientifically. The files didn't point to anything helpful. What would she need to prove that it wasn't suicide? If everyone's prescriptions were registered and stored here, that meant that Hutch's Oxy might still be here if it was legally administered to him. A stretch, but at least Devon could cross Hutch's possible legitimate need for Oxy off her list. But where were the meds stored in here?

The one locked cabinet in Nurse Reilly's office was a giveaway. Why attempt the security unless it was something worth securing? Devon tried to imagine where she would keep the key if she were Nurse Reilly. Opening and closing the drawers on Nurse Reilly's desk would be loud, and she didn't want to waste time guessing.

The top of the desk was clean. Nurse Reilly had to open that cabinet every day when students came to take their medication in the mornings, so she would want easy access. Devon patted her hand along the bottom of the cabinet, along the sides . . . nothing. The "When Mama Ain't Happy, Ain't Nobody Happy" needle-point hung on the wall, mocking her struggle. Did the needlepoint know something she didn't? Devon slipped the frame off the wall, careful not to let it make any noise. A sliver of gold fell to the floor with a slight *clink!*

With trembling fingers, Devon unlocked the cabinet.

Her eyes widened at row after row of labeled orange pharmaceutical canisters—easily over a hundred. This didn't even account for the kids taking pills that didn't have prescriptions. There had to be a system to this cabinet, otherwise it would take Nurse Reilly all day to find everyone's designated meds. Devon scanned the labels; they appeared to be organized by student last name. The first row, A–D. Nothing, just a lot of Ritalin and Adderall. E–K. More of the same. An asthma inhaler or two. L–R. Asthma medicine. Eczema cream. Valtrex. Devon made a note never to make out with Park, Robert. The last shelf, S–Z had more Adderall than the other shelves, insulin pills, and . . . nothing. No Oxy. No prescriptions for Hutch sitting unused.

It seemed the only Oxy at school was hiding from Isla in Devon's dresser drawer.

CHAPTER 7

Name: Isla Martin
Session Date: Sept. 18
Session #2

"You been feeling any better?" Devon asked. Isla sat in the leather chair opposite, winding her hair into small braids.

"I don't know, whatever," Isla said with a shrug. "Fine, I guess."

"Kind of a gnarly week, huh? Last session you wanted me to hold onto your pills, Hutch's funeral happened, and classes kicked into full gear. You handling everything all right?"

"How else would I handle it? Smile and be perfect, isn't that the mandate around here?"

Devon returned her stare as gently as possible. "Did someone say that to you? Because if you're not feeling like smiling, you don't have to. There's no mandate like that around here, with me."

"Well, look who's been drinking the Keaton Kool-Aid. Are you going to report me if I say anything anti-Keaton?"

Devon cleared her throat. "I didn't see you at his service on Sunday."

"What was I supposed to do? Play the grieving girlfriend? Comfort his mom, sit in the front row, and cry the loudest like a good girl? When meanwhile there's some slut in the chapel carrying his baby? No way, I'm not doing that for him."

Devon swallowed. "What do you mean?" For the first time, it occurred to her that she had no idea how much Isla knew.*

"Looks like Hutch knocked someone up. Cleo Lam-bitch thought it'd be funny to leave a pregnancy test on my bed. I thought maybe she heard something about the night Hutch died, but whatever. I caught her doing it, you know. She shouldn't have been in my room."

"I'm sorry." Devon took a deep breath. "Start from the beginning. What would Cleo have heard about the night Hutch died?"

"Nothing. It's nothing. She shouldn't have been in my room. She said she saw Hutch getting a freakin' pregnancy stick for someone, can you believe that? She thought he was getting it for me and she wanted to help, yeah right. Crazy Francophile bitch. She knew Hutch wasn't buying it for me; it was just her passive-aggressive way of telling me what she knew. I hate that freak." Isla scratched at her arm, leaving red streaks along her pale white skin.

Devon kept silent. No way would she try to fill in the blanks here.

"The scary thing is, she was probably telling the truth. It was too random for her to make up. Cleo's good at stirring up shit, but she's not quite creative enough to invent it, ya know? Hutch was seeing someone this summer, after me. I know he was."

"Did you see him with someone?" Devon asked.

"No, I didn't . . . why do I have to prove everything to you? I just know it, okay? I talked to him before school started, you know, just to see where we stood before all the rumors started about us being broken up. And he was distant, like he had moved on to someone else after me."

"So, you and Cleo think he moved on to someone that he got pregnant?"

"I don't care what that bitch thinks. I got her back though, crushed up an Ambien and put it in her little Frenchie water carafe she keeps next to her bed. She passed right out in Chem that day. It was awesome." Isla laughed a little.

"That's . . . um." *Devon paused to make sure she phrased this the right way. "Isla, I'm not here to tell you what to do, but slipping anyone a prescribed drug is extremely dangerous. They could have an allergic reaction, for one thing. After what happened to Hutch—"

"What do you mean 'what happened to Hutch?' It was suicide. The asshole did it to himself and left us to pick up the pieces." Isla's dark blonde eyebrows pushed toward the center of her face.

"Okay, but do you understand what I'm saying about slipping people prescriptions?"

Isla chewed on the inside of her cheek and stared at the Rorschach poster behind Devon.

"Isla. Seriously. I have to refer to you to Mr. Robins if this could happen again. I really don't want to narc on you." Devon tried to keep her voice steady. She wouldn't let this turn into one of those moments that people regret for the rest of their lives. *If only I'd intervened.*

Isla eventually brought her eyes back to Devon. "Fine. I hear you. I won't slip pills into anyone else's water. You've gotten really boring you know. Or maybe you've always been boring and I just never knew it. "

Devon sat back in her chair. "I'll take boring, just as long as you hear me on the prescription thing. Speaking of, do want to tell me any more about the Oxy you asked me to hold onto last week?"

"Why, what's wrong with it? Did you flush it or something?"

"No, I still have it. Keeping it safe like you asked. It's just . . . I'd like to know where it came from."

---

* "It is up to the Peer Counselor to determine if the subject is a danger to themselves or others."—*Peer Counseling Pilot Program Training Guide* by Henry Robins, MFT

Isla leaned forward in the creaky leather chair. "I told you. I got it at home before coming back to school. It's not that hard in Portland. Doctors are pretty lax about pain meds."

"And there's no chance you shared any pills with anyone when you came back to school?"

"I had them and then I gave them to you. That's all there is to it. Why are you so obsessed with this?"

Devon stared back down at her notebook. She realized she hadn't taken nearly as many notes since she'd lost her Mont Blanc pen. Of course, the cheapness of her Pentel had nothing to do with the lack of note-taking. "The thing is, before you gave them to me, Hutch overdosed on the same drug. So, you can see why I'm interested. Just trying to make sure that there wasn't a chance Hutch got into your stash or something like that."

"Well he didn't, okay?" Isla picked at her split ends. "You wanna know where I was on Sunday? I went to the Cove. I couldn't see Hutch in a coffin. I watched the surfers floating out in the waves and pretended that Hutch was one of them. When we were together, I would watch him catch a wave and he would wave back to me on the shore every now and then. Even though we weren't next to each other, I could still feel him." Isla absentmindedly scratched at her arm again. Her eyes brimmed with tears and she let them fall from her lids and skate down her cheeks. "There's nothing to feel now."

Devon nodded. She envied Isla's memories. To feel that connected to someone, even from afar. . . . He'd wave to her on the beach. She'd wave back and return to her homework, smiling, feeling that warm glow spread across her body, the warmth of knowing someone loved you. . . .

"Whoever she is, she doesn't get to have Hutch's baby." Isla's words pulled Devon back to the session.

"Well, we don't know what it's like to be in this girl's shoes. Maybe she doesn't—"

"No!" Isla slammed her hands on the arm of the chair. "It's not her choice. I get a say, too. It's Hutch. There can't be a baby. "

Devon stared at Isla. She was breathing heavily. Her cheeks turned a splotchy red. She didn't want another panic attack on her hands.* She ripped a blank page out of her notebook, hoping to catch Isla's attention. It worked. Devon started folding the paper into halves. Isla watched, curious.

"You know, Isla, in normal counseling we could keep talking about this, your feelings, blah, blah, blah. But normal is boring, and that's not you. You think outside the box. Want to try something a little different?" Devon had no idea where she was going with this, but at least Isla was breathing evenly again, and her cheeks were no longer flushed.

"Yeah. Sure. Different is good, I guess," Isla conceded.

"Okay, close your eyes. Take a deep breath. Inhale. Exhale." What to do with the folded piece of paper? She wasn't sure. She tucked it under her thigh.

"You feel calm throughout your body. It moves from your toes, up your legs, up the back of your spine, behind your eyes."

Isla leaned back in her chair, eyes closed.

"Now imagine you're a girl who's scared, alone, not sure who you can turn to," Devon continued. "Now imagine you're pregnant and alone."

Isla's eyes popped open. "I'm not stupid, you know."

So much for subtle manipulation or phony meditation. "No, you're not stupid."

"You're just trying to throw me off the scent."

"Isla, there's a girl who's probably going through a rough enough time right now. How about if we just focus on you and how you might be feeling?"

"You seem pretty focused on protecting this girl," Isla spat. "How do I know it's not you?"

Devon laughed. "Are you serious?"

Isla didn't respond. Her eyes turned to slits.

---

* "If the subject goes off track, it is up to the Peer Counselor to stop them and shift their focus to the task at hand."—*Peer Counseling Pilot Program Training Guide* by Henry Robins, MFT

"It's not me. Seriously, it's not. "

"Then why do you care so much?" Isla demanded.

"It's my job to care. No one deserves to be going through what this girl is probably going through. And we don't know what this had to do with Hutch."

"It's got everything to do with him! It's his fault. Why is everyone so busy making him out to be the perfect guy that could do no wrong? I'm so sick of it. Hutch acted like the world revolved around him, and now he's dead, and it still revolves around him! It's disgusting."

"Isla, death, especially a sudden death like this, can bring up all kinds of emotions. Denial, anger, depression . . . let's talk through it."

"No, I'm not going to talk through it with you. You're just as bad as the rest of them. You think I don't hear you defending him every chance you get. Let me tell you, Hutch was not the angel everyone makes him out to be, okay?"

"Isla—"

"No, you know what? I'm not going to sit here and listen to you defend him. You really want to know how I feel? I'm glad he's gone." Isla stood and turned to go.

"No, you're not."

"Stop thinking you know me. You don't."

"You loved him, Isla. That doesn't go away. I saw you with him last year. He loved you and you loved him."

"Oh yeah? It's your turn, prove it." Isla leaned against the door, her arms folded across her chest.

Devon hesitated. She was probably crossing all sorts of counseling lines. But Isla had to see the truth. "Last year. Spring. I was in Bio and you two had a free period. I remember looking out the window and seeing you two walk across Raiter holding hands. Hutch kissed your hand on the inside of your palm and held it there against his cheek. I saw that look in his eyes. He loved you, Isla. No one else mattered to him."

Isla was crying again, her mouth curled into a frown, pooling the tears around her chin. "You're sick," she whispered, then pushed the door open and let it slam shut behind her.

DEVON WANTED TO FINISH up her session notes before vacating her cramped office. At least in here she could count on a little silence. She debated whether or not to include Isla slipping Ambien into Cleo's bedside water in her notes. What was the worst case scenario? Isla drugs and possibly injures or even kills someone, and if Devon's notes were used to prove that the school was counseling Isla and *knew* of this dangerous activity, the school would be sued until the end of days for knowing about Isla's behavior, and not reporting it. Or, was it that Devon could be sued for not reporting it? Or could Mr. Robins be sued for overseeing Devon and not knowing about Isla's dangerous tendencies? If Isla drugged someone to the point of harming them, *someone* was getting sued, that was a guarantee.

Nope, that's a piece of her sessions Devon could keep stored away in a forgotten storage unit in her brain. Unit 24, reserved for potentially threatening activities by counseling subjects, in the box marked *Stuff No One Else Needs To Know, Seriously.*

"Hey, sunshine," Grant opened the door a crack and leaned his head inside. She wrapped her notebook around her chest and squinted at the sunny outline of Grant.

"Hey, you're not supposed to be . . . what if I was with. . . ?" Devon couldn't find a polite way to say: *What the hell are you doing here?*

"Don't worry, I saw Isla leave. I'd never barge into a session like that; I know what you look like when you get angry. No thanks," Grant laughed and Devon relaxed.

"Sorry, no one's ever been in here with me that wasn't a—"

"Nutjob?" Grant plunked himself down into the leather chair. "Tell me Doctor? Is it bad that I want to have sex with my mother and kill my father?"

Devon didn't laugh. "We should go."

"Wait, wait, I'm sorry. That was insensitive of me. Let's talk about you, your feelings. Any lingering emotions you want to confess to me?"

Devon tried to squirm out of Grant's way, but he held her hands and kept her in her chair. "Grant, I don't know. . . ."

"Isla's gotta be a real piece of work once you get her in here, huh?"

"You know I can't talk about that stuff." She pried her hands from his grasp.

"Right, right, of course. Heaven forbid Devon breaks a rule." Grant shook his head.

"You know, since you are in the chair, I have a question for you."

"Shoot, Doctor."

"How are you and Eric Hutchins so tight?" Devon was more curious how Grant would respond to the question that what his answer could be. He blinked, avoiding her eyes. *Hmmm, so telling already.*

"We're not really."

"So, why did he ask you to be a pallbearer?" Devon asked.

"Okay, you got me. It was Colonel Mustard in the Billiard Room with the lead pipe. Happy now?" The bell rang for the start of next class. "And I'm late to French." He stood and reached for the door.

"Grant, seriously."

He sighed. "Eric and Hutch and I went to the same lacrosse camp once, years ago. It was before Keaton. To be honest, I don't really know why Eric asked me. Now, can I be excused?" His voice took on a harsh edge.

"Hey, I didn't ask you to barge in here."

"Yeah I'll remember that next time I try to visit you." Grant slammed the door behind him.

Devon felt sick. *Keep this up and not only will your subjects quit, you'll drive away all your friends, too.* She grabbed her backpack and locked up the therapy room. How did an extracurricular start taking over everything in her life? There was nothing "extra" about it.

THANKFULLY, BAY HOUSE WAS quiet. Devon was grateful to have a free period. *Clean my room, catch up on homework, be a human again.*

As she approached her room, she noticed that Sasha's door was open at the end of the hall. Devon stopped and listened. No toilet flushing, no phone call chatter, no shower running . . . no Sasha. Devon poked her head inside the room. Sasha's dad had once played for the New York Jets. Apparently he was Hall of Fame material. Sasha's room looked like a Jets-themed sporting-goods store. But, Devon supposed it was why Sasha pursued her athletics and education with equal intensity.

On her desk Devon spied a pad of green paper. The same paper she had seen Sasha give Matt. "Sasha?" she called out to the empty room. Nothing. *A place that bases everything on an honor system leaves a lot of room for stupidity.* Devon darted toward Sasha's desk. The green paper had the Keaton logo at the top of the page. Now she felt like an idiot. She had the exact same pad. Everyone always got a pad of Keaton paper on their desks at the top of the school year. Nothing could go more unnoticed.

BACK HER OWN ROOM, Devon examined the paper she'd swiped from Matt before Hutch's funeral. It was hastily scrawled with *25Ad/15* in dark pencil. "Ad" probably was code for Adderall; that part wasn't too hard to guess. 25Ad probably meant 25 mg pills and /15 meant that person wanted 15 of them. Her heart thumped. If Devon ratted Matt out for selling Adderall, there would be a lot of angry classmates. As far as she was concerned, Adderall for homework was the same as steroids for sports: cheating. (How Sasha didn't make that comparison was beyond her.) But this was about Hutch. He'd died from an Oxy overdose. The Health Center didn't seem to be Hutch's source. Matt and Bodhi had both denied that they would ever supply a drug as hardcore as Oxy, but that was what they told her. Would they admit to something like that in person? To Devon of all people? What if the request came from another source? Devon grabbed a pen and wrote 30Ox/10 on a piece of her Keaton paper. Now she had to find the right person to give Matt the order.

"DEV, WAKE UP." THE flashlight glaring in her eye woke her up before Presley's whispering did.

"What time is it?" Devon covered her eyes with a hand. Presley stood next to her bed.

"It's almost two A.M. Come on." Presley pulled Devon's comforter down.

"Pres, come on. I wanna sleep," Devon said. She rolled over.

"Devon. Get up." Presley wasn't whispering anymore. "There's a thing for Hutch at the Nest. You should be there."

Now Devon was awake. She squinted up at Presley. "What?"

"Just put on your damn shoes." Presley flicked off the flashlight and tossed one Converse at a time onto Devon.

THE FIRE WAS THE first thing Devon noticed once they'd cleared the weed-entangled path to the Nest—the other Keaton hideaway for bad behavior, on the opposite side of the hill from the Palace. Funny, in all her time at Keaton, she'd never been here. It was nothing more than a tiny clearing with a metal trashcan at its center, now roaring with flames.

Devon could only see the dark outlines of other students until she wedged herself in the circle around the fire. Presley slid next to Pete, who wrapped a blanket around both of them. Allison Rice, Greta Lewis, and Taylor Pierce—all contributors to *The Keaton Hawk*, like Presley and Hutch—were writing on small pads of paper. These three had been on the newspaper since freshman year, and seemed to always have an article about something in the works. Devon was

amazed that in such a small community, where the same things happened all the time, they still found new things to write about. Well,
maybe this year was an exception. Taylor handed Devon a pad of
paper and a pencil.

"Here," she said. "We're all writing notes to Hutch. You know,
for closure."

"Um, okay." Devon looked down at the blank page. Across the
fire Allison ripped a page off the front of her pad and dropped it
into the fire. Her eyes filled with water and reflected the flames as
she watched her paper burn. Greta rubbed her back in a supportive
gesture. Allison wiped the tears from her cheek. Another subculture
that Hutch was a key member in, and yet once again Devon didn't
get the invite. At least Presley knew Devon would have wanted to
be there.

"I got one," Taylor said. She unfolded her piece of paper and
read aloud, "Dear Hutch, I remember the first day you walked into
the *Hawk* and wanted to join. You were so excited to interview
other students. Your love of writing a good story, or learning something new about someone was infectious. With you gone, I will try
to spread your enthusiasm to the rest of us. I'm sorry I couldn't be
there for you. With the utmost respect and love, Taylor."

She let her paper flit in a loopy spiral down into the fire.

Presley cleared her throat. The fire made her curly hair and pale
round cheeks glow like honey. "I'm not writing this one down." She
smiled at Devon across the flames. "Last year I almost got busted
buying vodka in Monte Vista. I was at the register and Hutch was
outside. Mrs. Ascher was about to walk in, and Hutch distracted
her so I could get out before she saw. Thanks, Hutch, for having
my back."

She ripped a piece of paper from a pad and watched it burn.

"Amen, sister," Pete chimed in.

"Amen, God bless America, and word up, homeboys."

A deep voice slurred its way into their circle. Someone was stum-
bling toward them through the brush. Matt? Devon tucked her chin

to her chest and tried to be invisible. He might not like seeing her at Hutch's secret memorial. He could make a case that Devon was a narc. If he did, everyone would see her that way—probably until well after they'd all graduated.

"What's up, children," Matt's glistening eyes skimmed past everyone and stopped on Devon. She looked back at the fire, hoping he would move on. "Seems like a pretty crappy showing for the Man of the Hour."

Greta tried to coax Matt into the group.

"We were all just writing letters to Hutch about the things we wished we could have told him. So he knows how much he's missed, you know, in spirit."

Taylor and Allison traded looks. Presley stared at the fire. Devon held her breath.

Matt took a swig from a leather-encased flask. "Oh right, in spirit. I get it." He laughed a little and then poured the rest of his flask into the fire. "Here ya go, buddy. Drink up."

"Matt? Is there anything you want to tell Hutch?" Allison asked.

"I dunno," Matt began. "I want to know what Devon has to tell Hutch."

All eyes flashed over the fire to Devon.

She swallowed hard. "I'd rather write it down, if that's okay," she said.

"Nah, come on. We'd love to know. What would you tell Hutch if you could? Something you've always wanted to say. . . ." Matt's smile curled up on one edge, twisting his charm into a devilish grin. "Come on, Devon. We're just here to talk, aren't we?" Devon's eyes flicked back to Presley for help, but Presley seemed to be waiting for an answer, too.

Great. This is how Matt gets to humiliate me.

"Okay, that's cool. Something I want to tell Hutch." *That I know about his secret lovechild? His illicit PharmClub? That I can't see a Nutter Butter without thinking of him?* "It's like Presley said. Hutch always looked out for everyone. I feel like we kind of dropped the ball on being there for him. So, I guess I would tell him that I've got his back. Better late than never."

Devon flashed to that first day of school this year when they spoke across the parking lot. She wished she could rewind to that moment and this time she'd press *Play* and tell him that she'd love to have pancakes with him; that those damn pancakes freshman year were always in the back of her mind. She'd tell him that what they felt that night in the kitchen wasn't just because of the moment; it *was* the moment and it was real, *they* could be real together.

Better late than never.

Devon closed her eyes and pulled her tears back into hiding. She saw Allison wipe her cheek again. Matt's grin faded across the fire.

Next to Presley, Pete pulled his sweatshirt over his head and dropped it into the can.

"Pete!" Presley squealed and backed away. The sweatshirt caught on fire in a mushroom cloud of smoke. Everyone else took a few steps back but Pete stayed put, his pale chest red in the light of the flames. "The shirt off my back. We all know Hutch would have given anything to anyone, including the shirt off his back. So, here, dude. It's yours."

Matt laughed. "Now we're having fun. Here ya go, Hutchins. The shirt off my back." He unzipped his crisp Patagonia jacket and tossed it into the fire. His white tank top followed into the growing cloud of smoke. The blue trimmed flames cast dancing shadows across Matt and Pete's bare chests. The Newspaper Squad traded shocked looks.

"Screw it," Presley said. She pulled her ratty Keaton hoodie over her head and dropped it into the fire. She stood there next to Pete in her purple bra. "The shirt off my back, Hutch."

"Nice," Pete said and kissed Presley's neck.

"Hot," Matt said as he ogled Presley's chest.

Everyone eyed everyone else.

What the hell? Devon pulled her sweatshirt off and tossed it into the fire. "The shirt off my back," she said, and then wrapped her arms across her chest. At least she had thrown on a sports bra from her floor before Presley dragged her here. It may not be the sexiest look, but she'd take unsexy over bare-chested in front of this crowd any day.

Matt raised an eyebrow at her. She shyly smiled back. If taking off her shirt proved to Matt how much she cared about Hutch, maybe she should have taken it off sooner.

CHAPTER 8

Name: Cleo Lambert
Session Date: Sept. 21
Session #2

"So? She totally deserved it." Cleo crossed her arms and glared at Devon. Her florescent pink nails were a stark contrast to her all-black uniform. "Besides, not like what she did to me was cool at all. I'm still debating about ratting her out to Wyler."

"Okay, let's talk that out.* You put the pregnancy test on Isla's bed, which, I think it's safe to say, hit a nerve with her. Isla retaliated by slipping an Ambien into your bedside water, causing you to fall asleep in a class. So, what are the pros and cons of telling Wyler what Isla did?" Devon waited, ballpoint pen poised above her notebook. She wanted Cleo to get a good look at her crappy replacement pen before asking about her missing Mont Blanc.

Cleo licked her lips, debating whether to jump in or not. "Fine,

---

*"Egan's Skilled Helper Model: Second stage: Help the subject identify what they want. Which options are open to the helpee?"—*Peer Counseling Pilot Program Training Guide* by Henry Robins, MFT

I'll play. Pro. I get to watch the bitch suffer. Con. I'm already on thin ice with Wyler, so why call more attention to myself?"

"Okay, sounds good so far."

"Con. The school's already freaking out about Hutch overdosing. If another pharmaceutical thing comes up you know there's going to be a crackdown."

"How would that affect you?"

"It wouldn't really. I don't do drugs, legal or illegal. But, it would certainly lead to a lot of kids freaking out, and I just can't be bothered with everyone in a constant state of PMS. It's bad enough already."

"How is it bad?"

"You haven't heard? People are getting cracked out around here. *C'est fou.*"

Devon blinked and wrote the words in her notebook. "That means crazy, right?"

"Freakin' Sasha Harris of all people comes into Calc yesterday. She's five minutes late, so of course, Mr. Lee calls her out on it. Sasha goes nuts, starts yelling at Lee like, 'I did your homework, what else do you want from me?' She threw her notebook across the room and then went to the board and wrote down all these insane equations. She wouldn't stop writing on the board and Lee totally didn't know how to handle it. Matt and Omar had to drag her out of the classroom and take her to Nurse Reilly. Totally crazy."

"Is she all right?" Devon wanted to know more. Was Sasha's meltdown because of her pill use? Was she having a bad reaction to something? Could it just be stress? Of course, none of this had to do with counseling Cleo. *Stay on target, Devon.*

"I heard Matt got royally pissed at her," Cleo went on. "Like she would draw too much attention to the pills, which could lead back to Matt. Any of his people freak out, you know that's going to bite him in the ass." She laughed. "Although, it is a hot ass."

Devon pushed the bangs out of her face and crossed her legs again. "You like Matt? That way, I mean?"

"Hells no. It's just an observation. Matt's staying busy anyways."

"Busy? With a girlfriend, busy?"

"Who knows if girlfriend's the right word? I just saw him walking back to Fell the other night close to curfew with a blanket over his shoulders, and we know what that means."

"The late night hook-up uniform." *Matt's probably hooking up with some unsuspecting freshman*, Devon convinced herself. Although, now it was going to nag at her until she knew whom it was.

"The thing that's weird about it is that Matt's keeping a low profile. Usually he's the biggest bragger of all the guys. But this one, this one he wants to keep quiet." Cleo gave Devon that smug smile of hers.

She's doing it again. Pulling me into the gossip circle.

"Well, I'm sure that's Matt's business," Devon said. "Let's get back to you. It seems like the cons outweigh the pros in reporting Isla to the Headmaster, right?"

"Yeah, it doesn't really make sense to rat her out. *C'est la vie.*" Cleo shrugged. "You know who else has been on something lately? Maya."

"Maya? Really? On drugs? But, she's like so quiet."*

"It's always the quiet ones, isn't it? I caught her the other night taking a shower at like two A.M. Scared the hell out of her I think, too. She wasn't expecting anyone to be in the bathroom then." Devon thought about seeing Maya in her robe around midnight the other night, too. But, Maya and drugs somehow didn't seem like the right fit. "She must be on a bender," Cleo continued, "because I've got first period with her, and she's fallen asleep in class almost every day this week, if she shows up at all."

"Let's try to get back to the subject at hand. Do we** want to talk about why you stole that nail polish in Monte Vista? I'm not sure we got to that last week."

---

* "The Peer Counselor should help the subject shift away from socializing after the first few minutes of the session to focus on the subject's emotional needs. A subject that continues to socialize is avoiding the real issues." —*Peer Counseling Pilot Program Training Guide* by Henry Robins, MFT

** "Using terms like 'we' and 'our', help the subject tackle issues that may be daunting to address alone." —*Peer Counseling Pilot Program Training Guide* by Henry Robins, MFT

"I love all this 'we' talk, when it's not your soul that's being poked and prodded."

"Is it possible that stealing was about getting attention? Or maybe just for the thrill of it?"

Cleo looked out the small window. "Not sure. You know the first time I stole something it was in France. When I was growing up there with my mom, we were in Lyon. I remember she took me to this little soap shop. It was, like, quintessential French. Everything was handmade and wrapped in wax paper. *Petites paquettes* my mom called them. *Little packages.* My mom wasn't paying attention but I knew I just had to have one of them. She was talking to the clerk and no one suspected me, so I just grabbed one and put it in my pocket. I still remember it, pink hand soap in the shape of a rose with a cream colored ribbon around the wax paper." Cleo now looked back to Devon, challenging her. "So, you tell me, Counselor: attention or thrill?"

Devon dropped her notebook on the floor next to her chair and folded her hands in her lap. "That's a very interesting story. I didn't know you grew up in France."

Cleo tossed her head back and laughed. "Mmmm." She nodded yes.

"Because," Devon continued, "I thought you said last week that you grew up in San Francisco going to the same golf club as the Hutchins family. Maybe I'm confused."

Cleo's eyes darted back to Devon. "No, that wasn't what I said. I said my parents belonged to the club, but we never went."

"Oh, but you weren't there with the Hutchins? Growing up with them?"

"No, I, we. . . ."

"Why do you feel you have to lie to me?" Devon kept her eyes glued to Cleo's face, not letting her off the hook.

"I wasn't lying. Okay, maybe I didn't *grow up* in France. But I spent time there." She sounded pissed off.

"That's the thing about lying. I mean, no one's perfect, we all do it from time to time. But it makes it hard to trust someone. If this is going to work at all, we have to trust each other."

"Whatever. That's like assuming that we're doing real therapy in here, which, let's be honest, we're not," Cleo said.

Devon ignored the sting. "But why not try to make it work? You were let off the hook for shoplifting in Monte Vista, and the only condition is that you complete five sessions with me."

"So?"

"So, it's kind of a waste of both of our time for you to sit here and lie to me for an hour. What if we end a little early today and next week, and for the two sessions after that, you come back with the truth?"

Cleo chewed on the side of her lip. "And what I say in here doesn't get out?"

"Not to anyone," Devon confirmed.

"Fine. I'll try." Cleo stood up with a sigh. "You know, I didn't know you could be such a ballbuster."

"I'm sorry. I'm really not trying to be a bitch here. But—"

"No, that's a compliment. You kind of needed to grow a backbone. Here." Cleo pulled Devon's Mont Blanc pen from the inside of her boot and tossed it to Devon. "Sorry about that."

Devon turned the silver pen over in her hand. It looked unharmed, plus Cleo offered the pen as opposed to making Devon ask for it. That was progress, right?

"Hey, I might have a favor to ask you." Cleo turned, her back leaning against the door, waiting. "If you wanted to make it up to me, that is."

"Depends. What is it?" Cleo asked.

Devon paused for a split second. She had to ask someone, and preferably someone she wasn't that close to. Devon pulled the folded green piece of Keaton paper from her notebook. Her Oxy order for Matt. "Would you give this to Matt for me? It's not for me, I swear. I just need to research something."

She tentatively held the paper out. Cleo studied Devon,

debating this new facet of their relationship. She took the paper and opened it.

"No, you don't have to—" Devon tried to stop Cleo from reading, but it was too late.

"Got it. Consider it done." Without the expected smirk, without the usual French exclamation, Cleo folded the paper and put it in her pocket. For a second, she looked completely unaffected. "See you next week."

"RIGHT ONE'S YOURS."

Devon caught the right speaker just as it tumbled off the dashboard. Raven's Volvo sped down the Keaton hill, taking the curves above the recommend speed limit.

"Got it," Devon yelled over the music. She wedged her speaker back into its place on the dashboard, and wiped off the layer of sand already sticking to her palm. "Thanks for the ride. I was dying to get off campus today."

Raven adjusted the speaker on her side threatening to slide out of position. Her black hair swirled in all directions as the wind whipped through the car. "No problem. Waiting for the van must suck."

"No kidding." Devon leaned her head against her seat and let the wind dance over her. Outside the pine trees fluttered in the breeze, making the green needles flicker and flash different sun-drenched shades of green. She could smell the dust from the road and the comforting smell of the pine.

"I gotta make a quick stop first, hope that's okay. Reed's computer is acting up and I'm his personal geek squad it seems." Raven looked both ways at the end of the Keaton road and took a left, away from Monte Vista.

"No problem. I'm just enjoying the ride." Devon closed her eyes again. It was true: She was happy to be moving, period, to feel the engine revving under her seat, to be away from school. The car twisted and turned, kicking up dust and spitting gravel out behind it. After what seemed like a very short time later, it lurched to a stop.

"Be right back." Raven hopped out and slammed the door behind her. Devon finally opened her eyes and saw the ranch house at Reed Hutchins's vineyard Raven had taken her to before. But this time, a rusted black Rover was parked in the circular driveway in front of the Volvo. Devon recognized it instantly: The car Hutch had been unpacking the last day she had seen him.

Raven disappeared inside the house.

Without thinking, Devon got out of the car and approached the Rover. The front window was open and the door was unlocked. Devon opened it and sat in the driver seat. She ran her hand across the cracked leather steering wheel. Hutch had driven this car to school. Somehow it had gotten back to his grandfather's house. She'd ask Raven about that part. The floor and seats of the car had leftover dirt and twigs and grape stains. It smelled like a mix of dried dirt and men's aftershave. In the cup holder next to her, Devon found a crumpled up piece of paper—white, not Keaton green.

"Ready?" Raven called from the front door. "Great car, huh?"

Devon quickly pocketed the piece of paper. "Yeah, really cool. How old is it?"

Devon casually ran her hand across the dashboard, around the wheel, like she was interested in taking it for a test drive. Maybe Raven would take the bait.

"Who knows? It's Grandpa Reed's. Kind of the junk car for all the heavy lifting and hauling around here." Raven got back in the Volvo and Devon followed, even though she would have preferred to sit in the Rover all day. That aftershave, though . . . maybe Grandpa Reed wore it? It smelled almost old fashioned, musky, too overt for Hutch.

Raven started the Volvo and Devon held onto her speaker again as the car bounced back down the hill. "Feel like surfing?"

Devon shook her head as the beach swam into view through the trees. The waves boomed. Seagulls coasted on the wind above, not flapping, surveying the water below.

"You sure?" Raven asked, turning into the parking lot. "I've got an extra board."

"No thanks."

Raven pulled her surfboard off the roof rack and shimmied into her wetsuit in the parking lot. Waves crashed like thunder. The gulls squawked and squealed.

Devon pulled the hood of her sweatshirt over her head as she eyed the rocky beach for a place to sit. She grabbed her backpack and a towel from the sandy backseat.

"Oh, can you grab my board wax? I think it's on the floor back there." Raven used the long string hanging from her wetsuit to zip the suit up her back. She tied her hair into a tight knot.

Devon reached back into the car. She dug past a damp towel covering the seat, protein bar wrappers, aged sunscreen tubes, a few loose homework assignments, some pamphlets. One of them caught Devon's eye. *Pregnant? You Have Options.*

Devon froze. Did this mean that Raven was the one Hutch stole the pregnancy test for? Had her brother gotten Hutch off the hook for shoplifting because Hutch was stealing for his sister? Devon's mind raced with questions. She had to ask Raven about this, but how?

"Found it?" Raven called from the outside.

Devon looked below the pamphlet and found a round hockey puck-sized mound of wax. *Sex Wax,* the label read. Sex Wax under the pregnancy pamphlet. Jesus. If that wasn't irony, Devon didn't know what was.

"Got it," she called back. She tossed the puck to Raven over the top of the car.

"Thanks." Raven started scraping the wax against her board. "Oh dude, I forgot to ask. What's up with you and that lacrosse guy?"

"Grant." Devon couldn't make eye contact with Raven. Not now.

"Yeah, Grant. I wouldn't have called that one. He doesn't strike me as your type. But you never know about people, huh?" Raven tossed back the wax. "See ya in a bit."

She strapped the surfboard leash to her ankle and ran down to the beach, over the rocks, and skidded into the surf like a rock skipping over water.

"Yeah, you never know," Devon said as she watched Raven duck under a wave.

DEVON DUG *A TALE of Two Cities* out of her backpack, but there was no way she was going to get any reading done today. Instead she stuck her bare feet into the warm sand and watched the surfers out on the water. They sat in a cluster behind the breaking waves, straddling their boards and bobbing along with the tide. In their full-body black wetsuits, they looked like a family of ducks out for a swim. Devon couldn't tell anyone apart, except for Raven's signature nest of hair atop her head. Devon watched as Raven paddled next to a blond dreaded surfer. Bodhi, no doubt.

So. Raven knew about Devon and Grant. Was it public knowledge? Were they officially a couple now? She was going to have to remember to make peace with Grant if this "official" label was going to stick. That is, if she wanted it to stick. Why didn't Raven think he was her type? She hadn't exactly had enough boyfriends to identify a *type* at this point.

Off to the side of the group of surfers a figure bobbed alone. He ducked under a wave and when he came up he shook his head, sending water flying from his blond shaggy hair. *Was that Matt?* Devon smiled. It was another chance to see a side of Matt most people didn't get to see at Keaton. He spent so much time surfing and now she got to see him in his element. She envied him his surfing. To have something that he craved every day, something that he loved that much. Although he would probably never admit it, Matt must get that buzz that surfers talk about. The idea of battling roaring waves on a piece of foam; the chance to be a part of the water, to bring everything you are and throw it into the ocean, and to come out cleansed by it. . . . Before her days at Keaton were over, Devon promised herself she'd at least give surfing a try.

A wave approached the group and Devon watched Raven pop up on her board and weave expertly up and down the wave, while other surfers paddled out of her way. Before she got too close to the rocks near the shore, Raven dropped down to her board and paddled back out for another wave. She was graceful, and she clearly had the respect of the other locals. Having an older brother at the center of the surfing community didn't hurt either.

The pamphlet in her car, though. Devon wished she had grabbed it. She wasn't jumping to conclusions, was she? *Okay, what do you actually know?* She had to get her thoughts straight before talking to Raven. Hutch definitely stole a pregnancy test for someone. And she knew that someone was not Isla. She also knew that Raven bonded over peanut butter products with Hutch over the summer— while he was broken up with Isla, so the opportunity for them to hook up was definitely there. She cried more often than not at the mention of Hutch's name.

Was this a bunch of coincidences, or was this a time where her mother would say, "There are no coincidences?" If Raven was pregnant with Hutch's baby, would that be enough to drive Hutch to suicide? And, if Devon's theory was correct, what if it *wasn't* suicide? Was it enough to make someone want to kill Hutch? Like a protective older brother, perhaps? Could Bodhi have killed Hutch because he got Raven pregnant?

Okay, so maybe there was a lot of speculation here.

Devon resolved to talk with Raven on the ride back to school. She would be the comforting-older-sister type Raven probably wished she had right about now. And she could ask about Bodhi. Did Bodhi really have murder in him? Something about surfers, so attuned to the tides and harnessing the ocean—no. But a pissed-off older brother could be capable of a lot. And Devon still didn't know why Bodhi left MIT. Could he have been kicked out for violent tendencies? Now she was just making stuff up. Forget about all that; she'd start with confirming if Raven was pregnant with Hutch's baby.

Another wave approached and Devon saw Bodhi and then Matt both turn and paddle for it. The wave swelled and Bodhi stood up. He aimed his board toward the wave break and drifted to the top lip of the arcing wave until Matt dropped in on Bodhi's wave, cutting him off, and riding it the rest of the way. Bodhi yelled something at Matt and then quickly let the next wave push him to shore. Matt was walking through the rocky shallow water when Bodhi caught up to him. "Dude!" Bodhi barked at Matt.

Devon shielded her eyes from the sun with her hand. Bodhi didn't sound happy.

Matt reached into the water and unhooked his foot from his leash. He nodded at Bodhi, oblivious. "What's up, man?"

"Did you not see me there, 'cause you'd have to be freakin' blind to miss what you just did." Bodhi was carrying his board toward Matt now.

Deeper in the water, Raven caught a small wave to join Bodhi on shore. A few others followed her. Devon stood. This was bad.

"What are you talking about, dude?" Matt kept walking out of the water with his board.

"Are you kidding me?" Bodhi ripped the Velcro off his ankle and dug his board straight down into the wet sand. "You know better than to take my wave. Or do I have to teach you again?"

Matt turned. "Hey, chill. I support you, remember?"

Bodhi laughed, incredulous. "You support me? That's hilarious. I told him it was a mistake to go into business with you. And from what I hear, he should have listened to me."

"What are you saying?" Matt didn't back off.

Devon noticed that both of them were puffing their chests out, and she could see a red patch growing up the back of Matt's neck spreading to his ears. She crept toward them, careful to not draw attention to herself.

"I'm saying that if you can't respect me out there, then I know you're not respecting me up there." Bodhi pointed to the looming mountains behind them. "We're done."

Matt pushed at Bodhi's chest. "That's not your call, local."

Another surfer—shaved head, lots of tattoos—leapt out of the water next to Raven. They both quickly unhooked from their boards, and dropped them on the sand.

"You don't want to do this, man," Bodhi said. Now he had backup, but that didn't seem to faze Matt.

"Oh no, I do. I really do." Matt unzipped his wetsuit.

Shaved Head moved in front of Bodhi. "You're lucky we let you surf here this long. Tourist." Before Devon could process what was happening, the guy took a swing and connected with the side of Matt's jaw.

Matt stumbled back momentarily, but came back quickly with a hard punch to Shaved Head's ribcage. Bodhi's right hand jabbed at Matt and caught him in the eye. Matt reeled back and then prepared to lunge at Bodhi until Raven appeared between them.

"Stop it!" she shrieked. "Seriously, stop. It's not worth it. This is stupid." More surfers stood behind Bodhi now. Devon could see their muscles bulging underneath their wetsuits, and they eyed Matt like a dog waiting for a treat. Devon realized she was holding her breath, digging her nails into her palms. Just one word from Bodhi and they'd spring into action.

"Don't make the mistake of thinking this is over," Matt said with a hand over his eye.

He turned and took off across the beach with his board, through the parking lot. Devon watched him go. Had he seen her there? She wanted to run after him, help him get back to school, get some ice, but he was already out on the road. This crowd was entirely Monte Vista locals, and Devon was nervous about outing herself as a Keaton student.

She looked down and realized she was wearing a sweatshirt with KEATON blazed across the front in huge letters. *Too late for that.*

The surfers gave Bodhi pats on the back or quick nods before getting back in the water. Bodhi flashed Devon a slight smile, which she took as a sign that it was okay to join their group. Raven was focused on Shaved Head, who had a hand clamped around his rib cage and his eyes squinted in pain. As she stepped closer Devon could hear Raven talking in a small, sweet voice.

"It's going to be okay, baby. I'll take care of you." Raven said to Shaved Head.

She kissed him on the lips and wrapped her arms around him. He wrapped a hand around her waist and pulled her closer, nuzzling her neck.

Time stood still on the hot beach as Devon watched them. *So,* she thought, *that's what an official couple looks like.* Almost like Hutch and Isla had once looked, but even more tender and intimate. Maybe Devon was wrong about everything. Maybe Hutch wasn't Raven's type.

CHAPTER 9

Name: Devon Mackintosh
Session Date: Sept. 24
Session #2

Mr. Robins was already writing notes in his notebook when Devon sat down.

"Devon, right on time. Have a seat," he nodded in the direction of the chair across from his desk. Devon sat down and pulled out her own notebook. Her Mont Blanc pen wasn't in the pocket she left it in. *Damn, Cleo strikes again!* This game was getting old. Devon reminded herself to get her pen back during Cleo's next session. "So? How's it going this week?" He scrunched his nose, pushing his glasses further up.

"Good, I think. I mean, I guess it's normal counseling stuff, two steps forward, one step back." She smiled politely and sat up straighter. The more committed and serious she could seem the less he would question her, was the hope.

"Glad to hear it. But, I've got to admit, I have some concerns with the work we're doing." He folded his hands and leaned on his desk. *Uh-oh.* "It's Matt Dolgens. Apparently he's been skipping a lot of classes the last week or so. I'm thinking I should take over working with him. He might be a little more than you're ready for."

Devon arranged a smile on her face, but it felt plastic and crooked. "That's an interesting idea." If Matt suddenly had to stop seeing Devon and start seeing an actual faculty member, she'd come off like the enemy he'd been trying to make her out to be. "But, isn't missing a few classes here and there somewhat expected given what he's been going through? Hutch was his best friend."

"We've been told that Matt has been seen talking with Bodhi Elliot in Monte Vista lately. I'm not sure if you know him, but Bodhi is an alum with a troubled past. The concern is that if Matt gets in with the wrong element, his behavior could take a turn for the worse. I'm sure I don't need to tell you how vulnerable he is right now."

Images of Matt and Bodhi—smoking a joint behind the pharmacy, fighting on the beach—flashed through Devon's mind. Exactly which one of them was the wrong element was difficult to discern. She kept her head down, studying her fingernails. *Next question. Next question.*

"I take it from your silence you know something about this," Mr. Robins said, leaning back in chair. Devon wanted to tell him to lose the smug grin; he didn't know a fraction of what he thought he did.

"I've met Raven, Bodhi's sister. As far as I can tell, she's a smart girl and excited to be at Keaton. I've never met Bodhi, so I can't really say much about him."

"I'm not at liberty to go into details, but Bodhi didn't leave Keaton with the best reputation, and we weren't exactly happy to see him back in Monte Vista."

"But that doesn't mean anything about Matt. Maybe they just surf together or something?"

Mr. Robins took off his glasses and rubbed his eyes. "Devon, we've got to watch out for peer sympathy getting in the way of you making informed decisions. That's an inherit blind spot with this program."

"But I'm not. . . ." Devon stopped herself. Getting too defensive right now would only confirm Mr. Robins' theory. "I understand the concern. It's just that I feel like Matt is finally starting to trust me, and to open up, and to make some progress in working through his grief. I'd really hate to cut that off now. You mentioned in your training how important it was so establish a good rapport with your subject. Can I try one more session with Matt? See if I can help with this attendance thing?"

Mr. Robins glanced at his watch. He pulled a handful of pages from the back of his notebook. "Fine. But if we see any other red flag behavior from him, I'll be meeting with Matt personally."

"Okay, I'll see what I can do."

"Now, if we could take a minute to review your notes." He stole a glance at the clock on the wall behind Devon. *What's he waiting for?* "Everything looks good. You say Matt presented with anger and disbelief about Jason's suicide, all perfectly normal." He flipped to the next page. "Isla with feelings of guilt, and Cleo ashamed of her behavior in Monte Vista. Everything sounds good." He scrunched his glasses up his nose again. "On paper."

She swallowed, her heart picking up a beat. "Great. Glad you think so."

"But there's more than what you're telling me, isn't there?"

"What?" *Play dumb. Play dumb.* Devon tried to force herself not to blush. *He knows you're lying.*

"Matt's absences indicate that he's going through more than anger and disbelief. And I think you know what it is." He let the words hang in the air while Devon's insides squirmed.

"Really, I'm not sure—"

"Devon, if you and Matt are dating, I need to know about that," he interrupted. "I realize counseling can often bring people closer together, so if you two have. . . ." He waited for her to fill in the rest. *Ha! Devon: 1; Mr. Robins: 0! He has no idea.*

"Mr. Robins, that's not what's happening. Matt and I, we really don't see each other outside of our sessions."

There was a knock on the door. Headmaster Wyler walked into the room without waiting for an answer. "This still a good time?" he asked.

Mr. Robins pulled a chair for the Headmaster. "Yes, glad you could make it."

What is he doing here? In his ever-present khakis and sweater vest and perfectly cropped salt-and-pepper hair, Devon wondered if Wyler looked the same as a Keaton student years ago. She pictured a seventeen-year-old version: soccer legend, bio whiz, and sweater vest collector. And now living back at the school he attended three decades ago. *I'll bet the outside world wasn't all that kind to the Sweater Vest King.*

"Devon, I'm glad I didn't miss you," he said, scooting his chair around to face her.

She nodded and half-stood up from her chair. "Headmaster Wyler. Good morning."

"Have a seat, please."

Devon realized both men were now staring at her. This wasn't an impromptu interruption, was it? They had planned this, whatever *this* was. She braced herself.

"Devon, I wanted to be here along with Mr. Robins to thank you for your hard work serving our student body. Your commitment to this program has not gone unnoticed."

She breathed a little easier. *Okay, that's not bad news.* "Thanks. It's been a good experience so far."

"Because this program is the first of its kind for Keaton, or for California for that matter, it's important that we can really quantify our results. After all, if this proves successful for our students, hopefully the state will allow more programs like this in other schools. What this could do for bullying, depression, substance abuse—the possibilities are really inspiring." Headmaster Wyler used his hands in a practiced, political way. *He must rehearse in front of a mirror,*

Devon thought. "Which is why we're installing a camera in your 'office.'"

Putting her "office" in finger quotes was immediately annoying, a paper-cut kind of annoying. But the video camera was a nearly-slicing-a-finger-off *beyond* annoying. It enraged her. Everything Devon had promised Matt, Isla, and Cleo about protecting their secrets, about creating a safe place, would be ruined. They'd become characters for Mr. Robins and Wyler to take to their School Board meetings: a twisted Show and Tell. She could almost make it work by typing up fake notes for Mr. Robins, but now the evidence would be impossible to deny. Devon felt her neck getting hot. Her palms started to sweat at the thought of Matt being exposed, of Isla's twitches and ticks and tears being used as textbook material, of Cleo being labeled as a liar.

"I don't get it. Why do you have to do that?" Devon asked.

"We don't need to go into all the boring details, but suffice it to say, boarding school students are legally under the guardianship of the school. *In loco parentis*, as they say. Because this is all new and untested thus far, our insurance would prefer if we handled the program this way going forward. I'm sure you understand." Headmaster Wyler nodded his head at Devon, as if confident she would not push back.

"We're going to tell them we're filming the sessions, though, right?" She asked the question in a way that didn't make it sound like a question, but an assumption.

Headmaster Wyler shot a look at Mr. Robins, who sat up straighter in his chair and cleared his throat.

"For the moment, we'd like you to say nothing. These sessions are going to be used for research purposes only, so there's no real need to alert your subjects. Not to mention, we'd hate to tamper with our results by alerting them to the presence of a camera. Getting authentic emotions is imperative. Otherwise, how can we gauge our success levels? You understand, don't you? It's for the good of the program."

"But. . . ." Both Wyler and Mr. Robins were watching her closely. Devon realized that this wasn't a discussion. What she thought didn't matter. The fact that they'd even told her about the cameras was lucky. She could have been filmed this whole time and these two wouldn't have had the conscience to tell her. But, no . . . they told her as a warning that they were now watching her as closely as her subjects.

First they'd needed her to sit in that chair and get her peers talking. The scale of power was tipped ever so slightly in Devon's favor. Wyler and Robins could take away her status in a second, but they knew students would talk to a peer in one way, and an authority figure in another. For all the backlash and attitude she got from Matt, Isla, and Cleo, they *were* still talking to her. The same might not be true if Mr. Robins sat in her chair, and he and Wyler knew it. She had to be smart with her ounce of power.

"Whatever you think is best for the program," she said with a warm smile.

CHEMISTRY WAS KILLING HER. Devon let her pencil drop to her desk and rubbed her eyes. *One more molecular equation might cause blindness.* She stood up and stretched her back out. Her eyes drifted to the single rose resting in a water bottle near her bed. Yellow petals with blood red tips. The makeshift card that came with it; a piece of green Keaton paper scrawled with "I'm sorry. Let's start over. —G " in one line across the bottom.

When Devon had returned to her room from classes, she found the rose and note lying on her pillow. Grant was trying to make peace with her. Devon knew she should accept it. He had gotten mad when she asked him about knowing Eric Hutchins. Who could blame him? Hutch's death affected everyone here, and in a million different ways. She had to stop treating all her friends like they were subjects ready to be dissected. Grant was just trying to be supportive. Maybe she should have been the one delivering apologies.

"Hey, George Whore-well," Presley called out, throwing herself on Devon's bed. "How was your weekend?"

Devon slumped in her armchair. "The Queen returns," she said, relieved at the distraction. "My weekend was blah, I want to hear about yours. I'm sure it was *much* more interesting."

"It was. Pete's parents were great. They took us out for dinner. His mom and I played tennis."

"Blah, blah, boring. What aren't you telling me?"

"Let's just say there are two kinds of people in this world, the ones who are on the pill, and the ones who aren't. And some are having way more fuuuu-n."

But Devon's hearing was stuck on '*two kinds of people in this world.*' The supposed-tos and the not-supposed-tos. The ones who like peanut butter and the ones who don't. Devon had a new distinction to add to the list now: the ones who'd slept with Hutch, and the ones who hadn't. Which one did Presley fall into?

Presley threw a tube of hand lotion at Devon. "Yo, J.D. Slutinger, you hear me? Besides, you make something happen with Grant yet?"

"Yeah, I mean, no. I don't know." Devon walked to her mirror and tried to figure out what to do with her hair. "Pres, you didn't hook up with anyone when you and Pete were broken up, did you?"

Presley furrowed her brow, still smiling. "No, why?"

Devon tried to sound casual as she brushed her hair. "Just wondering. Cause you weren't on the pill until recently, so it's possible—"

"Dev, cut the shit. I know that weird tone in your voice, what are you getting at?"

She sighed, turning to face Presley. "You didn't hook up with Hutch did you? I know it sounds out there, but you two were on the newspaper together, you were barfing. You didn't get pregnant did you?"

Presley's face softened. She shook her head, got up from the bed, and stood behind Devon at the mirror. They looked at each other in the reflection. Then Presley's lips tightened. She ran her fingers through Devon's hair and started to pull it into a loose braid. "Devon, I'm saying this because I love you, because you're my best friend, and you don't talk to ton of other people. So someone has to say it. You have got to get over this Hutch thing. No, I never slept with Hutch. Never even kissed the guy. Thought about it, yes. Did anything about it, no. But you? You're obsessing. It's annoying. But more than that, it's disturbing. Go find Grant. Go make out with that hot boy and forget about the dead one. You hear me? This is for your own good." Presley finished the braid and gave Devon a supportive smile in the mirror. "King Slut-ankhamun," Presley added, and slapped Devon on the butt, then ran from the room with a laugh.

"William Slutspeare!" Devon called down the hall.

Presley poked her head out of her door. "That one sucked."

Devon turned to the mirror again. Presley had a point. Devon didn't think she could stop thinking about Hutch, or his possible murder, but Grant wanted nothing more than to take her mind off things. Maybe she should let him.

AFTER THREE KNOCKS SHE opened the door to Grant's room. No one there. A huge American flag was tacked to one wall, and a large iPod dock took up most of the remaining space on his book-strewn desk. His bed was still unmade and dirty clothes formed a trail from the bed to closet.

She'd try to find him later.

Down the hall, Devon passed a door that stood out from the rest. Carved, inked, painted, scribbled all over it were messages to Hutch. *RIP. We'll miss you, bro. Always in our hearts. Keaton forever, Hutch! Wish You Were Here.* And on and on, covering almost every inch of the dark wood. Devon ran her hands over the writing, the deep grooves in the wood, the gloppy white-out hearts and stars around his name. When her hand brushed against the metal doorknob she couldn't resist. The door was unlocked. She would just look and get it out of her system. This wasn't obsessing; it was closure.

Devon ducked into Hutch's room, quietly closing the door behind her. The mattress was bare and wire hangers hung in the empty closet. The poster from *The Godfather* still tacked to one wall and ripped corners of photos on another were the only sad remnants of the boy who'd lived here. Surely another student would be claiming this room at some point—someone thrilled to be taken off the waiting list, to be given the chance to attend the prestigious The Keaton School, only to discover they'd be sleeping in a dead student's bed. The wait list might not look so bad then.

Devon reached for the light switch, but stopped. She could almost feel the weight of Hutch's hand and his whisper in her ear, *"No lights. It will give away our position."* Devon inhaled, trying to find a scent of Hutch, but the air only smelled of dust and floor disinfectant. She lay down on the bed and closed her eyes for a moment. When she opened them, she spotted letters carved into the underside of a shelf behind the bed. She scooted closer, the words seemed out of order, and then she realized: *miles to go before I sleep* written backward. Next to the words was a circle with what looked like three branches stemming from it. She ran her hands over Hutch's carvings, brittle slivers of wood dropped away at the touch. Her breathing got shallow and quick and she felt her ears burning. Anger was creeping in and taking over. She had to get out of here.

ON A CLEAR DAY, with the sunset over the Pacific Ocean, the Palace had one of the best views on campus. Deep shades of orange and pink bled into purple as the sun vanished, and the ocean turned a dark blue as if pulling a comforter around itself to sleep for the night. But now the vista was ruined. The decaying concrete bunker was sectioned off by *police tape—do not cross*. Bright yellow and rippling in the wind, it threatened to snap off and drift down the mountain any second. The gravel and broken glass crunched under

Devon's shoes. Again, she wasn't obsessing; she just wanted to see where it had happened. Returning to the scene of the crime—out of curiosity alone.

Devon sat on the bench wedged in the back of the bunker, with the graffiti-smothered walls all around her and nothing but the view below. Here was where he'd drawn his last breath. But for Hutch to be murdered, someone else had to have been here with him that night too. What were they doing? What brought Hutch out here? Matt said Hutch got a phone call that night. Could someone have called him to meet at the Palace? The police found a body and pills so they assumed suicide, which meant they probably hadn't looked beyond this spot.

Devon walked behind the bunker. Only a single narrow trail through overgrown plants led to this spot. Anybody going to the Palace had to come through the Keaton campus and down the hillside. She walked up the trail, tucking her arms close to avoid getting scratched by the dried branches. The top of the trail opened to a gravel driveway where the school left outdated landscaping equipment. The driveway then eased into the lawn, where 100 yards up the hill, the gray rooftop of Spring House appeared. Devon stood in the gravel driveway. It must have been dark when Hutch had come here.

The sun was getting lower over the ocean, a half circle of golden orange light casting long shadows through the trees. If Hutch was angry about a phone call he got that night, did he come down here to blow off steam? But why *here*? Did he want to smoke a cigarette? Pot? Drink? It had to be something illicit to take him away from his dorm after hours. To Devon's left she noticed an old tractor, rusted, tucked away by the hillside. *Where Keaton farm tools go to die*, Devon thought.

Something else caught her eye. Her feet crunched in the gravel as she walked toward the tractor. Three small green bottles were lined up next to the dirt-encrusted wheel. They looked oddly clean. Devon picked one up; it was small and round in her hand, not lean like a soda or beer bottle. She sniffed; the sharp smell of stale alcohol hit her. She studied the front of the bottle. The label was peeled off; only streaks of white paper remained. Was it possible Hutch drank from these bottles? Or better yet, his murderer? She tucked the bottle up her sleeve. Even getting caught with an empty was an offense punishable by suspension. She would have to hide it well back in her room.

Behind the tractor Devon saw a metal bottle cap: dark green with the ridges poking out and a white G printed on the top. It fit her bottle. Now she just had to figure out what the G stood for. It was possible other students had snuck to the Palace and had a beer or two in Hutch's honor, but these were too far away.

Devon peered around the tractor to the hillside behind it. A wide patch of dirt cut a path down through the scrub brush—marked with fresh tire tracks. Is this how the tractor maintained the hillside? Devon glanced back at the wide, zigzag tires. The pattern didn't match, and she doubted the tractor had actually moved from that spot in months. Could a car have driven up here? The tracks disappeared around a bend in the mountain. While anyone going to Keaton had always used the paved main road leading up the hill, Devon wondered if this was a secret fire road only certain people knew of. The opposite mountainside was draped in grapevines extending long shadows, like an army of scarecrows guarding their fortress. Grandpa Hutchins's vines. He had ridden a horse up the hillside to Hutch's funeral, and he had somehow left Devon's room without taking the main road. . . .

It was getting dark. Devon knew she would have to be checked into her dorm for study hours soon. With her green bottle and metal cap, she trekked back up the hill. So, who besides Grandpa Hutchins might have access to that fire road? Hutch, Raven, and Bodhi probably knew about it too. A car door slamming in the parking lot near Spring House snapped Devon back to attention. It was that same silver BMW she had seen idling there before, Maya was walking away from it. Actually, more like stomping away from it. Devon saw her swipe at her cheeks, as if wiping away tears.

"Maya, come on! It's not that big a deal." A familiar-sounding guy with brown hair tucked behind his ears was yelling after Maya from the driver's seat. He yelled again, "Maya!" but she didn't turn around. He slammed his fist on the steering wheel, then turned, noticing Devon walking by.

She locked eyes with Eric Hutchins.

CHAPTER 10

September 10, 2010
Freshman Year

"Want another?" Hutch dipped a Nutter Butter into the gallon of molten chocolate and careful to catch the drips, he fed the cookie to Devon. "Amazing, right?"

"Reh. Ah-mreh-zrhing," was all Devon could muster in between chews. Hutch smiled, watching her chew. He wiped at a drizzle of chocolate on her lip and leaned in and kissed her.

"Chocolate," he explained.

Devon self-consciously wiped a hand across her chin. "I'm probably a total mess right now." She hopped off the counter and started washing her hands in the sink. If only there was a mirror in here, she could at least fix her hair. It was probably too dark to see her reflection anyways. *Please, don't let me have cookie and chocolate all over my face.*

"Hey, I need your help," Hutch said. Devon turned and saw

Hutch had a glob of chocolate on one cheek. "I think I got some chocolate on me, could you tell me where?"

Devon laughed. "Right there." She pointed to her own cheek.

"Here?" Hutch put a glob on his other cheek. Devon laughed more.

"No, here," she wiped at her own cheek again.

"Oh, I get it. Here," Hutch left a streak of chocolate across his mouth.

She kept laughing. "Nope, that's not it."

"I need you to show me then," he said. He reached out and grabbed her hand, pulling her against him.

Devon used the paper towel in her hand and wiped at Hutch's cheek. "Right here," she kissed his cheek. She wiped the chocolate off his other cheek and kissed that spot too. "Right there." She wiped the towel across his lips. "And right here." He leaned over and kissed her on the lips. She lifted onto her tiptoes to meet his kiss again. But this time, both of his hands were around her waist, the small of her back, pulling her up against him. *Now this is making out,* Devon thought. Goosebumps ran down her arms. She felt his fingers slip under her bra strap.

"Whoa, wait a sec," Devon said pulling away. "What if someone comes in?"

"I'm sorry. Do you want to stop?" Hutch ran his fingers along Devon's cheekbone, her jaw, over her shoulders.

"No, I mean, it's just. . . ."

"It's fine. I get it." Hutch smiled softly, his eyes inches from her own.

"You don't think I'm like some prude now, do you?"

"Devon, there's a lot of things I think about you, but that is not one of them, okay?"

"A lot of things? Really?"

"Really."

"Just from tonight?"

"Not just from tonight. You sat in front of me in that Orientation assembly."

"You kept kicking my seat."

"You got bitchy about it."

Devon laughed and felt her cheeks go red. "I did, didn't I? But you were pretty annoying, you have to admit."

He shrugged, his arms still around her waist. "Hey, I would have hated me too."

"And you stood up all proud when they called out the legacies."

"Proud? Are you sure it was me you were looking at? Not some other handsome legacy?"

"No, pretty sure it was you. What? You're not a proud Keaton legacy?"

Hutch let go of Devon and poured himself a glass of water from the sink. He sat on the counter opposite her. "You know, before I was even born, I was going to Keaton. It was a given. Nowhere along the way did anyone ask me what I wanted."

"Sounds familiar. My mom sent in my application and had an interview set up before I knew this place existed. And once I got the scholarship there was no debate; I was going. And any time I try to talk about it with my mom she just thinks I'm being ungrateful. I'm not ungrateful, I just . . . "

". . . would have liked a choice in the matter," he finished for her. "I get it. The freaky thing is that our parents were easier than this place. Every minute here is accounted for, regimented. It's like this creepy ooze that just gets in everywhere, and eventually takes over your life. I hate it. I'd take public school, or even just being a day student any day. When you live here you can't escape it."

"But, you can go into town and stuff on weekends? At least there's that, right?"

"Not really; even there you're still in it. You think if we ran into a teacher in Monte Vista they wouldn't note what we were up to, who we were with, and what flavor ice cream we eat? All of it is noted. Filed away."

"That sounds a little paranoid. It can't be that bad."

"I saw my brother go through it. His friends, their parents, his teachers, everyone knows all this random stuff about him. He's in the bubble for the rest of his life and he can't get out. None of us can."

"Okay, so let's say we're all in the bubble. What's tonight then? Part of the bubble too? Because, it can't be all bad if there's Nutter Butter pancakes, right?"

He flashed a crooked smile. "This? This is a blip in the bubble. A glitch in the matrix. This is the ultimate not-supposed-to."

"Right, your favorite group, the not-supposed-tos?"

"Something like that. You know, I was hating this week so far. I mean, I guess my roommate Matt is pretty cool, so that's lucky. But, when you walked into the dining hall, that cute bitchy girl, Devon, from assembly, this week stopped sucking."

"Yeah, you're kind of the only good thing about this week."

"I have a feeling you're the only good thing about this whole place."

Devon laughed off the compliment. "We just got here."

"But what if I'm right? What if tonight is the best it will get around here for the next four years and everything else is just downhill?"

"If getting locked in the kitchen together is the best it gets, that doesn't bode well for the next four years."

September 26, Present Day

THE GREEN BOTTLES CLINKED together at the bottom of Devon's T-shirt drawer. The stale beer smell was worse than she thought and she grabbed the plastic bag from her trashcan to wrap them. The white torn labels caught her attention again. Were they purposely torn off because someone didn't want it known what they were drinking? A Keaton student would take much smarter precautions than just ripping a label off a beer bottle. Vodka disguised in water bottles, flasks in the shape of cell phones, travel-sized perfume, extra shirts, and breath mints were all basic items everyone used for concealing drinking and/or smoking. Over the summer at a barbeque Ariel hosted while her parents were away, Devon drank a few beers. They were fancy, apparently appropriate for Ariel's beer connoisseur friends. But, Devon remembered not liking the taste very much and she peeled the labels off the wet bottles while she watched Ariel flirt with a new guy.

Maybe this person was an absentminded label-peeler too.

All at once, a thought occurred to her. Devon found her jeans from the other day at the beach on the floor of her closet and dug into the pocket. The balled up paper she found in Hutch's car. Carefully she unraveled.it A label. *Gersbach* written in white letters on a gold background. The G matched the lettering on the metal cap Devon had found. She wrapped the paper over one bottle but the torn paper didn't match. She tried the second and the label matched the tears from the bottle perfectly. Her pulse picked up. This put Hutch's car at the Palace, didn't it? Hutch could have driven up the hill from his grandfather's, had a beer or two, left the bottles on the hillside. But somewhere along the way he had torn off the label on his beer and dropped it inside the car. But, when? The car driving up the hill, the beer drinking, and the bottles left behind could have happened at any time. *You haven't really solved anything*, Devon thought.

"Bee-yotch! We're gonna be late for the game, and I'm not running extra laps because of you." Presley barged into Devon's room wearing a short plaid lacrosse skirt and her cleats. She spotted the green bottles in Devon's open drawer. "Oh, what are you hiding, Miss Mackintosh? Anything good?"

Devon slammed the drawer shut. "It's nothing. Just a project. I'll be right behind you." She reached for her lacrosse skirt and started changing clothes.

"Whatever. See you out there." Presley slapped Devon's butt with her lacrosse stick on her way out the door.

The first game of the season, Devon thought. Nothing could seem less important.

As Devon jogged across the parking lot, past the rival school Lewis Academy's bus, she spotted a black Range Rover parked next to it. Devon stopped. *The* black Range Rover. She peered in the windows. The doors were locked, dirt still streaked the seats and dashboard. Why was it here? How did it get here?

"Sweet car, huh?" Grant said behind Devon. She quickly turned, caught.

"Hey," she said.

"You get my flower?"

"Yeah, totally. I tried to find you last night to thank you. It was really nice of you." Devon's cleats clicked on the pavement as she shifted her weight from foot to foot.

"So, are we cool?" Grant asked, his eyes sheepish below the brim of his white hat.

"Mackintosh! You're late! Five laps! Let's go!" Mrs. Freeman yelled from the lacrosse field across the parking lot to Devon.

"I gotta go, but yeah. We're cool. Wanna come by tonight?"

"I'll be there." Grant's smile returned. Devon started jogging toward the field. "Hey, Mackintosh," he yelled after her. "Kill 'em."

"I'll try," Devon yelled back over her shoulder.

Both teams were already warming up on the field: Keaton in its green-and-white plaid skirts and Lewis in their blue skirts and tops. Devon started her laps, jogging around the field. Weird: The Keaton cheering section wasn't just a few over-eager parents on the sidelines. What seemed like every guy in school sat on the wooden bleachers. Girls in short skirts battling it out on the field did have a certain attraction, she figured.

Devon spotted a blond head of dreadlocked hair. Bodhi. Why was he here? *Raven . . . right.* She rounded the bend for her first lap and saw Raven putting on the hockey-mask sized helmet worn by lacrosse goalies. Raven must have worked her way up to becoming their second-string goalie. Smart way to get on the Varsity team; play the position no one wants. Raven warmed up with the assistant coach on the sidelines.

"Go, Devon!" Bodhi whistled as she passed, smiling and watching her finish her laps. Devon gave him a half-wave and kept running.

The black Range Rover crept back into her mind. Bodhi and Raven had access to the Range Rover, didn't they? Either one of them could have been up to the Palace, although it seemed much more likely that Bodhi was the one with the taste for rare German beer.

AT HALF-TIME KEATON WAS winning 5-2. Devon, Raven, Maya, sat on the bench.

"All right," Mrs. Freeman lifted her wraparound sunglasses onto her head and leaned her clipboard against her round belly and khaki shorts, "Let's rotate a few of you in this half. Raven, you wanna get some goal time? Suit up. Maya, how you feeling?"

Maya smiled weakly, "Not great."

"Fine, let's not push it. Devon? Feel like a little defense?" Mrs. Freeman's sunglasses balanced precariously on her spiky blonde hair.

Next to Devon, Raven wiped the sweat off her hands as she put on her shin and arm pads. "Come on, Dev. I could use all the help I can get."

"Yeah, I'll go in," Devon said. She stood up and jumped up and down a few times to get her blood flowing. The other team took the field and the ref blew the whistle. Presley scooped up the ball first and charged across the field. Devon watched her go, staying on Keaton's side of the field to protect the goal, but the crowd bustling in the bleachers caught her attention. They weren't cheering for Presley.

"Yo, you don't have the right to do this!"

It was Bodhi. And there were two cops from Monte Vista pulling him off the bleachers and struggling to pin him to the ground.

"Bodhi!" Raven threw down her stick and ripped off her pads, sprinting to her brother. At the other end of the field Devon could see the Lewis players were also distracted by the commotion. Presley kept running and whizzed her ball passed the goalie into their net, but she was the only one still playing the game. Devon ran to the sidelines as the ref blew the whistle.

"You're under arrest for trespassing," one of the cops announced. "You have the right to remain silent; anything you say can and will be used against you in a court of law."

Raven burst into tears, crouching next to Bodhi as he lay in the dirt. "What do you want me to do? Why is this happening?"

The other cop, a younger guy with a military buzz cut, wrapped plastic cuffs around Bodhi's wrist and pulled them tight.

"Call Reed," Bodhi gasped, spitting out dirt. "He'll know what to do."

The cops pulls Bodhi up and walked him toward the parking lot where their cruiser was parked, the red lights silently spinning around and around.

Raven cried as Bodhi was folded into the back seat. Devon put an arm around her. "I'm sure it's just a mistake, right?"

"I've got to call Reed," Raven choked out. She ran to her backpack near the player's bench and pulled out her cell phone. Devon watched the police cruiser drive away. Trespassing? At Keaton? Was Bodhi caught for being here now or possibly for another time? The beer bottles, the prescription pills. Maybe Mr. Robins hadn't been so far off base in his worry over Bodhi.

Behind the cruiser, Devon noticed Eric's silver BMW sitting idle in the lot. The passenger door opened and a tall guy with shaggy blond hair stepped out. *Matt.* Even from this distance she could see that he had a swollen black eye. Probably from his fight with Bodhi on the beach. Behind her, Devon could hear Raven crying into the phone talking to Grandpa Reed. She wanted to help Raven; she truly did—no matter what was going on with Bodhi. Raven was on her side when it came to Hutch.

And maybe Raven could help her, too.

CHAPTER 11

"This should do the trick." Raven placed a small metal box on Devon's bedspread. She zipped her backpacked closed again while Devon inspected it. Nothing but brushed metal and a single switch on one side of the palm-sized device. They had only ten minutes until first period. For Devon, first period meant doing a session with Matt. But after her last meeting with Robins and Wyler. . . .

"This little thing will jam the camera?"

Raven gazed into Devon's mirror, rolling her nest of hair into one organized spiral at the nape of her neck. "It's just a frequency jammer, super basic. Once you bring it in the room, it will automatically find the frequency the camera is recording on, set itself to the same frequency, rendering your video feed useless. They'll record you, but it will all be static." She turned her head toward Devon. "My hair look okay?"

"Yeah, it's cool. And seriously, thanks. You're totally saving me.

I had no idea how I could still do sessions without selling everyone up the river." Devon tucked the jammer into her backpack. She noticed Raven twisting the hemp bracelets around her arm, her eyes on the floor. "Any update on Bodhi?"

Raven forced a smile. "Reed's lawyers are working on it."

"Did you find out who reported him?" *Matt. It had to be him. What other enemies could Bodhi have?*

"Don't know yet. But he should be home today."

"That's great. That should make your parents happy, right?"

"Our dad, sure. If he even noticed Bodhi was gone."

"Oh, does he work a lot or something?" Devon realized she had no idea where Raven and Bodhi actually lived or with whom. If she wanted to know more about Bodhi, that seemed like an obvious place to start.

"Not really. He's just not that present. Our mom died when I was five. Reed is kind of the best parent we've got. He's looked out for us for years. That's why we're at the guest house at the vineyard most of the time. Reed always needs help with something, the wine, the land, security, you know." Raven slung her backpack over her shoulder. They walked outside together and up the hill toward the classrooms. "You should come over sometime. Like, take a weekend to the guest house or something. Reed would sign you out. If you wanted."

"Yeah, that'd be cool. Thanks."

"Gotta make it to Spanish before the bell goes. Good luck with the session. And remember, turn on the jammer before you go inside so the camera doesn't catch you doing it. See ya." Raven quickened her pace up the hill.

"Wait, how will I know it's working?"

Raven was already yards away. "You won't!" she called without turning around. "But when it comes to this sort of thing, I don't mess up."

∞

Name: Matt Dolgens
Session Date: Sept. 27
Session #3

"WHY DON'T YOU TAKE my seat today?" Devon crossed her legs in the bigger leather chair, and held out a stiff arm toward her upright desk chair.

"Whatever," Matt said as he sat down across from her. His eye was still conspicuously bruised. She let her eyes quickly dart around the room before landing back on Matt. The small camera had been installed behind her old seat, wedged between the ceiling and the wall so Mr. Robins and his cohorts would have a clear view of Devon's subjects. But, no one said her subjects *had* to face the camera. Hopefully given how small it was, obscured by the soundproofed walls, nobody would notice it.

"Does it hurt?" Devon couldn't think of anything to say beyond the painfully obvious bruise staring back at her. Her thoughts were focused on the frequency jammer turned on inside her backpack, sitting below the camera. *Sorry, Headmaster Wyler. I guess the monitor malfunctioned. Too bad there's no footage from the student sessions, Mr. Robins. Bummer.*

"Feels great, actually," Matt said. His good eye glared at Devon.

"Do you want to talk about how it happened?"

Matt shrugged his response.

"Okay, how about I tell you what I saw at the Cove last weekend?"

"You were there?" Matt asked. His head hung a little lower. A witness he probably would have preferred not having.

"I got a ride down there. Wanted to get off campus for an afternoon. I saw you argue with Bodhi." Devon paused, giving Matt ample opportunity to jump in. He didn't. "And I saw Bodhi give you that black eye."

Matt kept silent.

"So, then to get even with Bodhi you had him arrested on campus. Am I right?"

His head jerked up. "You think I did that? That's funny. I thought *you* were the rat."

'Why did you think that?"

"Duh! Because you're all Miss Anti-Drug Crusader. So you'd make an anonymous call about Bodhi, knowing he would be on campus for the lacrosse game."

She blinked, hurt, even though she knew she couldn't blame Matt for thinking that way. "Wow, that's what you think of me?"

"Look, I didn't make that call. Why would I?"

Devon's mind raced. *If it wasn't Matt, who did?*

"Come on, think it through," Matt said gruffly, with a cruel smirk.

"If Bodhi goes to jail, he's likely to tell them about your business up here. I get it. Mutually assured destruction. You rat on him, he rats on you. Okay, so it wasn't you that called the cops, it wasn't me. Who was it then?"

"Look, I don't know and I don't care who ratted out Bodhi. What I'd like to know is who had Cleo give me this." Matt pulled a green slip of paper from his pocket and flicked it at Devon. It hit her arm and landed in her lap. Devon felt the blush coming to her cheeks. *Oh, no. Please don't be. . . .* She opened the paper to find her handwritten 30Ox/10. *It was.* "I told you, I don't deal with this stuff. Not for you. Not for Cleo. Since when do you have Cleo doing you favors, by the way? All this power seems to be going to your head."

"Look, Matt, I realize this was probably unprofessional—"

"Unprofessional? Really? That's the first word that comes to mind? I got one. Two actually. City. College. Because that's the only college that will take you if you keep trying to throw me under the bus. My dad will make sure Stanford burns your application next year."

She shook her head queasily. "Matt, I wasn't trying to throw you under the bus. No one else knew, okay? It was for Hutch. I needed to know."

His eyes held hers, one injured, one blazing. "Let's just draw this line right here so there's no confusion. When it comes to Hutch, you don't need to know anything. He's gone, Devon. That's all there is to know." Matt leaned back in his chair, his chest heaving up and down. "Missing him doesn't make you special," he added quietly.

"I really am sorry. It was totally stupid of me. I was still debating about whether or not to give you the paper, but then I heard what happened to Sasha in Calc. I didn't want anyone else to get hurt."

"No one's going to get hurt. I didn't know how much she had, okay? She was squirreling the pills away because normally we, Hutch, would keep tabs on how much they were taking. I guess I wasn't paying enough attention. It got away from me." Matt swallowed hard.

"You know, I looked it up. It is possible to die from an Adderall overdose. Someone could get seriously hurt here. And, if I was you, I'd be worried that 'It got away from me' wouldn't really hold up in court."

"I know, okay?" Matt yelled. He banged his hand on the chair. "Not like it matters anymore. Bodhi and I are done. He's in jail probably ratting me out. Everyone here's going to hate me for dropping the ball. It's done." He chewed at a cuticle on his thumb. "You know, if this gets out, people are going to think it was you."

"Me? But, I've had nothing to do with you and Bodhi. That's your thing."

"Yeah well, people are talking. This little position hasn't made you a lot of fans."

Devon felt queasy again. "What are you talking about?"

"What do you think? No one trusts you anymore, Devon. Word is you're telling Robins everything that happens in here. So, I'm going to go. They can't require me to be here for this bullshit." Matt brushed his stringy hair out of his face, wincing when his hand swiped his black eye.

"But. . . ." Devon started. *But nothing, he was right. It was better if he didn't tell her anything.* "Matt, who said I was telling Robins anything?"

"Why would I tell you that?"

"Just curious."

"If I was you, I'd drop this counseling thing completely. Stop talking to me, to Isla. We don't need you poking your head in our lives, okay?"

"Wait, did Isla tell you to say that? Did she tell you that I'm telling Robins everything? That's not the truth, Matt. I swear it isn't." She knew she sounded as if she were begging, but she couldn't help it. She *was*. "Let's keep talking."

Matt was already opening the door. "I can't tell you anything else," he said over his shoulder.

HEADMASTER WYLER PACED ACROSS the gravel circle at the bottom of the amphitheater. A vast semi-circle of stone steps and wooden benches sunk into bright green grass, the amphitheater was used whenever the weather was good enough for the school to conduct their daily assemblies outside—about 80 percent of the school year. But why this special assembly had been called out of the blue had everyone guessing. Wyler silently watched students file into their seats.

Devon saw Presley and Pete squeeze onto a bench near the top. Their arms were intertwined, as if sitting next to each other wasn't close enough. Devon was glad she hadn't chosen a seat yet. They would be completely annoying to be near right now.

"How'd it go this morning?" Raven asked, popping up next to Devon.

"I turned it on and chilled. After that, who knows, right?" She spotted Grant taking a seat on a middle bench with Raj. Grant nodded to Devon, beckoning her over. "Wanna sit down?" She asked Raven. Raven followed her and they sat down next to Grant and Raj.

"Ten bucks says it's a new drug rule," Raj Kahn leaned in and whispered to Grant and Devon. His eyes landed on Raven. "Raj," he said, extending a hand to shake Raven's. She smiled, shaking hands.

"Raven," she said.

"Raven has a boyfriend, Raj," Devon said. "Watch yourself."

"I'll consider myself warned then," Raj said with a smile.

"You been in session?" Grant whispered in Devon's ear. He directed his eyes at Raven. She shook her head, no. "Just a friend," she whispered back. *Whose brother I am trying to investigate.* Raven was spinning her bracelets on her arm again, lost in thought.

Grant wrapped an arm around Devon's shoulder as Headmaster Wyler cleared his throat and tapped the microphone. "As you are all well aware, our community has suffered a terrible tragedy already in this short school term," he began. "We, as the faculty appointed by your parents are here to protect you." Raj slapped Grant's arm. Other students mumbled and shifted in their seats. Wyler continued. "But, with that in mind, we felt as if we could all use a little break. A way of looking forward." He smiled. "So we're going to have a Pop-Up Party. No sports this afternoon. The party will start at six P.M. Dinner will be served on Raiter Lawn."

Students jumped up and cheered. Grant slapped Raj's arm. "You lose, dude! Ten bucks!"

Raven laughed and put a hand over her heart. "I don't know why, but I was really worried he had bad news or something," she whispered. "I don't think I could have handled it."

Devon nodded, even though she felt unsettled. Maybe wallowing in misery wasn't the best response to the Hutch "tragedy," but maybe it was a bit too soon for a party? On other hand, she appeared to be the only student who felt that way. "It's perfect timing," she heard herself say. "Now you can get out of here early and go meet Bodhi when he gets home. I'm sure he'll have a lot to tell you." *What are you doing, Devon? She's not your spy.*

"Yeah, that's what I'm going to do. I'll call you later." Raven hoisted her backpack over her shoulder.

"Wait, Raven," Devon said. "Thanks again for helping me this morning. It was sort of above-and-beyond of you."

Raven smiled and suddenly pulled Devon into a hug. "I'm happy we're friends. It feels like Hutch would approve, you know." She walked away, leaving Devon with a pit in her stomach. Raven was right, Hutch would approve of their friendship, while he would completely disapprove of Devon's second guesses about Bodhi. Wouldn't he?

"So, you wanna make good use of this Pop-Up?" Grant's question brought Devon back into the celebratory chaos.

"Good use?"

Grant wrapped an arm around her waist. "You can't tell me that now, when the whole school is stopping to have fun for the night, that you have other things to do."

"Don't you have the same classes I do? I've got crazy amounts of homework." But even she could hear how thin that excuse sounded.

"Devon, there will always be homework. Always. But you and me? If that's not better than homework, then I should just give up now. Seriously. If you'd rather do homework, then I won't stand in your way." His eyes searched her face for an answer.

Devon smiled. "You're right. I'm sorry. It feels like I haven't had free time in so long, I don't really know what to do with it."

"Yeah?" Grant's smile spread across his whole face. His eyes crinkled into smiling lines.

"Yeah. You and me is definitely better than homework."

"Cool. How about you go do what you gotta do for a bit. I'll come by and get you when it's dark, okay?" Grant kissed her on the lips and stood.

"Okay," Devon said back.

Grant turned and disappeared into the jubilant crowd, filing out of the amphitheater. She fell in line, her head reeling. What did she just agree to? She had to find Presley. Devon turned toward Bay House and saw Cleo walking across the lawn toward her. Devon gave her a slight wave. "Hey."

"We gotta talk," Cleo said. "*Faire une promenade?*" Devon squinted in response. "Wanna go for a walk?" Cleo explained, steering her toward Bay House.

"Oh, okay sure. Why? What's up?"

"You and Grant are a thing now, huh?" Cleo asked.

"Yeah, I guess. Why?"

"I don't want to rain on your parade or anything, and seriously, you're a little high strung. You deserve a parade. But, just keep your eyes open with Grant. I don't know that he's everything he fronts."

Devon stopped walking. The wind picked up and she wrapped her arms across her chest as a chill rippled through her body. "Why are you saying this? Grant's been really great."

"*D'accord.* I'm sure he has been, but I'm just looking out for you." Cleo smiled and walked away. Devon scowled. Why would Cleo say that to her? It had to be because she was jealous? Grant was a good guy. Devon wasn't sure she wanted a boyfriend, but she trusted Grant. He had earned that after two years of being her friend. Cleo was probably laughing at her ability to mess with Devon. *Don't let her get in your head, Devon. She's just playing with you.*

"WHEN IT'S DARK? THAT'S what he said? Oh, baby!" Presley squealed, applying eyeliner in her dorm room mirror before dinner.

"What? Why 'oh baby?'" Devon muttered from Presley's striped duvet.

"Because someone's gonna get laaa-id!" Presley sang. "You ready for that?" Presley moved onto mascara.

"But really? How did you know just from that?"

Presley paused and arched an eyebrow. "Simple. 'Cause guys don't actually go to the trouble to make plans about anything unless there is sex in it for them. Grant wants to seal the deal. So the only question is, do you?" She turned and waited for Devon's answer. "Well, bee-yotch? Do you?"

Devon slumped over to her side. "I don't know. I mean, how do you actually know?"

"Good point," Presley turned back to the mirror. "You don't know necessarily. I think mostly it just happens and then you decide afterward if you were ready or not."

"That's not the most romantic thing I've ever heard."

"Look, my theory is that losing your V card is like taking the training wheels off a bike. You gotta lose it first to know what you're really working with. Then you can start having fun and all the romantic stuff you think comes along with. Should I wear black and sexy, or pink and lacey?" Presley held up two different bras.

"I don't know. Clearly I'm out of my depth here." Devon stood and shuffled to Presley's door.

"Hey, slutface." Presley stopped her. "Don't stress. Don't over-think, 'cause I know you will. Grant's a good guy. Just relax and enjoy the ride. And if you don't do it, that's cool, too. I've seen the way Grant looks at you. He'll still like you afterward no matter what." Presley squeezed Devon's hand.

"He is a good guy, right? Like, I can trust him?"

"Totally. He's crazy about you. Of course you can trust him. Duh. Now stop being lame and go find some matching underwear."

Two hours, five outfits, and one barely read chapter of *A Tale of Two Cities* later, Grant knocked on Devon's window. As usual he wore the LAX baseball cap, brim pulled low, but he had changed into a fresh shirt and jeans. Devon immediately spotted the green blanket tucked beneath his arm.

"Ready, sugar?" he asked.

Devon stepped out her room. She had decided on a blue dress that Presley said made her boobs look good, and matching black bra and underwear. "Yeah, let's do it—I mean, I'm ready."

"I got a good place in mind, come on." Grant wrapped an arm around her shoulder and walked her up the hill. Screams came from Spring House next door, and they could see water balloons being tossed from trees and behind bushes.

"Freshman." Grant laughed.

"Remember that bread fight when we were freshman?"

"There was no toast the rest of the week because we swiped so much bread from the kitchen."

"I remember I even found bread in my hair the next day," Devon said.

"I think Matt hit me over the head with a baguette," Grant added.

"I got hit with a pita pocket in the eye. Hutch was flinging them like Frisbees," Devon said. She hadn't even realized it, but the mention of his name stopped them both.

"Hey," Grant said, turning her toward her. "I know you're still going through a lot of Hutch stuff. But, I'm the one that's here. And I like you, Devon."

"I . . . I know. And I'm sorry. But why? I mean, that sounds stupid, but I kind of want to know why."

"You really don't know? Okay, well. You're hot, but you don't know that you're hot, which makes you hotter."

She laughed, her face suddenly warm. "I guess that's a compliment?"

"You're smart, like really, scary, smart. You're a good kisser." He leaned forward and planted his lips on hers, then withdrew.

"I didn't know that," she whispered.

"It's true," he said. "And, you are really selfless, which most people aren't, and that's kind of amazing." He kissed her again. "Is that what you wanted to know?"

"Thank you." She looked at Grant, his smiling face, his long nose, and the stubble on his chin. *He's here, and he likes me*, she thought. *And I like him. Screw Cleo.*

They turned and walked over the hill, past the Dining Hall. The kitchen staff had set up barbeques, grilling burgers and corn on the cob outside. The gasoline-y smell of charcoal reminded Devon of the summer, now gone. Movement down the hill near the History classrooms caught Devon's eye. A flash of red: Matt holding a blanket. Followed by . . . Isla? Yes. Definitely. They disappeared behind the classrooms. So, Cleo was right about Matt hooking up with someone. But Devon would have never guessed Isla.

"Hey, you coming?" Grant was pulling Devon down the hill.

"Yeah, sorry," she said. *You can process that later*, she told herself. But her mind wouldn't let her. Matt and Isla? Together? Maybe it made sense in a twisted way since they were the two closest people to Hutch.

Moments later, Devon found herself being led into the art building. Grant opened a door to a student's studio and led her inside, closing the door behind her. It reminded Devon of her therapy room. A wooden easel held a half-painted bowl of fruit on canvas, and a tall closet took up the corner. Devon shuffled her feet against the cool cement slab floor.

"Hold on," he said. Grant laid his blanket on the ground and then pulled two pillows from the closet, placing them next to the blanket.

"Who's studio is this?"

"Raj's. Don't worry, it's cool. I brought the pillows down here, they're not his." He reached into the closet and brought out a candle. "A little mood lighting." And then he brought out his iPod and pressed play. "A new playlist. What dya think?"

"You really thought this through." Devon was kind of impressed. It was a valiant attempt at boarding school romance, all things considered.

"Come here," Grant said. He pulled her close and started kissing her. Devon let herself enjoy the kiss, enjoy Grant holding her tight. Slowly, carefully, he lowered her to the floor and put a pillow behind her head. "Are you okay?" he whispered.

She nodded. Her heart thumped. So. This was it. The training wheels were going to come off. Grant lay on top of her, the weight of his body pressing the air out of her chest.

"Hold on," he said. He rolled to the side and pulled a keychain from his pocket. "These don't feel so good." It rattled on the floor next to Devon's head. He started kissing her neck and she could feel him searching for the zipper to her dress.

"Wait," she said and rolled to the side. Grant pulled back and watched as Devon reached behind her and unzipped her dress. She pulled it over her head and placed the pile of cloth on the floor next to them. As she lay back down, Grant's keychain caught the light from his candle and metal flashed in Devon's eyes. A bottle opener. Familiar-looking. A green bottle opener with a white cursive G at the top. Not "G" for Grant . . . no, that same beer bottle G. The part of Devon that was enjoying the moment, that was keeping other thoughts at bay because kissing Grant felt so good, whooshed from her like air out of a flat tire. She sat up and reached for her dress again.

"What is it? Are you okay?" Grant asked.

"Um, sorry, I. . . ." She tried to put it all together. The bottles near the Palace. The label in the car. Grant with the same opener. Most of all: Cleo's being right about Matt. If she was right about Matt, she could be right about Grant, too. It wasn't a coincidence. There was no such thing.

"I gotta go."

CHAPTER 12

Name: Isla Martin
Session Date: Oct. 3
Session #3

"I wasn't sure if you were going to show up today or not," Devon said. "I'm glad you did."

"Yeah, well, it's not like I'm going to talk to you about anything." Isla stared up at the ceiling. "I know you're just here to rat on us to Wyler."

"But you're here anyway. Is there something you want to talk about?"

Isla shrugged and turned the window, pretending to be bored. *Let her talk first.* She picked at her nails, which were even more ragged and chipped than usual.

"Okay, fine." Devon gave in. "There is something I want to talk about with you. You and Matt? How long has that been going on?"

Isla pressed her lips together. The veins in her neck seemed to tighten.

"Did you hear what I said?" Devon asked, purposely being overly polite.

She slowly brought her eyes back to Devon. "Matt? We're not like a thing or anything. It's just that, since Hutch, you know, Matt's the only person that really gets what it's like."

"What it's like to lose someone close to you?"

"Yeah, that. And. . . ." Isla looked out the window again.

"And. . . ." Devon tried to draw out the answer.

"Forget it. It's nothing." Isla snapped. She lifted up her sleeve to scratch at her arm, and Devon noticed a series of scratches scabbed and hidden underneath Isla's shirt. "I know who it is," she added, answering an unasked question.

"Who what is?"

"The slut that Hutch was with. It's your little freshman BFF, Raven."

Devon forced herself to look down and pretend to write something in her notebook, frightened her face would betray her feelings.

"After Bodhi got arrested at the game, Matt told me that Bodhi and his little sister worked on the Hutchins vineyard over the summer," Isla went on. "That little day student with her crappy Volvo. Just cause she surfs, she thinks she's all local and cool, but they're just a bunch of losers." She glared at Devon as she spoke, daring her to defend Raven and Bodhi.

"I heard that they worked there this summer. But that doesn't—"

"I knew it! I knew you would defend the lying bitch." Spit flew from Isla's mouth as she yelled.

"Isla, I'm not defending anyone. I just want to help."

"Spare me, Devon. You're not my shrink. That's why Hutch got the pregnancy test for her. She was too afraid to tell her pharmacist brother because he and Hutch were tight. Bodhi would have killed Hutch if he found out." But all Devon heard was *killed Hutch*. Even though she didn't want to believe it, Raven could have been, could even still be, pregnant with Hutch's baby. And when she factored in that Bodhi had access to the car and the beer and the Oxy—and could have easily met Hutch at the Palace by driving up one of Reed's fire roads—Isla's theory wasn't too far from the one Devon had been halfway to forming.

"What makes you say that? I mean, 'kill' is a big word." What did Isla know about Bodhi that Raven didn't let on?

"Please, you saw Matt's face. All those Monte Vista guys are the same. They're not smart enough, so they think beating everyone up is the solution to their problems."

"Yeah, I was wondering what happened to Matt." Devon tried to look curious.

"Duh. They jumped him. Of course they see some rich Keaton kid walking down the beach, so they think it's cool just to beat him up and take his money. Anyway, Matt told me that you saw the whole thing. Let's just stop bullshitting each other, okay?"

Devon let the slightest laugh out.

"What?"

"Nothing. It's just, I'm not sure that's the only side to that story. Bodhi did get a scholarship to MIT. Is it possible that Matt told you what he wanted you to believe?"

"What does that mean? I'm actually telling you something here and you think I'm lying? Nice work, they teach you that in therapy school?" Isla scratched at her arm again.

"I'm sorry, that was rude of me. Forget I said anything."*

"Look, I trust Matt, okay? He wouldn't lie to me." Isla laughed to herself. "He wouldn't."

"What are you laughing at?"

"It's just our thing. We don't lie to each other. When we got together we promised that over the summer we wouldn't lie unlike everyone else in our lives."

"Wait? Over the summer? So you got together last year?" Devon sat a little straighter in her chair.

---

* "Never lose trust with your subject." —*Peer Counseling Pilot Program Training Guide* by Henry Robins, MFT

Isla looked out the window again. Studied her nails, trying to look nonchalant. But Devon could see the raised veins in her neck again. Finally she sighed. "Whatever. It's not like Hutch is around to be all shocked now. Yes, Matt and I started hooking up a little last year while I was still technically with Hutch. We didn't see each other over the summer or anything, so it's not like we *totally* stabbed him in the back."

"Right. You just *slightly* stabbed him in the back?" She bit her lip. *Stupid.* Above all, a peer counselor was never supposed to condemn a subject for any behavior, but Devon's mind wasn't on her training right now.

"I don't have to take this from you," Isla said.

Focus on the session. "Hey, I'm just trying to put all the pieces together. Like, when Cleo got you that pregnancy test you thought it was because she heard something about the night Hutch died? What would she have heard, Isla? That you were sleeping with his best friend on the night Hutch died? Was that it?"

Isla shook her head, but she wouldn't meet Devon's eyes. Devon shifted in her chair. Maybe she was playing "bad cop" now and yelling at Isla until she owned up to her mistakes, but she knew she had already crossed any counseling boundaries and there was no "good cop" to save the day. Isla had disrespected Hutch, lied to him, cheated on him. Devon couldn't change that no matter how much she hated her for it. She steadied her breathing and tried to bring herself back to the moment. This was all about how to help Isla. How to help lying, cheating, drug-abusing Isla.

"No," Isla said after a long silence. "You're spinning this to make me look like the slut here when it was that freshman who went behind *my* back and slept with Hutch and got herself pregnant. It's her fault. All of it."

"Isla," Devon sighed. Isla wasn't making sense. Her illicit relationship with Matt had been exposed but instead of justifying it, or even lying about it, she was fixated on Raven. This pregnancy had really hit a nerve for some reason. That's what Devon needed to help her with. "Whoever Hutch may have gotten pregnant doesn't have anything to do with you. That was Hutch's business. It's not a judgment about you."

"No, no, it's all connected." Isla shook her head, sure of herself, getting worked up. "It's all part of the same thing. Hutch always thought he was better than me." Isla scratched at her arm again, digging deeper into her skin without flinching.

"Okay. Let's just calm down for a second, take a few deep breaths."

"And you. You sit there thinking you're better than me, too. You just wish it was you with Hutch last year, don't you? Yeah, that's it. You're jealous I got to screw him all year long and you sat in your little room holding onto your virginity like you were a princess or something. Well, you and your little friend Raven better watch your backs because Hutch isn't here to protect you anymore." Isla's hands were shaking now. She squeezed her eyes shut and fell back into her chair. "I don't feel good," she whispered.

What do you do when your subject freaks out? Where was that in the training book? "Isla, are you on something right now? I know this isn't you talking; it's the drugs. What are you taking?" Devon reached out and held onto Isla's hands. Devon couldn't watch her scratch herself up anymore. "We're going to find Matt. Okay? Matt can help you."

"I don't need any help," Isla said as her chest heaved.

"It's okay to ask for help if you need it." Did she have a reason for not wanting to accept help or was this simply denial that she actually needed it? Isla ripped her hands away. She stood up Devon could see the beads of sweat along her hairline. "I'm fine. I don't need you. I can see what you think about me. And you know what, you and this counseling shit can fuck off. You don't know anything."

"Isla," Devon stood up but Isla turned back with a growl.

"Stay. Away. From. Me."

∞

MATT WAS ALONE, OUTSIDE the Dining Hall eating a banana, when Devon spotted him. She debated approaching him; was it violating Isla's confidentiality to tell Matt about this morning? No, this was for Isla's safety, she needed to tell someone.

"Matt, wait!" Devon clutched her backpack straps as she hurried to catch up.

Matt's shoulders slumped when he saw her. "What?" he said. His voice sounded sharp. He threw the banana into a garbage can.

Devon waited until she was close enough to talk quietly. "It's Isla. Would you check in on her. I'm worried, and she doesn't exactly want to hear any lectures from me. Figured you might know best what to do."

"I'm sure she's fine," Matt said. He looked over Devon's shoulder at a gaggle of freshman girls exiting the Dining Hall.

"Matt, I don't think she's fine." Devon stepped closer, invading his personal space. "She needs help." She made a point not to blink, not to act like Matt was a full foot taller. She couldn't flinch now; Matt had to know that this was important. His eyebrows pushed together for a brief moment and he blinked.

Raven in her Volvo honked the horn from the driveway down the hill.

"I gotta go," Devon said. "Just make sure Isla's okay, will you?"

Finally he nodded, "Okay, I will. Thanks. Good looking out." Matt gave her an awkward pat on the shoulder.

"HOP IN, WE GOTTA pick up Bodhi." Raven's Volvo spit and sputtered as it pulled out of the parking lot. Devon tossed her backpack into the pile of towels in the back and hopped in the car. "Right one's—"

"I got it. I got it," Devon muttered, gripping the speaker in front of her. She and Raven smiled at each other. "I'm a pro, remember?"

The Volvo bounced down the hill into Monte Vista. Devon closed her eyes and tried to organize her thoughts. She liked Raven. They were even friends. But, she still needed to find out more about

Bodhi. She hoped the arrest was all a simple misunderstanding, and that the various things that seemed to connect Bodhi to Hutch's death in her mind could be easily explained. Wouldn't that be the best case scenario? That Hutch's murderer was still out there? She sighed. The best case scenario would be Hutch, still alive. It was a downward spiral of thought with no end in sight.

Past town, the ocean swept into view at the end of a winding suburban street. The houses got bigger the as they neared the water. Newly remodeled balconies and rooftop decks were positioned for the optimal sunset views. The car turned down an alleyway lined with garage doors.

Raven parked the car in front of a guest house with sun-bleached coral-painted wood and a splintering front porch. "I'll be right back," she said. "Better if you stay here." She slammed the door behind her and Devon watched her glide up the stairs in two long steps. Raven and Bodhi lived here? Just as quickly as she had gone in, Raven came bounding out. Devon caught a glance at a man standing near the door.

"Bodhi's already at Reed's. Let's head there," Raven said starting up the car again.

"Was that your dad?" Devon asked. "This is your place, right?"

Raven rolled a cigarette as she steered with her knee down the alley. "Technically, yeah, that's my house. My dad is, well, he's not really going to coach anyone's Little League team anytime soon."

Devon nodded. She didn't understand completely, but she knew enough to let the subject drop there.

THE BLACK RANGE ROVER was sitting in the driveway when Raven pulled in. Bodhi was unloading a duffle bag from the back and for an instant Devon thought with a pang of Hutch taking his bags out of the same car. Raven parked and jumped out. "Hey, missed you at Dad's. He's always such a pleasure."

"Yeah, I got outta there pretty fast," Bodhi said. They walked inside and Devon followed. "Hey, Devon."

"Hey," she said back, quietly. It was awkward to be so close to Bodhi in person. She didn't want to look back two weeks from now and think, *I spent all that time with a murderer*. But it was a stretch. For one thing, Raven couldn't be that blind to that possible side of her own brother. On the other hand, she knew all too well that people saw what they wanted to see, especially in someone they loved.

"You're okay, right?," Bodhi asked Raven. She nodded and Bodhi wrapped an arm around her shoulders and drew her close. "We don't need to go back there. Never again."

"Never again," Raven said, nodding at her brother.

The dark wood floors and window frames of Reed's guest house gave it a classic craftsman house feel. A kaleidoscope of colored glass wrapped around the lighting fixtures in the hallway and dining room. In the living room, floor-to-ceiling windows overlooked the Athena vineyards. It was breathtaking. Devon felt herself relax instantly. The silence of his living room, the organized rows of vines, the empty blue sky—all of it created a sense of calm.

"Sorry, Dev," Raven said. "You gotta take your shoes off."

Devon slipped out of her Toms and padded down the thick carpet. Raven stepped into a bedroom and shoved a pile of clothes off the bed, then plunked herself down. School books and notebooks covered a nearby desk. A tall chest of drawers on the other side of the room had make-up, nail polish, and surf wax scattered on top.

"This is me," Raven said.

Photos taped to the wall made Devon step closer. Raven and Hutch were smiling at the camera in one, screaming at the camera in another, glaring at the camera in the last. "We took those this summer," Raven said.

"What were you doing?" Devon's throat went dry.

"When Reed didn't need help with his computer or security system, we'd go for walks in the vineyard. Hutch said the vineyard was a horror movie waiting to happen. We were the victims in that one, getting hunted in the other, and then we did the twist ending where we were the killers in the last one." Raven laughed. "Crazy Hutch, huh?'

"Yeah," Devon said. It seemed like a very Hutch-ian game. "So, do you basically live here?" Judging from the clothes in the open closet, this didn't seem like a weekend stopover.

"Really couldn't live with my dad anymore. It got ugly. I dropped out of school in Monte Vista."

"Ah. So that's why you're a freshman who can drive."

"Yeah, this is my second attempt at high school. That's also why Bodhi came home from school. He couldn't be across the country while everything last year was going down. We got hooked into Reed's world, hung out with Hutch when he came down this summer. After Hutch died, Reed seemed to like having us around. It's kind of a mutually beneficial thing."

Devon nodded, her curiosity prickling. "So, will Bodhi go back to MIT? I heard he got a full scholarship." This was the stuff she needed to find out. Ask questions, but don't be too obvious.

"Don't know. He's working with Reed now, not sure he has to go back. I mean, you've got this crazy famous scientist right here, what else could MIT offer him?"

"Scientist? I thought Reed grew grapes and rode horses."

Raven laughed. "Nah, the vineyard was like a retirement project. Reed made all his money ages ago in the bio world. But he's always been a cowboy. Come on, you gotta see the hub." Raven led Devon further down the hallway, and down a flight of stairs, which opened into a large room. Windows covered two walls in an L-shape, and a counter crammed with security cameras and computers wrapped around the other two walls of the room.

"I don't get it," Devon said.

"Reed's a bit of a nutty professor. He's got projects going all the time. You should see the patents he's got in the works. Major." Raven sat in a fancy ergonomic chair at one end of the desk and typed a few things into a nearby computer. "You didn't know he was like a famous scientist at one point? I thought knowing that was a Keaton requirement."

"Reed? Um. . . ."

"Cell proliferation," Bodhi said coming down the stairs—followed by Reed Hutchins, himself. Devon recognized his silver belt buckle with the three trees on it. "Reed was one of the first guys to identify the various stages of cell proliferation. In the bio world, he's kind of a rock star. He's practically Elvis."

"Don't bio dork out on us," Raven said to her brother.

Reed stopped when he reached the bottom step and spotted Devon. Their eyes met. His were the same blue as Hutch's, though rheumy and crinkled. He took a long, raspy breath. "So, Devon," he started. He had to catch his breath before continuing, "We meet in better circumstances."

"Hi. It's nice to meet you properly, Mr. Hutchins." Devon managed, extending a hand. He shook hers with a surprisingly strong grip. He sat himself in a nearby armchair and gestured to Devon to grab a seat. She swiveled an office chair around to face him.

"Please call me Reed. Besides, I owe you an apology," Reed began. "When I went to your room, I know I must have given you quite a scare. I should have called first. Or waited outside until you arrived. I'm embarrassed. I needed to lie down to rest a moment. That's why I was in your bed."

"I'm sure I could have acted better," Devon said sheepishly. Seeing Reed's beautiful house here, his high-end office setup, it was embarrassing to even consider that she had thought he was an asylum escapee who'd accidentally wandered onto campus.

"Hutch mentioned you. That you two were good friends." Devon felt her ears get hot. That's how Hutch had described her? It was shocking and flattering at the same time. Maybe Reed was confusing her with someone else? "A fellow not-supposed-to," he continued. *Wow,* Devon thought, *maybe he was talking about me.*

"Yeah, I guess so. Hutch and I talked about that once." Devon relaxed into her chair a little more. She was a welcome guest in this house; she could feel that now. Reed was trying to reach out to the people in Hutch's life, and Devon was one of them.

"There's something going on at Keaton we wanted to tell you

about," Reed started. Devon noticed Raven and Bodhi were both staring at her, their faces serious. Had Raven planned this when she invited Devon over for a Wednesday afternoon excursion off campus?

"Oh?" Devon's throat felt dry. "What is it?"

"Headmaster Wyler is the one that had Bodhi arrested," Reed stated. "His camp is claiming that Bodhi was selling drugs on campus and they had him removed."

"Of course Bodhi wasn't holding so they looked like idiots," Raven said. "But the arrest pissed off the pharmacy and they axed Bodhi yesterday."

"Whatever, that wasn't meant to last anyway," Bodhi said with a huff.

Reed's craggy face darkened. "I've told you. You're far too talented to be wasting away there. I think our arrangement now is much better."

"So true." Bodhi nodded.

"Devon, that's why it's important that you keep your wits about you," Reed continued. "Your counseling puts you in a rare position. And we're not the only ones that know it."

"What do you mean?" Devon asked.

"You're the only one with all the puzzle pieces," Reed said. His eyes flickered back and forth between Raven and Bodhi.

"The Isla and Matt puzzle pieces," Raven added.

"We don't trust them anymore," Bodhi said. "And we think they might have had something to do with Hutch's death."

CHAPTER 13

Name: Cleo Lambert
Session Date: Oct. 4
Session #3

Cleo crossed her motorcycle-booted ankle over her knee and bobbed her foot in the air. She leveled her eyes straight at Devon. Silence. Devon shifted in her seat. Normally she should let the subject start talking, but "normally" also implied that the subject hadn't given the counselor sincere advice which said counselor had then ignored and then suffered for. Cleo sighed deeply. More silence.

"Okay, you were right," Devon finally said. "I don't know what it is, but I totally can't trust Grant anymore. You've got to tell me what you know about him."

"I didn't mean to hurt you," she said, even though she was smiling. "I know everyone thinks I'm a sieve and get off talking shit behind everyone's backs." Devon waited for her to continue. Cleo frowned. "Isn't that where you're supposed to tell me that I'm wrong, no, everyone really likes me and doesn't think that about me?"

"Um, is that what you want me to tell you?" *Was this a counseling question or a regular person question? Ugh.*

"Whatever. No, don't say anything. I know that's what people think. It's totally true. I do get a secret thrill talking behind people's backs. I love knowing things before someone else does. Usually. But, I saw Grant in Monte Vista last weekend with Eric Hutchins. I guess Eric has been staying at the Four Seasons outside Santa Cruz, but he's been around here dealing with Hutch family fallout. But, why is he hanging out with Grant, I'm thinking, you know? Kinda weird. And then it gets really weird. I saw Grant use your pen."

"Wait, my pen? My Monte Blanc pen? I thought you stole it again."

"No, I gave it back to you. I wouldn't go back to something I already stole, where's the fun in that? No, Grant used your pen. I know it was yours. But he used it to sign something, like it was his pen he casually had in his pocket. He wasn't waving it around or making it a trophy or anything. Kleptos know the difference." Cleo tucked her short hair behind her ears. It gave Devon a second to catch up. Grant had clearly lied about his relationship with Eric. But why, unless there was something to hide?

"So, if he stole my pen, you don't think he. . . ." Devon didn't want to finish the sentence.

"He's totally looking at your notes. Guaranteed. Messed up, huh?"

The breath left Devon's body, and she sat there, empty. Of course, Grant had known which notebook she used for her session notes. Stupid to leave them alone in her dorm room. Behind her chair, in her backpack, a small metal box was scrambling some signal—or *something*—so she could keep what was said in this room quiet. She had rewritten her notes for Mr. Robins. And it wasn't enough. Because she was careless, or too trusting, or maybe both, what happened in here was out in the open. And Grant was also probably sharing it all with Eric Hutchins. It made sense. Wouldn't Eric want to know what was being said about his own brother's mysterious death? And even worse . . . she inhaled sharply and felt the blood rush to her cheeks . . . Grant's feelings for her must have been a complete lie, as well. The flirting, the late night visits, the compliments; he had manipulated her, and she'd let him.

"Why did you try to warn me?" Devon asked.

"That's the thing," Cleo said. "Having the drop on someone is a total power trip. But when I saw Grant something kind of clicked. Like I could use the power for good and actually help people instead of hurt them. And since you're one of the few around here who actually tries to help people, it seemed fair that someone should help you. I mean, I'm not like turning into a nun or anything."

Devon didn't know why, but she wanted to cry then and there. After all her time in these sessions being yelled at, berated, and despised for trying to help—finally, a glimmer of acknowledgement. From Cleo, of all people.

"I really appreciate that. I just feel so horrible. Everything I've been trying to protect in here has been leaked. Who knows what other people know? And it's my fault."

"Look, if everyone, especially Robins, really knew what being said in here, you would have been shut down already. My guess is, either they haven't seen anything interesting enough in your notes yet, or, they don't want this stuff to get out any more than you do."

Devon blinked a few times and looked Cleo in the eye. "Cleo, I'm so sorry that our sessions got out. You trusted me, and I messed it up. That should never happen in a proper counseling session."

Cleo waved her off with a smile. "Nah, that doesn't matter. I got caught shoplifting, it's not like those notes had anything that personal. Besides, isn't this session still about me?"

"What? I mean, it is, but you still want to talk?"

"That's why I'm here. I mean, your boyfriend betraying you totally sucks and all, but last time you told me to come back with the truth. So, is this a proper counseling session or what?"

Devon sat back in her chair and cleared her throat. She had been ready to watch Cleo slam the door on her way out. She had been ready to watch the whole program and all her work disappear like the puff of phony smoke in a magic act. But here was Cleo actually wanting to talk. Maybe it *was* a magic act. A real one. "Okay, yeah, we can do that. What do you want to start with?"

"I normally wouldn't be into all this shit, but once I started thinking about coming back in here, being honest with you, honest with myself, I kind of started seeing things differently."

"How so?" Devon wanted to reach for her notebook; this was the time to start taking notes. But, no. Those needed to be left alone, especially now.

"It was at that Pop-up Party the other day." Cleo flicked lint off her black jeans. "Everyone rushed off to go do something they couldn't normally do. Skip homework, dance, eat dinner on the lawn, hook up in a classroom. . . ." she raised an eyebrow again at Devon. The smugness of Cleo was still there, and in this case, rightfully so. Devon kept her eyes down and nodded, hoping she'd just move on already with the story. "But I remember I sat down on my bed and I didn't know what to do. Like, what was it I wanted to do now that I could do anything with this free time? And nothing came to mind."

"What did you end up doing?"

"That's the thing. Nothing. I sat there running through all the things I've done already in my life. I've been to the Louvre. I've met the Dalai Lama. I've skied the Alps, been in a hot air balloon over Holland during tulip season. I've gone sky diving, skinny-dipping in the Mediterranean under a full moon. I have a tattoo of my initials on my butt. I lost my virginity to a gorgeous surfer named Ocean in Hawaii *after* I swam with dolphins. And, I couldn't come up with one stupid thing I wanted to do while sitting on my bed in my ten-by-ten dorm room."

"Maybe everything pales in comparison to all that other stuff?"

"But, it's always been that way. My whole life has been full of 'you're gonna love this,' or 'you have to do that,' but no one ever asked what I really want to do. It's like I've been living someone else's bucket list. And now that I have the chance, I don't know what's on my own list." Cleo tugged on a buckle on her boot.

"No one told you that you *had* to steal that nail polish, or you're *gonna love* stealing nail polish, though, did they?" Devon emphasized Cleo's own words, but her tone was soft.

"No, I guess not."

"Stealing the nail polish was fun because it's something you're not supposed to do. Right?"

Cleo looked up. "Yeah, I guess."

"And everything you've done before that is a supposed-to."

"Yeah, that's right." Cleo sat up straighter. So did Devon. Was she actually making progress?

"A smart man once told me that there are two kinds of people in this world. The supposed-tos and the not-supposed-tos, and you, my dear, are a not-supposed-to."

"I am?"

"I mean, this is completely off-book, but hear me out." Devon leaned in, excited. Screw Mr. Robins's *Pilot Training Guide*. "You've done everything right, everything your parents wanted, everything the tour books say to do, the whole upper class society thing you're supposed to do, and the thing that excites you the most was stealing a five dollar bottle of red nail polish. My guess is it's not even a color you would wear."

"They took it from me, but yeah. It was that horrible tacky red from the '80s, like it belonged in a Billy Joel video."

"See? That's all this is. And Cleo, this is very cool."

"Why is it cool? I am totally depressed and have no idea what to do with myself."

"Because. Look what happened when you took away all that clutter. All the gossip. The chit-chat about everyone else. Without all that in the way, without a Keaton schedule to adhere to, there's only you left. And it can be totally freaky to look into that abyss of nothingness, but the amazing thing is, you can do anything you want with it. Your life is there for you to make it what you want."

Cleo rolled her eyes. "This is getting a little new age-y for me. Did you, like, watch *The Secret* lately or something?"

"See, there you are. I'm getting close to something otherwise you wouldn't be bringing out your bitchy self."

Cleo laughed shortly. "Did you just call me a bitch?"

"No. Well, yeah. It's like your persona, your armor. It's much easier to be bitchy and judge than it is to actually be a part of something and believe in it."

"Maybe."

"I do it, too. I mean, I don't turn into a bitch, but my armor is that I have to dissect everything into a million pieces for it to make sense. But really that's just me buying time before I have to commit to anything. We all do it in our own way."

Cleo was silent. Her lips twisted in a smirk, but Devon could see her chin quivering a little. Then a lot. The smirk disappeared and her eyes welled with tears. Cleo brushed them away.

"Honestly, I don't even know who I'm supposed to be." Cleo sniffed and sat up straight. "I'm just living the schedule they want me to live, you know? And here we wake up at seven A.M., class by eight A.M., lunch at noon, sports, homework, dinner, more homework, and bed, and then do it all over again. And there's no end in sight. I'm just going to go to whatever college they want me to, marry the guy they want who also has enough money so we can afford to put our future kids on the same schedule when it's their turn. I know I sound like some spoiled brat that doesn't appreciate anything, but I would give it up just to make my own choices. To live my life. Like, really live."

Devon handed a tissue to Cleo. *Finally, the tissue comes in handy.* "Look, we're all kind of stuck in the same thing here, some of us more so than others. But, even within that schedule there are amazing opportunities. You *can* live how you want." She bit her lip. She'd nearly added: *Hutch did.*

"Yeah? Like what?" Cleo blew her nose.

"Well, let's start at your definition of living, really living. What does that look like? Then we can find a way to get more of that in your life."

Cleo laughed and wiped her eyes. She shook her head. "It's stupid. You know, what just came to mind. No, it's too dumb."

"I doubt that. What is it?"

"Okay, well last summer my parents took me to Florence. It was supposed to be some big art history kind of tour. We saw the statue of David, the *Birth of Venus*, walked the Ponte Vecchio, you know, all the supposed-tos in Florence. On the last day my parents went with some friends on some winery tour. I was supposed to go on some tour of an art academy or something. Had the tickets and everything. I walked toward the academy thing that morning. On my way I saw this guy who looked about my age playing the guitar and singing in some piazza. He had this really cute dark curly hair, totally Italian cute. He sat on the steps near a church with the guitar case open, trying to make some money. I tossed him a Euro and he smiled at me and suddenly started playing a different song. The Rolling Stones. It was kind of cool to hear him sing in English with that accent, so I hung out for a minute to listen."

Devon nodded, encouraging her. "Did you go on your tour?"

"That's the funny part. I don't know how, but he kept singing, and I went from standing there to sitting on the steps. He started talking to me between songs. Franco was his name. His accent was so hot, he had these chiseled cheekbones, it was like hanging out with the statue of David, if David wore Levi's and was an emo guitarist. We chatted in his broken English and my guidebook Italian for a while. At one point he took a break and we got lunch at Burger King, which you're totally not supposed to eat because, hello, you're in Italy, try the spaghetti! But, I swear it was the best Whopper ever. We hung out together the whole day. We walked along the Arno River talking about everything, but nothing at the same time. He had to catch his train home before it got dark. I remember I was sitting on this stone wall right near one of the bridges, and he kissed me and said, '*Ciao, Cleo*,' and then he was gone."

She paused. Devon nodded for her to continue.

"I never told my parents about it. Or anyone, actually. But, that was probably the best day in my life. Unscheduled, no agenda, just going with it. It felt like that's what life is supposed to be like. Not museums or guidebooks, but just feeling the sun on your skin, or hearing a song you like, flirting with a cute boy. That's what it's supposed to be." Cleo sat back and smiled, her eyes still moist. She let out a long breath.

"I think we just had an actual proper therapy session," Devon said, smiling back.

"Yeah, I guess we did. See ya next week, Counselor."

DEVON THOUGHT THAT GETTING her homework done in the library would make it easier to concentrate. Plus, she doubted she would run into Grant here. But all she could think about was her stolen pen. At least now she knew to carry her session notebook everywhere instead of worrying about Grant sneaking into her room. She kept Cleo's words in her head. If anyone had found anything wrong in her notes it would come back to her. But the pen! Her mother had given it to her. It was sacred, in its own silly way. And Grant had violated a lot more than her trust by stealing it. She'd have to get it back.

She found herself drifting away from reading *The Rebirth of America Post WWII,* and writing notes in the margins of her notebooks. Pregnancy test = Hutch + ~~Presley, Isla,~~ Raven? At this point, was she to assume that Hutch had gotten Raven pregnant? Is that why he stole the test? So Bodhi wouldn't find out? But, Bodhi had helped Hutch evade his shoplifting charge. Bodhi had to know something more. He was the only other person to see Hutch that day in Monte Vista. Even with Bodhi and Raven's suspicions—not to mention Reed's—about Matt and Isla . . . still, that didn't exactly cross Bodhi and Raven off the list of people with secrets around Hutch.

Across the room two freshman girls were whispering back and forth about their Spanish homework. A senior, Archie Chan, read

Sports Illustrated in the magazine area. Behind Archie stood a monument to Keaton History: a display case full of old photos of Mr. Keaton in the 1940s, the shovel he broke ground with for the first Keaton building: this library, in fact. The display case had a logo carved into the top of it: the Keaton logo, but slightly different. Three trees, instead of one, inside a circle. Devon looked closer. Where had Devon seen that before?

THE HALLWAY OF FELL House was empty. In ten minutes study hours would be over and the halls would be full of guys roaming around before curfew. Devon said a silent *thank you* only after she'd slipped inside Hutch's room unnoticed.

She had to lie on her back on the mattress to see Hutch's writing underneath the shelf. But it was dark. She didn't want to turn on the light; she couldn't risk attracting attention to the room. Next to the closet was a mirror mounted to the wall, held to the wall with plastic clips. Maybe there was a way to get the mirror to reflect enough outside light to see what Devon needed.

These dorm room basics had passed through years of students, so it was no surprise that the clips didn't put up an argument when she pulled the mirror off. Devon lay on the bed again and she tilted the glass until she caught the light from outside. She saw the words Hutch had written on the underside of the shelf backward—*miles to go before I sleep*—now plain to read in the reflection. And next to them: the logo she had seen in the library. The circle with three trees, a variation on the Keaton logo. Could it also be the same logo from Reed Hutchins's belt buckle? It had to be, although why and how, Devon did not know. She also saw now that *Tres Abbatis* and the three-tree logo was scratched into the black mirror backing. Was this carving also from Hutch? The scrawl of the logos matched too well not to be from Hutch. What was he trying to communicate? Devon repeated the works to herself. "Tres abbatis, tres abbatis," probably Latin, meaning three of something. She'd look up *abbatis* back in her room.

As Devon slid the mirror back into the clips on the wall she heard muffled voices in the room next door. "Matt, you're being paranoid," a girl's voice was saying.

She held her breath, listening.

"I'm being paranoid? You need to be a little more paranoid if you ask me. You're certainly taking the pills for it. He knows I have it, Isla. "

"Calm down, you've kept it on the DL. He thinks everything went down in flames with Hutch."

"If anyone finds this do you know how busted I'll be? I'm not going down for this. You know what? Hutch isn't here anymore, he can take the heat."

Devon heard the door squeak open. There were footsteps in the hall—and the handle on Hutch's door turned. She barely had enough time to pull the closet door shut before Matt stormed into the room. She couldn't see what he did, but she heard a squeak of bedsprings. Then Hutch's door closed again. Devon took a deep breath. She counted to twenty, praying she wouldn't faint. She was alone. Hutch's mattress was still empty, the shelves still bare. She lifted the mattress and saw a small black moleskin journal like Hutch used to carry. Devon flipped it open to find pages and pages of initials with numbers and letters next to them.

SH: 15/mg/AD
MD: 25/mg/RT
RK: 10/mg/VC

Hutch's records of the pharmaceuticals. Cleo mentioned he was good at keeping track of how much people had. That's because he kept a notebook of everything. No wonder Matt wanted to hide this. He and Isla sounded worried about someone finding this notebook. Reed and Raven and Bodhi were right; they *were* hiding something. Maybe they knew where the Oxy came from that had killed Hutch. Maybe this book had that answer. Devon felt her hands clenching into fists. She tucked the book into the back of her pants and got the hell out of Fell House as fast as she could.

DEVON'S DOOR WAS OPEN. Funny, she'd left it closed before going to the library. Seething, she picked up her pace down the hallway. If Grant thought he could sneak in without her noticing, he was sorely mistaken. Devon would love to catch him red-handed. Would she turn him in right away? Or enjoy letting him simmer in his guilt for a day or two, knowing that he could be called to the headmaster's office at any time?

She burst in, taking a breath to yell "Caught you!" but instead of Grant, she found Presley sitting on her bed next to Mrs. Sosa. They both looked worried, sad—guilty, even. "Pres? What's up?" Devon asked. She dropped her backpack on the ground and noticed her dresser drawer was open. The drawer with the green bottles. Mrs. Sosa spoke as the dread snaked its way down Devon's back.

Oh, God, no.

"Devon? We need to have a talk. Have a seat." Mrs. Sosa said, slowly and quietly.

"Dev, I'm sorry. I thought you had my hoodie. I looked in your drawer and I saw the bottles."

Mrs. Sosa pulled the plastic bag of the three green bottles onto her lap. Inside the bag was also the small bottle of Oxy from Isla and the stray blue Adderall pills she had taken from Isla's dresser. When the photo of Isla and Hutch poked through behind the bottles, Devon thought she was going to throw up. How was she going to explain this? The book she had taken from Hutch's room was still wedged into the back of her jeans. She could feel it press against her, getting sticky against her skin as she breathed. Presley had warned her to stop obsessing. Matt had said it, too. And now, here she was, looking so obviously like a complete psycho with even more damning evidence tucked in her pants! She would be sent to see . . . who exactly?

"I've already called Mr. Robins. . . ." Mrs. Sosa began. Oh yes, that's exactly who they would send her to.

CHAPTER 14

Name: Devon Mackintosh
Session Date: Oct. 6
Session #3

Campus was typically quiet on a Saturday morning. A thick fog had settled around the Keaton hill. Devon couldn't even see the adjacent mountainside from her window. She had bundled up in her thickest sweatshirt and sweats, and fluffy Uggs. Somehow looking present-able at this meeting didn't seem like a priority. She had accepted her fate and knew the school would not look kindly upon any student hoarding items like she was. She also knew that the presence of Hutch's photo in her stash made it worse. It made her a stalker, an obsessive, everything Presley had accused her of being.

Inside Mr. Robins's office she found him sipping from a silver travel mug of coffee. His curly hair was still wet from a shower, but stubble formed a thin carpet along his chin and cheeks. Devon and Mr. Robins had something in common; they both knew this meet-ing was going to suck and hadn't put on false airs for it.

"I don't understand how this happened," Mr. Robins began,

without even bothering to say hello. He shoved his black-rimmed glasses back up the bridge of his nose, only to have them slip down again. "You seemed to embrace the training. Your comprehension seemed well above what I had hoped. "

"I tried to follow the training guide as much as possible," Devon added.

"I should have seen how much you were affected by Jason's death. The denial. The anger." He seemed to be talking to himself more than to her. "I just never expected it to go this far. The drinking, the pills. . . ."

"Mr. Robins. I told Mrs. Sosa. I didn't drink from those bottles. I found them. Isla gave me those pills to protect herself. Well, not all of them, but I wasn't taking them."

He shook his head. "We have to shut the program down, Devon. We tried, but it's not working. It was taking too much of an emotional toll on you. Plus, the video footage never amounted to anything. Bad connection or something."

Even though she was being convicted of crimes she hadn't committed, Devon still found herself feeling bad for Mr. Robins. His vision of this program had vanished into the bottom of a teenager's found beer bottle. At least Devon knew that Raven's video scrambler worked. She had protected the privacy of Matt and Isla and Cleo. That was something. "I don't know if you were drinking, or if you were taking these pills. I can't prove that, and I'm inclined to believe you here. But, you were still found with these items in your possession. I've already spoken to Headmaster Wyler and we'd prefer not to make the failure of the program public knowledge. You were clearly not prepared for such a demanding position in light of Jason's death. You won't be suspended." He took a deep breath, letting the reprieve sink in. "The headmaster and I thought that twenty hours of yard work and the rest of the year under probation would be a sufficient consequence. And with that decided we can begin to put this business behind us."

Devon's cheeks burned. She knew he expected her to be

relieved, grateful even. Instead, she was pissed off. She wasn't some delicate flower, a basket case who'd fallen apart. She'd adhered to his training. Anything else was *his* fault. Except, none of that mattered now. Devon had gone too far. Hell, maybe she should have turned her notes over to Mr. Robins after their first sessions instead of thinking she could solve everything. Matt's control issues, Isla's addiction, Hutch's murder. . . . But looking at Mr. Robins slurp coffee, she knew she was in a better position to help than he'd ever be.

"What happens with Matt, Isla, and Cleo?" She hated the idea of him trying to get Cleo to be happy, or to convince Isla that she didn't need the drugs. They wouldn't confide in him. It was that simple.

"I'll continue the individual counseling," Mr. Robins said. "Now's the time to tell me anything I need to know about your subjects for their sessions. Anything you may have been hesitant to share before. It's for the good of your subjects."

She tried to make her face blank. If he wanted to paint her as incompetent, then that's what she would be. But inside her head was a whirring factory that kept churning out more and more things she couldn't tell Mr. Robins. Down the assembly line they went, little packages full of secrets: Matt was dealing drugs, Hutch had gotten someone pregnant, Isla and Matt were probably abusing pharmaceuticals together, Cleo was an obsessive gossip, the Health Center was far too easy to break in to, Mr. Robins's camera did work if only she hadn't intentionally messed with it. . . . Devon wished a bell would ring and the factory could shut down for the night. "I guess they'll tell you everything you need to know," she said as politely as she could.

"Now, I think you and I should schedule a few weekly sessions. Clearly you have not recovered from Jason's suicide—"

"Murder," she interrupted without thinking. It was not something she should have said out loud, but she refused to believe *suicide* was appropriate anymore.

"Suicide," Mr. Robins came back. "This tells me where we need to start in therapy. You know, Devon, denial can be more powerful than we realize."

"Hutch was murdered, Mr. Robins. And I'm going to prove it."

"Devon, this is very disconcerting. This murder mystery you've invented is the clearest sign of your inability to move on from Jason's death. It's time to let him go. Would a trip home for a few days help? Maybe a check in with your mom?" Mr. Robins eyes studied every inch of Devon's face. Was he looking for clues to how crazy she was?

Devon stood up. "I think our time is up, Mr. Robins. I'll see you next week."

PLAYING A LACROSSE GAME was not how Devon wanted to spend her Saturday afternoon. Crying alone in her room was her first choice. Not because she was watching everything she'd done as Peer Counselor go down the drain. No, there was also being blamed for the failure of the program itself. Taking the bus into Monte Vista and getting a double thick strawberry milkshake at the deli was a close second. Playing lacrosse didn't even make the list.

"Hey, Ryan Slut-crest, you coming to the game?" Presley asked, her voice quieter than usual. She leaned in Devon's doorway as Devon finished tying her cleats.

She pulled her laces tight with a terse, "On my way."

Presley hesitated. "How'd it go with Robins?"

"It was great. We talked the whole thing out, ordered brunch, then told knock-knock jokes." Devon shot Presley a glare just in case she had missed her sarcasm. She grabbed her stick and marched out her sliding glass door.

"Dev, you know I'm sorry, right? I didn't know what else to do," Presley pleaded, catching up with her. "You would have done the same thing, you know it." Presley walked sideways to look at Devon.

"I wouldn't, though, Presley. That's the thing," Devon stopped walking. "If it was you, I would have come to you first. When Pete cheated on you last year, I told you. I didn't wait to find out if he would or wouldn't tell you the truth, I told you because you deserved to know. Just like I deserved to know if you were gonna rat me out to Mrs. Sosa." Devon could hear her voice cracking. Being in trouble with Keaton stung enough, but having that perfect record shattered because her best friend turned her in . . . there would be no quick fix or easy forgiveness.

Presley bit her lip. "I tried, Devon. I tried to talk to you. But you don't know how it's been watching you. You've become totally obsessed with Hutch, while everyone else is trying really hard to move on."

"I can't, Pres. It's not that easy."

"You think it's easy for any of us? We all miss him. But he's gone and we have to keep living. You weren't listening to me, you were off in your world that seemed to revolve around Hutch, and then I found that stuff in your drawer. Don't hate me, seriously. I'm the only one that cared enough to do anything."

Devon shifted her weight on her plastic cleats. "Yeah, well, I care, too. Still do." She ran off toward the field. Maybe she was a nightmare to deal with right now. But she had her reasons. And she would prove them to Keaton.

THE BLEACHERS WERE LESS packed at this game. Either the thrill of the season opener had died down, or the arrest at the last game freaked everyone out.

Raven was tucked into her goal, defending warm-up shots from the Keaton team. Isla charged and took a fierce shot, aiming right for Raven's chest. Raven deflected. Devon smiled. *Good for her.* Isla scooped up another ball and launched another shot over her shoulder. This one whizzed toward Raven in a blur with a *splat!* as it ricocheted off Raven's chest plate.

"Ease up. It's just a practice run," Raven yelled. She rubbed at her padding; she was probably going to have a bruise from that shot. Isla didn't hear her, or maybe she didn't care. She lobbed another ball toward Raven's shoulder. Raven managed to deflect again, but hobbled back. With a scream, Isla suddenly threw down her stick and charged. Devon's jaw fell open. She could only stare, too shocked to react, as Isla tackled Raven to the ground. She ripped off Raven's goalie mask.

"You stupid whore! I know it was you. I know it was you," Isla growled. She slapped at Raven, pulled her hair, while Raven squirmed under her pinned to the ground.

"Isla, stop!" Devon finally came to her senses and dashed across the field. Luckily Maya swooped in and pulled Isla off Raven. Isla tried to push past her to tackle Raven again, but Maya held her back. Devon skidded to a stop just as Maya slapped Isla and pulled her close by her lacrosse shirt. "You leave her alone, Isla. It wasn't her. Do you hear me? It wasn't her."

Isla took a few steps away. She glanced around, breathing heavily, her face flushed. Everyone stared at her. She looked back at Maya, confused, like she had suddenly landed in this spot, unaware of the last minute everyone else experienced. Maya repeated quietly, so only Devon and Isla could hear. "It wasn't her, Isla."

Devon stepped in. "Let's get you to the Health Center, huh?" She reached a hand out to Isla, but Isla turned around and bolted— vanishing into the woods on the other side of the parking lot.

Mrs. Freeman walked Raven toward the team bench. "We still got a game, ladies," she called, but even she sounded shaken. "Let's get ready."

Devon noticed Raven's goalie pads were askew, strands of black hair stuck out of her ponytail, a red blotch was turning into a welt on her cheek. She turned back to Maya. "How did you know what she was talking about?"

"We both know it wasn't Raven, don't we?" Maya whispered. She brushed past Devon to the bench where Mrs. Freeman was gathering the team into a huddle. But Devon couldn't move. *We both know it wasn't Raven.*

CHAPTER 15

Sept. 10, 2010
Freshman Year

The cookie sailed past the metal coffee can and sent crumbs skidding across the floor.

"Take a sip," Hutch said.

Devon held up her nearly empty glass of milk. "I can't. So full." Her eyelids were getting heavy; even the cold cement floor was starting to look like a comfortable bed.

"Better start making some shots then," Hutch smiled at her and launched a piece of cookie into the canister. "Swish!" he said, arms raised to the ceiling, cheering his victory. "You're not falling asleep on me, are you, Mackintosh?"

"No, not at all." She tried to stifle a yawn. "Okay, maybe a little. What time is it?"

Hutch looked at his watch. "One twenty-seven in the morning." He squeezed his eyes shut and then blinked several times. "We've been in here for what? Almost three hours."

"They're never going to find us. We're going to be in so much trouble." Devon couldn't get through the sentence without yawning again. Her fatigue had become more overpowering than any fear about getting caught. She curled up on the floor, tucking her arm under her head as a makeshift pillow and allowed her eyes to close. "We should just give up and sleep here."

"Here, use this," Hutch said. He lay down behind her and shoved a paper towel roll under her head.

"Thanks."

"You warm enough?" Hutch asked.

Even half-asleep Devon could tell this was a flirtatious hint. She smiled and opened one eye. "Why, you gonna keep me warm?"

"Only if you want me to." Devon could hear the smile in his voice.

"Yeah, I want you to. But bring your own paper towel roll." Hutch crawled across the floor toward her. Devon felt him wrap an arm around her waist; he pulled her close to him. She relaxed into his grasp, feeling his knobby knees behind her calves, his chest inhaling and exhaling, and his breath on the back of her head.

"Isn't it weird that we just met?" Devon said.

"Technically we met earlier this week."

"You know what I mean. Three hours ago I wasn't sure if you knew my name. And now we're here, like this, and it seems like it's always been that way."

"Yeah, like we've been here this whole time. Not, like, in the kitchen, but comfortable like this."

"It's nice."

"It's better than nice." He ran his hand up the whole side of her body, stopping at her head to pull her hair back. He kissed her neck just behind her ear.

Devon opened her eyes. The flashing starbursts in her mind bled into the moonlight reflecting off the glossy floor. The locked metal door loomed large on the nearby wall. The metal hinge at the top caught the outside light. For the first time Devon saw words near the top of the door. REPLACE PIN TO UNLOCK.

"Replace pin to unlock?" she cried, suddenly wide awake. "Did you see that before?" Devon stood and scrambled to the door. She ran her hands along the frame. Hutch stood up and dug his hands into his pockets. "Maybe the pin fell out. I need your height over here," Devon said. Fully stretched her arms couldn't reach the v-shaped hinge at the top of the frame. "What? Did you see the pin or something?"

"Um. . . ." Hutch started, but Devon noticed he wasn't making eye contact.

"Hutch. Did you see the pin?"

"It's not like it matters anyways. Tino locked the door. We're still stuck."

"What do you mean, *still*? As in we weren't stuck until Tino came along? Hutch? What aren't you telling me?"

He reached into his pocket and fished out a slender metal pin with a loop at the top. He walked over and slipped the pin into the hinge. It fell into place easily. "That's what I wasn't telling you. I pulled it when you reached for the switch. I thought it'd be fun for a minute."

"You thought it'd be fun to lock me in a kitchen?" Devon pressed herself against the door. Even with the pin in the hinge, the deadbolt still kept the door firmly closed. "Do you know how freaky that is?"

"I know, I know, I'm a total asshole. I was only going to let it go on for a few minutes, until we got the milk, just for fun. But then Tino came along and kind of made that decision for me. Devon, I'm not some creepy rapist guy, really."

"This whole night then. . . ." she couldn't finish the sentence. Didn't want to finish the thought. Everything she had told him. Kissing him. It was all a lie. Feeling safe with him? Gone. She opened her mouth to speak but nothing would come out.

"Devon, seriously. Everything about tonight was true. I just wanted a little time alone with you without all of them getting in the way."

The ripple of moonlight on the cement floor made Devon feel dizzy. She slid onto the floor. "You know what really sucks? Meeting you made me feel like I could survive here. Like everyone wasn't always going to feel like a complete stranger and I had something to look forward to. But now . . . now all I can see is four years of being trapped with people I hardly know." She glared at him. She wanted him to know that he would be just another cog in the Keaton wheel to her.

Hutch sat across from Devon on the floor. He took her hands in his. "I know I screwed up. I missed my opportunity like three hours ago to tell you the truth and then it was too late. But you gotta believe me, everything about tonight was true. I really like you, Devon. I thought I had a really cool plan until you figured it out and now I look like a total stalker freak."

She felt his hands tight around hers. Could she believe anything he had said? Everything had been so great up until now. Maybe it was too great. Of course: it had all been one big joke.

"You thought you'd just lock us in for a few minutes? And that would somehow be funny?"

"I was going to put the pin back, I swear."

"But you were still going to make me late for curfew?"

"Yeah, I guess. I wasn't thinking about curfew. I was on a secret mission with you. No bell was going to take me away from that. Don't hate me. Please?"

Devon took in his eyes, wide, eager and fearful at the same time. "You didn't have secret creepy plans?"

He smiled and shook his head. "No secret creepy plans. Swear."

"I appreciate the apology and all." Devon took a deep breath. "Maybe you didn't have ulterior motives, but I'm not sure I can trust you again." She flinched at her own words. It felt like she was cutting out a member of her team, the only member. Without Hutch, it would be a lonely team of one.

"You know what? You don't have to decide now. I'm going to go to that corner over there and face the wall until you make up your mind if you want to be friends again. I just ask that you weigh all the good things that happened tonight against the one little, stupid, stupid mistake I made before we really started talking." He let her hands go. "Just consider it. Friends allow friends a mistake every now and then."

Devon wanted to smile, his desire to make things right did seem genuine, but it seemed too important to maintain her angry composure.

Hutch nodded, as if understanding, and went to his corner.

October 8, Present Day

RAVEN'S HAIR LOOKED PARTICULARLY rat's-nest-like today, piled high on top of her head. The rubber band keeping that black tangle together in one place deserved an award. Devon couldn't tear her eyes from it while sitting a few rows behind Raven in their morning assembly. She hadn't been able to get Maya's words out of her head. How did Maya know what Isla was talking about? And who was Maya to know anything about Raven? Devon had never seen the two of them exchange a word—even as players on the same lacrosse team.

The pregnancy test Hutch stole remained an unanswered question. Devon knew he wouldn't steal anything unless it was for a good reason. Not wanting Bodhi the pharmacist to know about his possibly pregnant sister seemed like a good reason. But now Maya seemed to be implying that Raven wasn't the mysterious pregnant girl. Had Maya seen the pamphlets in Raven's car? Who else explores pregnancy options except a pregnant girl? There was also Raven's shaved head boyfriend to consider. Was it possible she had gotten pregnant with Hutch if she was already with someone else? Someone who had a formidable right hook, if Devon remembered his beach fight with Matt correctly.

At the front of the assembly, Mr. Lee was saying something about the Chinese students having a traditional Chinese dinner if

anyone else wanted to come. Devon had been served a bad helping of orange chicken last year, so no, she would not be attending.
Across the assembly hall Devon spotted Maya's black hair in a
perfect French braid down her back. Even from across the room
she knew not a single hair would be out of place. There was more
Maya wasn't letting on. Her argument with Eric Hutchins was
only a piece of the puzzle. And Maya was keeping all the other
pieces to herself.

Headmaster Wyler called an end to the assembly and everyone
shuffled out of the auditorium to their next classes. Devon fell in
line next to Raven as they headed toward the circle of classrooms.
"Hey, you doing okay?"

"Yeah, it wasn't anything a few hot baths wouldn't cure." Raven
shrugged. "But, I think they're going to have to start paying me to
get in that goal."

"No kidding. They should." They walked in silence as the
crowd around them thinned out. "You know, Isla's not in a good
head space right now. What happened, I'm sure, had nothing to do
with you personally."

Raven stopped. "Damn straight it had nothing to do with me.
Why? Do you think I asked for it? I asked to randomly get attacked
by a chick I have zero relationship with? I don't even know what
the hell she was talking about."

*This could go two ways: keep Raven in the dark or actually try
to find out what you need to find out, Devon.* "Well, it's not like
you have *zero* relationship with her."

"Whoa, hold up. What are you saying?"

"It's just that you and Isla were both close with Hutch. That's all.
Isla's just got it in her head that you and Hutch. . . ." Devon looked
around. No one seemed to be in earshot, except Devon could see a
classroom nearby filling up with students. The bell would ring soon
and she and Raven should be inside.

"What does Isla have in her head?" Raven's teeth clenched.

"Hutch apparently got someone pregnant. And Isla thought it

was you. So. . . ." Devon let her words trail off, hoping Raven would pick them up. She didn't.

"And you think she's right?"

"I don't know. No, I don't think she's right, but I don't know for sure. All this Hutch stuff has made me question everything. Even you." Devon knew she sounded like a hypocrite. One day she's friends with Raven and the next she's accusing her of something horrible. No wonder she was short on friends these days. Then again, there was no easy way to accuse someone of a secret pregnancy with a dead guy who may or may not have been murdered.

The bell rang. They were late for class. Devon waited. Their conversation would soon become a welcome distraction for the students filing into the nearby classrooms. "Okay, for the record," Raven hissed. "No. Hutch was like a brother to me. I would never. Sure, I thought I was pregnant for a minute this summer, but that was with my boyfriend, Drew, not with Hutch. Anything else you feel like you need to know about the contents of my uterus?"

Devon nodded. She deserved that. "Raven, please don't be mad. I'm just trying to figure this one out." She kept her chin low, hoping her sheepish composure would soften Raven's anger. "There's still a pregnant girl out there that we don't know about."

Raven shifted her backpack to her other shoulder. Her long skirt swayed and the hem held onto a few dried leaves on the stone walkway. "Okay. You're right. And I'm sorry. Seriously, it wasn't me though."

"I know," Devon said quickly.

"But you really think Hutch has a baby out there?" Raven asked.

"Let's talk later," Devon said. Heads were turning in their direction. Naturally, it was time to be in class. But one of those heads was Maya's.

WE HAVE TO TALK.

Devon passed Maya the note as Raj stumbled through an answer about recurring motifs in *A Tale of Two Cities*. Maya tucked it in between the pages of her notebook without a glance Devon's way.

When Mrs. Freeman dismissed the class, Maya stayed in her seat to apply a fresh layer of coral lipstick on her lips. Devon stared, but Maya focused on smoothing her hair back into place. *She's going to ignore me as long as she can,* Devon thought. Devon was almost out the door when Maya whispered behind her, "Tonight. After curfew. We'll talk."

Devon paused, her back still turned. *Okay, at least that was something.*

AFTER THE FINAL RUSH through the Bay House halls, after Mrs. Sosa had knocked on every last door and said good night to each girl, Maya crept into Devon's room. Only her desk lamp was on, turned away from the door. Maya was wearing her robe and a plush pair of slippers. She stood in the middle of Devon's room, awkward, waiting.

"You can sit down," Devon whispered.

"I guess I've never been in your room before," Maya said. She sat in Devon's armchair and tucked her legs underneath her. Even with the bulky robe and fluffy slippers, Maya looked small and childlike in the oversized chair. "It's cool," she added automatically.

"I spoke to Raven," Devon started.

"I can't believe Isla did that." Maya sighed, casual, relaxed, like she and Devon were two regular friends chatting.

Was Maya stalling for some reason? It like a game of chicken. Who would reveal what she knew first? Devon sat up straighter in bed. It might as well be her. "Raven isn't the one that's pregnant with Hutch's baby. And like you said, we both know that."

Maya swallowed hard and stared down at the floor. *Let the subject fill the silences.* Devon had gone first, now she would let Maya finish. The words tumbled out of her mouth in a terrible rush.

"I'm ten weeks pregnant. I found out just as school was starting. Hutch got a pregnancy test for me because I was too scared to be seen buying one in Monte Vista. You're the only one that knows." Maya slowly looked up. "I don't know what to do."

CHAPTER 16

Wednesday, October 10

Devon wondered why she'd even bother coming to the library. Studying or concentrating was out of the question. She sat at one of the wooden tables with the old green lamps, the ones that burned so hot they threatened to singe the arm hair on anyone who dared to touch the power switch. So, Hutch had gotten Maya pregnant. Well, Maya hadn't said those exact words out loud, but it was clearly not Immaculate Conception. Instead she talked only about the baby. She was determined to keep it, but knew she would start showing in a few weeks. How would she explain it to her parents, the school? Who should she tell first? Mrs. Sosa? Nurse Reilly? Was there a Keaton hierarchy of whom to tell first? Would Maya be kicked out? Devon realized she was as clueless as Maya was. Once again, there wasn't a clear guideline on how to handle secret pregnancies. Maybe once this was all done Devon would submit a new chapter for the *Keaton*

Companion. Beyond Rules Anyone Could Imagine: A Guide for the Unexpected.

The Keaton display case kept drawing Devon's eyes. *Tres abbitas.* Three trees, according to the old Latin dictionary she'd consulted. Why had the logo for Keaton changed from three trees to one? Sighing, Devon stood up and approached the case.

1946: Francis Keaton broke ground on what was to become The Keaton School. A framed picture from the *Santa Cruz Sentinel* showed a smiling Francis, thick dark hair slicked back to a pointed widow's peak, with his foot on the edge of the shovel. Devon had never really looked at any of this Keaton history before. A portrait of him, much later in life, hung in the admissions office. But that gray hair was slicked back the same way.

She looked more closely at the picture. Nothing but lush mountains and open sky behind him. No vineyards on the hillsides just yet. Behind him, three people smiled and watched as he posed. The caption read, *Mr. and Mrs. Reed Hutchins, Edward Dover.* Edward Dover? As in Maya's father, Eddie Dover? No, this guy would be too old, wouldn't he? But, if he had a son, Edward Junior . . . yes, that could be Maya's father.

Next to Edward, Devon recognized a younger Reed Hutchins: cowboy hat in one hand, his arm around the waist of beautiful woman with light hair. She must have been Athena. Devon could almost see Hutch in his grandmother's smiling pose. . . .

"Where were you?" a voice barked.

Devon whirled to see Matt standing behind her. His black eye was fading into a greenish half-moon at the top of his cheekbone. He scowled. "I showed up for our session and *Robins* was sitting in your chair."

"Did he tell you why I wasn't there?" she asked meekly.

"He said you were out of the program. He thought I'd talk to him instead. Why the hell would I do that?" Matt wiped a bead of sweat from his forehead.

"I'm sorry I didn't say anything before you met with him,"

Devon said, and she meant it. "I wanted to tell you, but after our last session, I wasn't sure if you'd even show up."

Matt chewed on the inside of his cheek. "Don't you ever just want to disappear for a bit? Clear your head?" Devon wasn't sure how to answer that. Matt shook his head. "Whatever, don't mind me. I wanted to tell you something. In session. But here's OK, too." He sat down at Devon's table and waited until Devon was sitting, too. "I gave it up. All of it." He raised an eyebrow, waiting and holding his breath until she responded.

"All of it? Like. . . ." Was he saying what she thought he was saying?

"All of it. I'm not supplying anything to anyone. Bodhi wants to get back at me, rat me out. His loss. He's got nothing. I'm not taking anything either. Seemed like I maybe needed to get my head straight again. I don't feel great, but at least I'm clear."

"Wow. So, no more pills? Matt, that's. . . ." *Don't judge. Or was this about reinforcing positive behavior? No, that was dog training.* "That's great."

"It's all gone, except, I'm keeping one piece of leverage over Bodhi if he ever wants to mess with me." Matt smiled to himself. *He still thinks the book is under Hutch's mattress,* Devon realized. "But I'm out. So, stop asking me for drugs all the time, okay?"

His smiled widened, and Devon smiled, too. They sat there for a beat, holding each other's gaze. The tension between them in the Peer Counseling room was gone. Strange: Matt had been right; the last time they'd spoken was their freshman year camping trip. Then, it was a brief flicker of a friendship that never materialized, but now there was something new. Something tangible. *I think he respects me.*

Could that be right? The thought was unfamiliar, like trying a new language. Devon was used to being out of the loop, on the fringe of everything. It was almost comforting to know that her place would always be as an observer, not the observed. But now something had shifted. Matt wasn't looking for her to simply reflect his personality back to him. He cared what she thought. For the first time, she mattered.

He tapped his hands on the tabletop and stood. "Anyway, just wanted to tell you. You don't have to worry about me."

"Who said I was worrying?" Devon looked up at Matt, an eyebrow raised. Now that she wasn't in an official role, it was fun to play along. He patted her on the shoulder.

"We both knew you were," he said. "You suck at lying, Mackintosh. Hutch always said that about you. One of the things that made you different."

Devon watched as he walked out of the library. It was true, she had worried about him. But she was a better liar than he gave her credit for. Hutch was a liar, too, of course. She was still going to keep that book.

DEVON HAD DEBATED ABOUT whether or not to tell Raven about Maya's secret, but considering Raven already knew that *someone* was pregnant, it didn't seem as big of a betrayal. Maya had asked for Devon's help, yes. But Devon needed to talk with someone else to figure out how to help her. Preferably that talk could happen off the Keaton campus, away from prying eyes and ears.

The moment classes ended Friday afternoon, the red Volvo whisked her through the Keaton gates.

"I really don't believe it. Like, really don't believe it." Raven licked the end of a hand-rolled cigarette as the car idled at the bottom of the hill. Devon couldn't help but keep her eyes on the rear view mirror. Getting in trouble for smoking a cigarette or smelling like smoke was not another notch she wanted on her punishment belt.

"Why is it so hard to believe? Maya's pretty, really pretty. Their families probably know each other. Couldn't Maya have run into Hutch this summer? And Hutch could have stolen the pregnancy test for her. I did see her barfing that week, could have been morning sickness."

On instinct, Devon gripped the right iPod speaker as Raven turned up the road toward Reed's house.

"I'm sure in theory it fits, yeah, but I don't know." Raven exhaled a cloud of smoke out the open window. "There's more to it. I think the Hutchins and the Dover families totally hate each other. Like, full-on Montagues-and-Capulets hate each other. Reed mentioned it once, something about him and Edward moving to California together ages ago, but I don't know the history there. He wouldn't go into it."

"Seems like there's a lot Reed doesn't like to talk about."

Raven took another drag and shook her head. The car pulled into the gravel driveway and she cut the engine. "That's not true. He just doesn't waste words. Bodhi's the same way. It's a science thing, I guess." She and Devon sat in the car a moment longer, looking at the guest house. "Okay, say Hutch bought Maya the pregnancy test, how does that get Hutch killed that same night? They have to be related, right?"

"They don't have to be related, but it's hard to imagine the pregnancy didn't matter. Hutch didn't have enemies, but getting someone pregnant could change that." Devon tapped her index finger along her door handle. "It doesn't fit for some reason," she said. "Like there's another piece we don't know yet."

"Well, let's run it by Bodhi. He's always good for an idea."

Devon followed Raven through the front door, across the courtyard to the kitchen. French doors were opened on the patio packed with herbs growing in old wine barrels. The thick smell of the basil followed Devon inside.

"Anybody home?" Raven called out to the empty kitchen. She dropped her keys and straw purse on the wooden countertop. No one answered. "Bodhi?" She kicked off her flip-flops and walked down the carpeted hallway. "Help yourself to anything in the fridge!"

"Thanks," Devon yelled back. She wasn't hungry or thirsty, but the idea of opening a fridge just to see what was inside was a

pleasure she hadn't had since the summer. It was the small ways
that boarding school life was different from being home that caught
up with her every now and then. Her heart sank. A half-loaf of
sprouted wheat bread with organic peanut butter and seedless raspberry jelly were the only items on the shelf. The jelly looked sticky
with congealed globs caked around the lid. PB&J. Hutch probably
made his sandwiches for Raven from these supplies. Devon felt
sorry for the leftover condiments: pets waiting for a master that
would never return.

Bottles on the door shelves jingled. Devon noticed the small
green bottles, the cursive 'G' on the metal lids. The bottles from the
Palace, the imported German label from the car.

"When did you get here?"

Devon popped her head out of the fridge. Bodhi was walking toward her down the hallway, barefoot. He took a seat at the
kitchen table.

"Um, Raven brought me over. Weekend off campus." Devon
couldn't pry her hands away from the door handle. The cool air
snaked its way up her bare legs. *The bottles at the Palace had to
have come from this fridge. Right?*

"Lame off-campus weekend. Why not actually leave the mountain?" Bodhi kicked his bare feet up onto the table.

"Good point. I guess anything that isn't Keaton is off campus."
Devon laughed, hollow and weak. *Bodhi drank these beers at the
Palace with Hutch. It was him.*

"Hey, would you grab me a drink from the fridge while you're up?"

He wants to drink the beer! Theory proven! *Be calm, Devon.
Don't freak him out.* "Sure." She picked up a beer bottle. The cool
glass felt slippery in her sweaty palm.

"Oh no, sorry. I should have said. . . ." Bodhi's feet plunked
back to the ground and he plodded over. "I don't do alcohol. Not
my thing. Those are Eric's. Aren't there any more bottles of water?"
Devon moved away to give Bodhi the full view of the fridge "Damn,
I'll get some from the main house later."

"Hey, dude," Raven said as she joined them in the kitchen. "Oh, are those Eric's?" She reached past Bodhi and Devon and grabbed one of the beer bottles. She held the lip against the kitchen counter, and with a snap of her hand, popped the metal cap right off. "Don't tell him. I love stealing his shit." She took a sip of the beer, the bubbles slipping through her smile. "Dev, you want one? We are off campus."

"I'm cool, thanks," Devon managed. "Umm, can I use your bathroom? I don't feel so hot."

CHAPTER 17

Saturday, October 13

Devon,
I'm in the lower parking lot. Find me before I leave.
— Isla

Before I leave? DEVON found Isla's note on the dry erase board on her dorm door, but it didn't make sense. Where would Isla be going? Away for the long weekend? Why would she tell Devon?

She hurried down the Bay House hall to Isla's room. Empty. Beyond empty: stripped bare. Her bare mattress with its faded blue case was the only hint of color in the stark white room. Gone were Isla's bright and hypnotizing tapestries and pile of clothes. *Jesus. She's leaving for good.* When Devon dashed outside she immediately noticed the bright red Prius, crammed full with suitcases and shiny black garbage bags. The red reverse lights were on as it silently backed out of its parking space.

Isla was in the passenger seat. She and Devon spotted each other at the same time. Her hand reached toward the steering wheel, and the car came to an abrupt stop. Isla said something to the driver, a

man with pale arms—probably her dad—and she hopped out. The
Prius clicked off behind her.

"Hey," Isla said. "You got my note."

"Yeah, where are you going? Is everything ok?" Isla was looking
even skinnier than usual. Her hair was tied in a knot at the top of her
head, but she was smiling. Devon hadn't seen that smile in a while.

"I met with Mr. Robins."

"How'd it go?" *Obviously not so great if Isla was leaving school.*

"It was good. We talked about stuff."

"Oh." Devon couldn't help but feel a pang of something—regret
or jealousy or both. Isla had actually talked to Mr. Robins during his
first session, something she'd never been able truly to accomplish.

"Matt said I should talk to him. It was his idea. I used my Get
Out Of Jail Free card* and told Robins everything. He and I figured
I should take some time away from school. Get some things worked
out, ya know?"

"What kind of things? Grief things, or . . . ?"

"Or pills. Matt said it was getting out of hand. I don't know
how it happened, but I guess after Hutch it kind of spiraled out of
control. I see that now. I'm going to go to rehab for a bit, detox
from all this, figure my shit out."

Devon nodded. The bitter feeling melted away. She was genu-
inely relieved. "Wow, that's a big step. I'm impressed."

"Yeah, well, Matt said I should thank you. You were the only
one that really noticed how bad it got. It made him realize how off
the deep end it had all gone."

"I was just doing my job." Devon shuffled her feet and looked down.

"I know you were. And you weren't bad at it either. You were
right about me and Matt. I didn't want anyone to know, tried to
convince myself it didn't happen, but on the night Hutch died Matt

---

* *Keaton Companion* Rule #2c: Dangerous Activities: If a Keaton student feels that
he or she knows someone, or he or she is a danger to themselves or others, he or
she is encouraged to utilize a one-time emergency assistance to properly deal with
the situation. Fearing punishment or consequences when someone's health is at risk
should not be an excuse.

snuck into my room. We shared one of those Oxy hits and hooked up. Probably at the same time Hutch was dying from the stuff. It's totally fucked. I'm not quite sure how I'm supposed to deal with that, but that's something I'm going to have to live with for the rest of my life."

"Regret can be a real asshole, huh?" Devon said. Isla smiled and broke out into a laugh. "I just meant that if we could rewind time, there's probably a few things we'd all like to do differently. . . ."

"Even you? I thought you did everything just right?" Isla raised an eyebrow.

Now it was Devon's turn to laugh. "Even me."

"Anyway, thanks." Isla reached out and pulled Devon into a hug. Devon could feel Isla's clavicle poking into her shoulder. "I'll see you when I see you." She opened the passenger door and got in. The car started up and Devon backed up to give it space. The passenger window rolled down. "I left you something in my room. On the door handle."

"What is it?"

"You know Hutch and I weren't instantly a couple. He said he was getting over someone. Honestly, I'm not sure he ever did." Isla smiled at Devon as her eyes filled with tears. She leaned back in her seat. The window rolled up, and the car disappeared down the Keaton hill.

Back inside Bay House Devon opened Isla's door and stepped into the empty room. This time she saw the necklace hanging there, on the inside door handle: Hemp string threaded through two small shells, the necklace Hutch had given Isla. "Love, H," she said aloud. Devon ran her fingers over the rough thread and wrapped it around her wrist into a bracelet.

IT SEEMED LIKE EVERYONE was taking off for the weekend. Devon bumped into Cleo rolling an oversized silver suitcase out of her room into the hallway.

"Wow, where are you off to?" Devon asked.

"My car is coming in a minute. Going to San Fran for the week-end. Why are you here, anyway? I thought you were with the amaz-ing Elliot siblings in town?" Cleo hoisted an overstuffed messenger bag over her shoulder. "Walk with me," she said without waiting for an answer. Devon followed as Cleo dragged her suitcase outside onto the bumpy pavement path to the upper parking lot at the top of the Keaton hill.

"Yeah, I was with Raven yesterday but. . . ." She didn't know how to finish the sentence. *I pretended to be sick and bolted, basi-cally.* She walked besides Cleo past the ring of classrooms. Freshly mowed shavings of green grass clung to her shoes.

"But, what? *Dites moi.*"

"I don't know. There was something weird that I couldn't figure out. Thought it might be better to just come back here."

"Damn, girl. We have got to get that boring gene out of you. Why would you choose to come back when you were already signed off campus?"

"I don't know. Lack of imagination?" They arrived at the top of the hill and scanned the parking lot. A black Town Car idled in a corner.

"Well, you want to imagine a weekend in San Fran? You hop in the car before anyone sees you, we can get out of here, no questions asked." Cleo waved at the car.

A uniformed driver stepped out and approached.

A flash of silver caught Devon's eye. At the bottom of the park-ing lot Devon spotted Grant tossing a duffle bag into the trunk of a silver BMW. He slammed the trunk closed and got in the passenger seat. Eric Hutchins, his long hair tucked behind his ears, drummed his fingers on the steering wheel. Cleo followed Devon's stare.

"A hundred bucks says Eric's letting Grant hang at the Four Seasons with him in Santa Cruz this weekend. Those two are thick as thieves aren't they?"

Devon's chest contracted. If she was ditching Raven and Bodhi for suspecting them, the least she could do would be to look into Eric Hutchins. Raven did say those beers belonged to him after all.

"How do you feel about spending the weekend in Santa Cruz instead?" Devon asked before the thought had fully formed in her brain. "I mean, you did bet a hundred bucks. Might as well see if your prediction is true," she added.

Cleo's eyes lit up. "Now you're getting imaginative! Good thing I never leave home without this." She flashed a Black American Express card at Devon.

"*Mademoiselle Lambert?*" The driver extended a thick hand toward Cleo's suitcase. To Devon he looked like a giant sausage stuffed into the casing of his black suit.

"Bonjour, Nikolai. Slight change of plans. We're going to be headed to Santa Cruz instead. The Four Seasons."

As soon as they saw the silver BMW in the parking lot at the Four Seasons, Devon knew they had made the right choice. Cleo had Nikolai unloading her luggage into their suite within minutes of their arrival.

"Don't worry, you can borrow a change of clothes," Cleo said with a sidelong glance at Devon's saggy jeans and faded sneakers.

"What should we do? Call their room? Wait until they leave?" Devon kicked her shoes off. Across the room Cleo was draping her clothes over the king-size bed. A red-striped couch with matching pillows made up a mini living room set up, complete with a glass coffee table. Devon was pretty sure that the couch cost more than all of the furniture combined in her mom's house. The metal studs along the corners and the stiff fabric reeked of money. Cleo tossed a notebook from the bedside table to Devon. A basic three-ring binder with pages and pages of menu, room service and spa options.

"Let's order some food. Pick a few things."

"Room service? Now?"

"What? Isn't that what you do on stakeouts? Here, try this on." Cleo threw a dress across the room to Devon.

By the time the room service arrived, Devon found herself look-ing like Cleo's twin. "Beachy slutty," is how Cleo described the flowing dresses with tight straps that emphasized their cleavage.

"Next to the couch will be fine, thanks." Cleo led the waiter and his packed rolling table of food across the room.

Devon didn't know whether to feel embarrassed or enthralled. She'd had only wanted to order the cheeseburger, but Cleo had insisted they get at least four entrees and four appetizers to best experience the hotel's menu. "You have to know how good they are as a whole to properly review something. One dish doesn't really tell you enough about the place. That's how they do it in Paris." She winked. "Or so I hear, apparently."

The waiter stole glances at Devon as he waited for Cleo to sign the bill. Devon smiled back prim and polite, at odds with *beachy slutty*. Oh, well. She wasn't sure why Cleo had gone for this look, anyway.

The waiter peeked at the receipt and thanked her.

"I have another order for you," Cleo said before he reached the door.

"Did we forget something?" His smile widened, eager to please.

"No, everything is great." Cleo noticed the waiter's name tag. "It's all fine, Dave. But, I'd like to send a bottle of wine to a friend of mine staying here. Eric Hutchins. Your most expensive bottle of Merlot, preferably. And I'd like you to deliver it. You can see I'm a good tipper, so you can make that happen for me, can't you, Dave?" Cleo pressed her shoulders back and pushed out her chest and ran a hand down the side of her flowing dress, just enough to highlight her curves.

"Yeah, we can do that. Bill it to your room?"

"Of course," Cleo said. "Merlot to Eric Hutchins. Oh, and if you would keep it a secret who sent it, I'd really appreciate it. Thanks so much, Dave."

"My pleasure." The door swung shut behind him.

"Holy cow. That was awesome," Devon said, breathing nor-mally again.

"Guys can be so easy sometimes. Just say their name, show a little skin, you'll pretty much always get what you want. It's a power French women have been working for centuries." Cleo started to take the metal lids off the food plates. "Oh, is that lamb? And gnocchi? *Delicieux*." She picked a jumbo shrimp out of a crystal glass brimming with cocktail sauce and ate it. "These are awesome. Try one."

"Why are you sending wine to Eric's room? Am I missing something?" Devon found her cheeseburger plate and sat cross-legged on her bed across from it.

"In about five minutes, I'll show you. Eat up."

TRUE TO HER WORD, five minutes (and a Kobe beef and aged English cheddar cheeseburger) later, Cleo opened their door. Across the courtyard, their waiter Dave was knocking on a hotel room door holding a bottle of red wine and two wine glasses. "There's our Dave," Cleo said quietly. "Let's get closer. Grab the key."

Devon grabbed the key card and they carefully and silently closed their room door. Staying close to the walls, Cleo made it half way around the courtyard and ducked behind an ice machine. From here they could watch as Eric opened his hotel room. Except, it was Grant instead that opened the door up for Dave. Devon noticed his white LAX hat immediately.

"I didn't order this," Grant said.

They couldn't hear Dave's explanation, but it seemed to suffice. Grant took the bottle and glasses and let the door close on Dave.

"It's room 1705," Devon said. "Should we go knock and confront them?"

"Jeez, you have as much subtlety as hoop earrings. Now that we've got their room number, we get into position."

"Position?"

"Spying position. You really think I find out this much dirt about people by sitting out in the open?" Cleo rolled her eyes and led Devon to the other side of the building.

With the ocean at their backs, Devon and Cleo had a full view inside each hotel room. Some had curtains drawn, others empty, but Grant's white hat made him easy to spot. Luckily he had left the curtains open. Devon ducked below a patio table, and Cleo lay next to her in the manicured grass. The wind whipped at their hair as the waves crashed behind them. Goosebumps rose on Devon's arms.

"I'm going to watch the front. Stay here," Cleo yelled into the wind.

Devon lay flat in an attempt to streamline her body against the wind. There was Grant, lit up by the yellow glow of the floor lamp. Grant handed the bottle to someone sitting on a red couch. Someone who wasn't Eric Hutchins. Devon squinted and pulled herself forward a few feet to be sure. It was Raj. What was he doing here?

Both of them suddenly looked toward the door in their room. Was someone knocking? Devon darted from below the picnic table behind a tree to better see the entrance to their room. Eric Hutchins, holding a six-pack of Gersbach beer. He extended his arm to Grant, who took the beers. Grant opened up toward the room, like he was inviting Eric inside farther, but Eric declined. He and Grant did a brief handshake/high five combo move. Grant closed the door.

Devon had to see where Eric was going; she could always come back to spying on Grant's room. She raced across the lawn toward the courtyard and ducked behind the ice machine again. Eric walked to his car and opened the passenger door. He extended a hand, and Maya stepped out in a short dress and five-inch heels. Definitely a far cry from her usual business wardrobe. She kissed Eric on the lips. Not a quick kiss, not a peck, but a hands-around-the-neck, lips-smashed-together act of pure passion. Devon's jaw hung open. She watched as they slipped into room 1707, next door to where Grant and Raj were drinking their beers and expensive Merlot.

Devon dashed back to the suite. Cleo was changing clothes and holding an oversized towel for Devon.

"I was just going to bring this to you," she said.

"Maya is here. With Eric." Devon said. She sat on the bed and picked at a nearby plate of truffle oil coated French fries.

"You mean with Eric, or *with* Eric?" Cleo asked. She sat on the couch and waited for Devon's answer.

"I think *with* with Eric. They're together now." She shook her head. "Amazing. After Hutch, she moved onto his brother."

ONCE DEVON BROUGHT CLEO up to speed on Maya's pregnancy, and after Cleo had banged her hands on the couch yelling "*Merde!*" at least a dozen times, they came up with an idea. It was imperative they get Maya alone. Calling or texting was too risky; her cell phone could easily fall into Eric's hands.

Cleo made the call. "Excuse me for bothering you, Mr. Hutchins," she said, lowering her voice, sounding as professional and grown-up as possible. "We need to request that your car be moved to another parking spot. Why? A Premier Guest spot just opened up for you near the front entrance. Thank you so much." She hung up.

"Premier Guest spot?" Devon's mouth was stuck in a perma-grin.

"If there's one thing I know, it's rich people." Out their door they saw Eric step out of his room, car keys in hand. "You're up," Cleo said with a pat of Devon's back.

Devon ducked out the sliding door and ran around the back of the building. She could hear Grant and Raj yelling at the TV as she knocked on the window next door. The curtains parted. There was Maya, inches away from the glass. She jumped. Devon smiled, tried to look natural. *Don't stress, I'm normally outside your window.* Maya opened her door. "What the hell are you doing here?" she hissed.

"We need to talk. When Eric gets back, go get ice." Devon ducked onto the adjacent balcony when she heard the key card beep in Maya's door. She could hear the scratch of the curtain rod as Maya closed the curtains.

Cleo was waiting for her behind the buzzing ice machine. "She coming?"

"I hope so," Devon said. "Otherwise I'm a totally ineffective stalker."

"Just use your skills, Counselor," Cleo shoved an ice bucket in Devon's arms. "I'll use mine." With a wave of her dress Cleo hurried toward the ocean. The echo of a door closing brought Devon to attention. She put her ice bucket under the chute and pressed the button for ice. Cubes dropped into the plastic bucket as Maya appeared next to her, arms folded across her chest.

"What are you doing here?" Maya demanded again.

"What are *you* doing with Eric? Did you really get over Hutch that quickly?" Her eyes couldn't help but wander to Maya's belly. The slightest bump protruded from her fitted dress. It still wasn't something anyone would notice unless they were looking for it specifically. Soon enough that would change.

Maya leaned against the wall, out of sight from the courtyard. She pursed her lips and looked into the empty ice bucket in her hands.

"You can't tell anyone, okay?" she muttered. "I was never *with* Hutch. He was just trying to help me figure out what to do. The baby is Eric's. We've been seeing each other since June. I really love him and he loves me, but our families will disown us if they found out we were together."

Devon's head swam dizzily. She had no idea what she was feeling. "I don't get it. Why would you lie to me about Hutch? You made me think it was his baby."

"I didn't make you think anything. You assumed, and I let you. It was safer. If they find out about Eric and I . . . he's 21 and I'm 17. He could be in real trouble. That's why he wanted me to get rid of it. We were fighting about it and Hutch was the only person who knew. He got the test for me so I could be sure. He was talking to Eric about giving me the space to make my own decision."

Devon nodded. *That sounds like Hutch. The Hutch I knew. The Hutch I trusted. And who, as it turns out, actually was the real Hutch.*

"What are you thinking?" Maya asked.

"That your decision affects Eric, too."

"I know. That's why we were fighting. But, we're okay now. That's why he brought us here this weekend, to be together, alone, before we broke the news to our families. We're going to have this baby together."

Devon slid along the wall down to the floor. Her hand dipped into the bucket of ice and the cold raised the hair along her arms. "That's brave," she said. "But what are you gonna do about the age thing?"

"My birthday is in a month. We just need to last until then. Then we'll tell them. It's good news, Devon. You don't need to look so sickened by the whole thing. Eric really loves me. We can make this work." Maya tugged her shirt lower. "Not that I have to tell you any of this."

"You're right. I can't tell you what to do. It seems like you've got a plan, so that's good." She stood. "But . . . does this have anything to do with why Hutch died?"

"What are you saying? Hutch killed himself. That's his business. My baby had nothing to do with that."

"Sure, but what about Eric? Was he angry at Hutch for getting into *your* business?"

Maya's eyes narrowed to slits. "Be careful, Devon. Be very careful about where you throw your accusations. Eric's family will sue anyone who slanders their name."

"Fine. Just tell me that he didn't visit Hutch at school that night. Just tell me that he was with you and I won't say anything." Devon's question hung between them. The ice machine shifted and rumbled again before Maya spoke.

"He said he had to take care of something in the city," Maya said quietly. "And I believe what he said. He was in the city." She turned and hurried back down the hall, leaving Devon alone with her bucket of ice.

CHAPTER 18

Sunday, October 14

Cleo had Dave deliver a bottle of champagne to their room before the kitchen closed for the night. "Because it's a happy buzz," she said. By 2 A.M. Cleo was lounging in the empty bathtub, ensconced in red couch cushions from the couch, drinking champagne out of the bottle. Devon sat on the bathroom counter dangling her feet off the side. She decided to pass on the buzz, happy or not. One of them had to keep her head straight.

"So, Bodhi, Raven, Eric and Reed Hutchins all had access to the car that drove up the backside of the Keaton hill to meet Hutch that night?" Cleo set her bottle of champagne on the floor next to the tub.

"Yeah, but Bodhi doesn't drink beer."

"But, he could have access to the Oxy," Cleo pointed out.

"True."

"Isn't it not really about access, though? I mean, we're talking murder here, right?" Cleo tapped a finger against the neck of the champagne bottle.

Murder was a word Devon kept trying to avoid. It sounded so deliberate. But Cleo was right. That's what they were talking. In one version, Hutch took the Oxy just to get high and accidentally overdosed, or he took it deliberately to end his life. In another version, someone purposely slipped him a lethal amount.

"If it's murder then we've got to figure out who had enough of a reason to want Hutch gone. Raven and Bodhi and Reed might have had access, but Eric and maybe Maya are the only ones with a real motive. Murder is usually an emotional thing. And Eric seemed to have the most to lose if Hutch squealed about Maya's pregnancy."

"So we gotta talk to Eric then," Cleo said.

Devon's lips flattened. "That's the champagne talking. Like he would even give us the time of day. Besides, say it's true. Hutch was going to rat out Eric and Maya's relationship. We're still talking about Eric killing his own little brother. That's hard to imagine."

"Hasn't counseling taught you anything?" Cleo snorted. "People are crazy. Especially rich people, I'm telling you."

"I don't know. Still doesn't add up. I think I need Bodhi and Raven's help."

"I thought you weren't sure you could trust them," Cleo said between sips of champagne.

"Hutch trusted them. They're living with Reed. I'm not sure that doubting them is accomplishing anything. Besides, they're the only ones who actually believed in me when all this happened, from the beginning."

Cleo closed her eyes and leaned back in the pillows. "All right, but isn't this how you set yourself up to ultimately be betrayed by them? How many murder mysteries have you seen?"

"That's why you're coming with me. If you can't spot a liar, then we're really screwed."

Cleo's eyes popped open. She giggled and offered the bottle to Devon, who shrugged and took a sip. Bubbles oozed out the top.

It burned in her throat and the back of her nose. She winced and handed the bottle back.

"Did you look on the desk out there? I got you something." Cleo said, that smug smile returning.

"What?" Devon padded her bare feet out of the cool tile bathroom floor to the living room. Her Mont Blanc pen was lying in the middle of the polished wood desk. "How did you get this?" she yelled toward the bathroom.

"When you were with Maya I thought I'd say hi to Grant. See if he wanted to combine parties or anything."

"What'd he say?" Devon hurried back to the tub.

"I left you out of it. He has no idea you're here. You're welcome, by the way. Seems like Eric is paying for Grant and Raj to hang out for the weekend, drink all they want and watch football."

"Why would Eric do that? Oh. . . ." She looked at the pen in her hand. "Grant stole my notes for Eric."

"Eric's super paranoid about your counseling sessions. And apparently Grant can't hold his liquor either. Once that kid started talking there was no stopping him."

"You got him to give you the pen back?" Devon asked. Cleo tilted her head at Devon. "Right, you took it. Sorry, forgot who I was speaking to."

"Don't do it again," Cleo playfully slapped Devon's arm. "But, it was the least I could do. You put yourself out there for me, for Matt and Isla and Hutch. Seemed like someone needed to return the favor."

"Thanks," Devon said. She twirled the silver pen between her fingers. "I didn't exactly solve your kleptomania though, did I?"

"Oh no, you were totally right. Of course it's for attention, but not like I was going to admit that to you. Come on, let's get some sleep. We'll get Nikolai to take us back to the hill tomorrow morning."

THE NEXT MORNING, DEVON found the black Rover parked in the driveway in front of Reed's guest house, but no one answered the door when she knocked.

"They should have a sign that says 'Gone Surfing,' or 'Surfs Up,'" a hungover Cleo croaked behind her Jackie O sunglasses from the backseat of the town car. These were the first words she'd spoken since they'd gotten in the car an hour ago. "Or maybe, 'Life's a Beach and then you Die.'"

The security camera above the front door gave Devon an idea. "Let's try the main house." The car wound higher up the driveway. The guest house was bigger and more beautiful than her own house, it was hard to imagine something more. But when it swept into view with its three stories and multiple chimneys, the pointed roof and double wraparound balconies . . . all she could think was that it was a palace. A *true* palace. She could see a few of the windows had blue and amber stained glass designs. A massive redwood tree grew through the middle of the front porch; Devon couldn't be sure if the tree or the house was in that spot first.

"*Merde,*" Cleo whispered as the car stopped at the front door. Devon hopped out. Cleo jabbed a finger at a security camera above the door. It swiveled toward them. Someone was home, and someone was watching.

Devon's knees felt shaky. Well. No point in trying to hide anymore. She forced herself to march up the front walk.

Bodhi opened the door before Devon had a chance to knock. "We were wondering if we'd been ditched or what."

"I need to talk to you." Devon said.

"*We* need to talk to you," Cleo chimed in, appearing behind them. Devon's shoulders sagged. Wouldn't Cleo be happier back at the Four Seasons? "What? You really think I'm going to walk away from this? All the action's about to go down."

"What's going on?" Bodhi asked.

"Is Raven around?" Devon peered into the room behind Bodhi. She could see that the hallway led to a massive living room with one wall of windows facing the vineyard.

"Come on in. She's surfing. Be back soon." He eyed Cleo up and down. "Bodhi," he said, extending a hand.

"Cleo," she replied, shaking it. "Nice dreads, Bodhi."

"You should probably get Reed, too," Devon mumbled.

"Yeah, yeah. Nice to see you, too, Devon." Bodhi shook his head. He kicked off his checkered Vans at the bottom of the carpeted stairs and disappeared upstairs.

Cleo made herself right at home, lounging on an enormous couch with faded green and blue plaid cushions. "Ow, jeez. This thing is probably older than I am." Devon wasn't paying attention though. She spied an end table with framed photos. A young Hutch, smiling on the beach next to a large surfboard. Reed and Athena in an old black and white photo no bigger than a playing card. Reed, standing on a redwood tree stump wider than his outstretched arm. But where was the rest of the family? Eric? Hutch and Eric's dad, Bill?

"Devon? I thought that was you down at the guest house," Reed called from upstairs. With Bodhi at one arm and his wrinkled hand on the banister, Reed made his way down slowly. "And who is this young woman?"

"Cleo Lambert, Mr. Hutchins," Cleo said. She stood up and shook Reed's hand.

"Well, Cleo. Welcome. If you're with Devon we're happy to have you." Reed took a seat in a thick leather chair and draped a blanket over his lap. "So. Shall we proceed with or without Raven?"

Bodhi looked to the door one more time and at Devon, his eyebrows narrowing slightly. "She'll get here when she gets here," Bodhi said. He avoided eye contact with Devon and took a seat in a chair farthest from her. He seemed to be mad. Maybe her exit on Friday hadn't gone over as smoothly as she had hoped. If Eric was guilty, she would need Bodhi and Raven on her side to help convince Reed of his grandson's wrongdoings. If it wasn't Eric, but in fact Raven and Bodhi who were keeping darker secrets than she knew, well . . . then Devon would really be lost.

"I had to tell you this in person because it's about Eric." Devon began slowly. "He and Maya Dover are seeing each other. She's pregnant with his child. I think Eric saw Hutch that night. I think

Eric went to the Palace to talk to Hutch about the pregnancy. And I think Eric may have given Hutch the Oxy that killed him."

She'd expected to feel much worse. She'd been dreading saying her theory out loud. But all she felt was an enormous wave of relief. Even if she was wrong, even if people ended up hating her for it, she was finally free. No more secrets or lies. She waited for someone to say something. Bodhi looked to Reed, whose eyes darted around the room as if he were following a bird trapped inside. Reed coughed and used a white handkerchief from his pocket to dab at his mouth.

"Where would he have gotten the Oxy?" Bodhi asked. "It didn't come from the pharmacy."

"Where does anyone get anything," Cleo said. "If someone wants something, from my experience they'll find a way."

Bodhi raised an eyebrow at Cleo. "Wait, weren't you in the pharmacy that day?"

"Getting busted for shoplifting? Yes, that's my claim to fame."

Bodhi grinned. Devon wondered if there was some weird sense of respect between the two of them. Both were criminals, but honest in their own ways.

"I think I know," Reed said between labored, raspy breaths. He pushed himself out of his chair. Bodhi reached out a hand to help him, but Reed waved him off and shuffled to a room in the back of the house. "Raven's back!" he yelled from down the hallway.

Bodhi sent a text on his phone. "How did he know that?" Cleo asked.

"Camera at the foot of the driveway, the guest house, here, among a few others. We know everything and everyone that comes and goes from this property," Bodhi finished up his text. He put his phone down on the coffee table. Devon thought he seemed very nonchalant about Eric and Maya. Shouldn't that have been a bigger surprise?

"So, you know about Eric and Maya already? Why were you suspicious of Matt and Isla then?" Devon asked.

Bodhi shrugged. "We don't have cameras everywhere up there. Yet. But we know Matt was out of his room the night Hutch was killed."

"I'm here. What's up?" Raven barged through the front door in her usual red bikini, cut-offs, and flip-flops. She spotted Devon and stopped. "You're back? What the hell happened? One minute we're cool the next you're looking at me all weird and faking being sick and begging to go back to Keaton on an off-weekend."

"Yeah, I'm sorry about that." Devon couldn't hold eye contact. Raven was right; Devon had acted like a jerk.

"Rav, it's cool. Devon has something to tell us." Bodhi waved her over. She sat on the arm of Reed's leather chair. "It's Eric. He and Maya really are together."

"Jesus," Raven mumbled.

When Reed reappeared, he dropped a crinkled paper bag on the coffee table. "I didn't want to tell you kids this way, but . . . I should have said something sooner." He dumped the bag out and pill bottles rolled onto the wooden table. Bodhi sat on the floor next to the table and read the bottles.

"Vicodin. OxyContin. Demerol." Bodhi shook the bottles as he spoke. "This one's empty. The OxyContin."

Reed sat back in his leather chair and closed his eyes. "That's what I was afraid of," he gasped. Forming the words seemed to sap all his energy.

"Reed, why do you have these? These are some serious drugs," Bodhi said as he analyzed each bottle.

"I haven't been taking them. The doctor said I'd need them as the cancer gets worse. I've got bone cancer, kids." Bodhi and Raven locked eyes. Devon knew their fragile world was about to change all over again. "I probably won't see the end of this year. You're the first ones to know."

"So Eric. . . ." Cleo began. Devon and Raven and Bodhi were all still processing Reed's news.

"He was here that week. We were fighting. We all were," Reed said. "I was worn out by all the fighting and must have left this out in my bathroom."

"What were you fighting about?" Devon asked. "Maya's pregnancy?"

"No, I didn't know about that then. I changed my will over the summer. I had to make arrangements after I got the diagnosis. Instead of passing everything down to Bill and his sons, everything was going to go to Hutch. The land, the vineyard, the house and my work in the lab. Eric and Bill, they just didn't get it. They wanted to butcher the land and sell my property so Eddie Dover would finally own the whole mountain and he could rip it apart for his experiments. I won't let them destroy our land and the school. I promised Francis Keaton I wouldn't let them, and I intend to keep that promise from the grave if I have to. Hutch understood. He's the only one who really understood. Eric came down thinking he was going to talk sense into me. I can't believe that sonofabitch. His own brother." Reed shook his head and twisted his mouth into a grimace.

"These are forty milligram pills," Bodhi said. "It wouldn't have taken much. If Eric crushed them up—"

"In a beer?" Devon added. She didn't want to be right. Somehow if her hunches were wrong she didn't need to look at the brutality of the truth.

"In a beer," he agreed. His voice shook. "A strong beer like Gernsbach would have hidden the taste. If the pills are broken up they release the full dosage at once instead of over time as they're supposed to. He would have stopped breathing within an hour."

The room was silent as everyone absorbed what Bodhi said. *For once,* Devon thought, *it feels like the puzzle pieces are all starting to fit together.*

"What do we do now?" Raven asked. "Reed is the one with the pills in his name. If we accuse Eric and we're wrong, the cops will turn on Reed, won't they?"

"We need a confession," Cleo said. "And if there's one person who can get someone to talk. . . ." Devon blinked. All eyes in the room were on her. "You're up, Counselor."

CHAPTER 19

The last remnants of daylight were fading from the sky. The night was taking over, ushering the brighter colors off stage. Devon leaned back on the bench against the cement wall of the Palace. But the beauty offered her no comfort and with all the graffiti vying for wall space around her, she felt as if she were in a bathroom stall. Trapped. It was hard to imagine that seventy years ago soldiers sat here, scanning the ocean for incoming enemy activity. It seemed ironic. This used to be a place of safety, security. And now it was for rebellion and secrets, the worst of all, murder.

Tires twisted on the dirt path above. A door slammed. Devon checked the six pack of Gersbach beers at her feet, the notebook in her lap. Everything was in place.

"Babe? You down here?" Eric's voice called. He was getting closer. Devon exhaled long and slow. Looking calm and confident was key. This was her session. She was in control here.

Eric rounded the corner and stopped when he saw Devon. "What are you doing here? Where's Maya? She was meeting me here."

"I know. Maya called you. But I'm the one meeting with you." Devon stood up. "Have a seat. Pop a beer." She slid the cardboard pack toward Eric with her foot. The glass bottles clinked together.

Eric tucked his hair behind his ears and glanced around. "Nah, Maya wouldn't do that. Where is she?"

"Well, she did. And she's not here. Maybe you two have more trust issues than you thought." Devon sat back down and crossed her legs.

"Excuse me?" he said. "What's this about, Devon? You wanted to have a beer with me in honor of Hutch or something?"

"I've got something for you." Devon tapped the hard edge of her notebook. "Heard you were itching to get a look at my session notes." Eric eyed the notebook in her lap. "Figured, if you were gonna pay someone to steal them from me, we could just cut out the middleman. I make a little cash; you get what you want. That is what you want, isn't it? To find out what everyone's been saying about Hutch. About you."

The crickets filled in the silence as Devon leaned down and pulled a beer from the six-pack. With one deft move, like she had seen Raven do, she snapped the metal cap off with a pop of her hand and the bottle against the stone bench. Devon took a long pull from the bottle like Eric's answer didn't matter to her. The beer tasted sour and the bubbles were thick in her throat. *Just try not to hurl in front of him.*

Eric broke the silence with a short laugh. "Listen. You could get suspended for being out here, doing what you're doing. You should walk back up that hill and check yourself into your dorm like a good Keaton kiddie." He stood, arms crossed, towering over Devon. *Okay, maybe staying sitting down wasn't the best idea.* "Whatever you think you know, you don't."

"Probably not. Want to explain it to me?"

"It's not in your notes, I can tell you that." Eric reached down and grabbed a beer and used a lighter to snap the cap off. He took a sip and looked out over the distant ocean. "Besides, I don't need your notes to know what happened. Hutch committed suicide. We had some family stuff go down and he was upset."

"Upset that he was set to inherit everything? Or, was it you that was upset?"

Eric glanced at Devon and then turned his gaze back to the horizon. "You spoke to Reed? He tell you how he was going to betray my dad and me? How I only found out about it by accident?" Devon didn't answer. She let him fill the silences, as she was trained. "Yeah, he wasn't even going to tell us. His lawyer's secretary screwed up this summer and gave me the wrong envelope with Reed's revised will in it. Reed wanted to give all the land to Hutch to make sure it becomes a nature preserve or some shit like that. He has no idea how much money we could make if we just let the Dovers drill. He's sitting on a goldmine and what does he want to do with it? Keep away the one person that is willing to pay him for this stupid land."

"You're smart," Devon said.

Eric turned to her. "What?"

She lifted her shoulders. "It's a smart move if you want to get in with the Dover family. I mean, you're looking at a potential statutory situation with getting Maya pregnant, but bringing something the Dovers want to the table could help your cause."

"Yeah, well, it wasn't going to matter. Reed wouldn't budge. And that same week Maya found out . . . we found out she was pregnant. I lost it when she said she wasn't sure what she wanted to do with it. You know it's my life that would get screwed too. I'm the one that's supposed to become this great doctor. And then, to find out Hutch was helping her get the pregnancy test? How much more could he turn against his own family? Against me? That's not how brothers are supposed to act. I was raised knowing this land would one day be mine. And in one week Hutch takes the land and tries to turn my girl against me?" Eric tossed his bottle over the hillside. "He probably killed himself because he couldn't live with the betrayal."

Still clinging to the lie. "Reed is dying. That's why he changed his will. He's going to be gone in a matter of months." Devon looked at him, calm and assured.

"How do you know that?" He tucked his hair behind his ears again. "That's true? Shit." He shook his hands out and flexed his fingers like he was warming up for a fight.

"That's why he had those pills in his house. The ones you found and slipped to Hutch in a beer like the one you just finished. Did you regret it all? Because, you still sent that text to everyone in his phone book, so you were probably around to watch your own brother die at your feet. What do they call that? Fratricide? It's a good SAT word."

Eric said nothing. The hairs on the back of Devon's neck rose as he stood still looking at the view below. *How could he not react? How could he not fill* this *silence?*

Finally Eric spoke. "My knee was killing me. I was at Reed's. We were arguing, and the pain was making it all worse. I found the Oxy in his bathroom. I put it in my pocket to take with me back to the city. I was going to go back to the city that night, but I called Hutch to try to talk it out again. He wouldn't listen to me. He wasn't going to listen, but he agreed to meet me here. I waited for him, and I don't know why, but I started crushing up the pills and put them in his beer. I didn't wake up wanting him dead that day. Really. This wasn't easy for me. I loved my brother."

Eric turned and looked at Devon, his eyes exploring her body up and down. She suddenly felt gross, exposed much too casually to someone so foul, so dangerous. He kept his eyes set on her as he reached for another beer. But in one swift move, he darted toward her and yanked her to her feet by the front of her shirt. He spun her around and broke his beer bottle against the wall of the Palace. He was strong, even stronger than he looked. Devon's arms flailed behind her, but she merely slapped and pecked at Eric. He held the broken bottle to her throat.

"What's to stop me from shutting you up right here? I killed my brother, you really think I wouldn't hesitate to kill some nosy little bitch?"

"People know I'm here," Devon whispered. Her voice quavered. "They'll know it was you. Maya will know. Please." She tried to dig her nails into his arms, but they didn't break skin. He didn't flinch.

"Oh, that's not a problem. I'm thinking that you were so distraught over Hutch's suicide, everyone knows it, everyone's seen you obsess about him, that you came down here where he killed himself and slit your wrists. It's romantic but it's also a slow death. Gives me enough time to text your suicide note."

Devon was crying now. She tried to kick his legs behind her but caught air.

"The common misconception about slitting is to go across like this," Eric used the glass and cut a thin line across Devon's wrist. The blood sprung to the surface, as if making a jailbreak from her skin. "But really, the way to do it is to cut upwards, severing the artery like this." Eric dug the glass into the center of her wrist. Devon screamed. But the glass didn't go any further. Eric let go and Devon fell to the ground.

Above her, she caught a blur of someone wearing a white hat. *Grant?* He pulled Eric away from Devon and punched Eric in the center of his jaw. Eric's head spun from the impact. It moved so fast it looked like it could spin a full rotation.

"Leave her alone," Grant choked out, his voice thick. "You've done enough." He punched Eric again and Eric fell to the ground.

"You suddenly going to do the right thing?" Eric said as he wiped at the blood running from his nose. "She's never going to be into you. Don't you get it? It's my brother she's wanted this whole time."

Grant's chest heaved. His right hand was clenched, ready to strike again. He looked at Devon, still sprawled on the ground clutching her wrist. "Yeah, well, Hutch was a better guy than you or me." Eric stood up.

"Give it up. You've taken too much money from me to suddenly switch sides. Let's go." Eric turned to walk away dismissing Grant as a credible threat.

Grant looked at Devon again. And then he stepped forward and leveled Eric with another right hook. "I should have done that when he asked me to steal from you."

Eric lay on the ground, passed out and bloody. Dirt streaked across his face. Devon could feel shards of glass on the ground digging into her thighs but the pain was remote. Nothing seemed to hurt. Her wrist bled and she held onto it, watching the blood ooze down her arm in long tendrils. Grant sat down next to her. He looked at his own hand, the skin on his knuckles torn and already swelling.

"How did you know. . .?" she began.

Grant shook his head. He was still breathing heavily. "Maya told me you were down here. I didn't trust Eric." Grant spotted the notebook on the bench. "You were really going to hand those over?"

"What do you think?" Devon said, trying to smile despite the pain. Grant flipped the notebook open. The Four Seasons room service menu was inside. Grant smiled.

"Nicely played, Miss Mackintosh." He smoothed back a strand of hair from Devon's cheek.

"Devon?" Raven's voice called from behind the Palace. "You down there?"

Devon mustered a tentative, exhausted smile. "The cavalry," she said.

Raven and Bodhi ran down the hill, flashlight beams waving. "We're fine," Devon called.

Raven crouched next to Devon and examined her wrist while Bodhi stood over Eric. "I think you'll live," Raven said.

Devon looked at Eric lying near her feet coming back from his knockout. "We get it?" Raven pointed to a corner of the Palace bunker. A small camera was wedged in the corner.

"We got it. Good work, Counselor. Oh, and I should tell you. You know how we jammed the camera in your therapy room? Yeah, well, we didn't really jam it, we just re-routed the feed to our monitors at Reed's."

"You got all my sessions?"

"Yeah, fascinating stuff." Raven shrugged.

Grant rubbed Devon's shoulder. "Looks like I'm not the only one screwing with your confidentiality around here." He stood up and helped Bodhi zip-tie Eric's wrists together.

"This is for you, by the way." Raven pulled a thumb drive from her jacket. "Copy of the confession. Might want to give it to Maya. She can hear it from Eric this way. Figured she deserved to know."

Devon looked at the small drive. The adrenaline was still coursing through her body. She felt tears running down her cheeks. "Thanks," she murmured. "Being here with him made me think about Hutch. He was just trying to do the right thing."

Raven sat in the dirt and wrapped an arm around Devon. Despite her bloody wrist, Devon buried her head in Raven's shoulder and sobbed. The tears came in a pulsing wave. "I miss him," she said.

"Me too," Raven said, holding her tight.

CHAPTER 20

Monday morning. The zillionth of how many zillions of Mondays? When Devon walked into the dining hall, students were shuffling through the food line, standing at the door chugging a glass of milk, or scarfing their morning cereal. The same old sea of sweatpants and unwashed hair. But this morning it felt different. For the first time Devon saw the Keaton world for what it was. It didn't feel like a factory for the Ivy League anymore, a sci-fi colony breeding The Perfect Student, organs and all. For the first time, Devon didn't feel like an outsider. She was a piece of this world. Keaton had been here for her this whole time, but she'd needed to strip away the lies and fakery around Hutch's death to see it. It was murder. Hutch wasn't a "troubled young man" with problems "beyond our control." He was complicated and sweet and rash and tried to do the right thing, and his own brother had killed him for it.

"Yo, Whore-issa Explains it All." Presley sidled up to her. She chewed on a piece of toast and held out another piece out for Devon. "I put raspberry jelly on it, just like you like."

Devon took the piece of toast. "Thanks."

"Um, so I'm sorry and stuff." Presley shrugged. "I know you want to smack me. I want to smack me. You were following your instinct and it paid off. I'm sure somewhere Hutch is glad you believed in him."

Devon swallowed and smiled. "I hope he is. But, I had to do it for me, too. To prove he was the guy I knew too."

"What was the deal with you two, anyway? I didn't know you were so tight." Devon took another bite of her toast. "Oh, I get it. You think you can keep a seeeecret. That's not going to last." Presley smacked her on the butt and walked away. "I gotta get to Chem. See ya later, hater."

Name: Devon Mackintosh
Session Date: Oct. 15
Session #4
Reason for Session: Peer Counselor Review

MR. ROBINS SIPPED FROM a white ceramic mug, stolen from the dining hall no doubt. The *Santa Cruz Sentinel*, with Eric Hutchins's mug shot splashed on the front page, sat on his desk between him and Devon.

"The truth about what Eric may or may not have done has yet to be determined," Mr. Robins began. Devon looked at her hands. Why had he called her here if he was just going to lecture her? "But, you did a brave thing. I shouldn't have put you in session with something this difficult. The good news is, now, everything else in counseling will probably seem easy in comparison." He laughed a little, and Devon looked up. *Okay, he was trying to be nice.* "Isla told me what was happening, with her, with Matt. You were keeping secrets, Devon, you shouldn't have had to keep. And as much as some of your choices went against policy, you showed a lot of strength. Your subjects were lucky to have you."

"Are you going to keep doing sessions with them? Matt and Cleo?"

"Matt left school last night."

"What?" Devon stiffened. "What do you mean 'left?' Like he just decided to walk away? How does that happen?"

"He wrote Headmaster Wyler a resignation letter of sorts. Said he was leaving school to clear his head." Mr. Robins took another sip of coffee and leaned back in his chair. "But the question you're here to answer, Devon, is what do we do with our program?"

"Our program? I thought it was *your* program at this point."

"Yes, well, in light of recent events I may have come to that decision too hastily. I'd like us to try again. And you've got more experience this time." Mr. Robins scrunched his nose, pushing his glasses up.

Devon wanted to gloat, but she forced her expression to remain neutral. *It's your session*, she thought. "Well, that's a nice offer, Mr. Robins. I appreciate it. A couple of things might have to be added to the Training Guide going forward. I'll help you with that. Whether I'm interested in sitting in that chair again? I'll let you know next semester."

Mr. Robins's eyebrows lifted slightly. "Well, I'm sure there's room for discussion."

"If that's all you needed to see me about. . . ?" Devon reached for her backpack.

"Actually, I just wanted to tell you that you did a good job. You'd make a good therapist one day. If you still want to be one, that is." Mr. Robins stood up and held out a hand to Devon. It took her a minute to understand. He wasn't asking her to hand him something or reaching for something across his desk, he wanted to shake it. Devon put her hand in his, and Mr. Robins's grip tightened around hers. "You stuck to your beliefs, Devon, and I respect that."

The smile flickered and she allowed it. "Thanks."

∞

WHEN THE DORMS CLEARED out for afternoon sports, Devon still hadn't gotten Matt out of her head. He seemed happy when she had seen him in the library. Maybe Isla's departure was harder for him than he expected? She still felt like he could show up any moment running to the soccer field or hosing down his wet suit outside Fell House. She had to know for sure. The shower was running at the end of the Fell House hallway. Hutch's door was still adorned with graffiti, but the words *Eric=Traitor* were scrawled in a thick black pen across the top. Matt's door was closed. His room looked as if he had never been there. Amazing how that happened so quickly. Stripped mattress, empty walls; the closet door hung open, also barren. As Devon closed his door behind her, white letters caught her eye. *MAVERICKS OR BUST!* scrawled in a thick, white paint on the wooden door. Devin smiled. The maintenance crew hadn't reported this one to the headmaster yet. Surely Matt's family would be billed for a new door. Not like they would care. Devon ran her hands over the writing, still sticky as it dried. As sad as it was that Matt was gone, he had gone surfing to the place where he and Hutch had wanted to live out their days. Maybe Matt would come back to Keaton, maybe not, but Devon knew he was honoring Hutch and figuring his own stuff out the best way he knew how: on the water. That was Matt's version of therapy, his Nutter Butters.

Devon noticed his desk had dust outlines around his books, computer, pencil holder. But there was a CD in a blank case sitting in the middle. It looked like it had been left deliberately.

Devon picked it up and saw the handwriting on the CD. Her throat caught. Devon's Prom Mix.

September 10, 2010
Freshman Year

"COME ON, COME ON, come on." Hutch wedged the butter knife in the door against the lock. "No, no, no, ahhh." The knife came out bent, the lock still in place. "If I get this open will you talk to me then?" He threw the knife in the sink next to the other failed lock picking devices. A spatula, a wooden spoon, a broken glass, a can opener . . . all busts.

"I don't know. Why don't you open the door and find out." Devon placed another plastic glass on her growing tower of glasses.

"I'm going to open this thing. I just need something else. Strong but thin." Hutch opened drawers, scanned shelves around the kitchen. "No, no . . . oh," he held up a cake cutter. "Maybe."

"Have you tried a credit card? That always works in movies." Devon didn't take her eyes off her tower.

"Do you have a credit card on you?"

"No."

"Then thanks for the suggestion, idiot." He said the last part quietly under his breath.

"Did you just call me an idiot?"

"No."

"You totally did." She put another glass on the tower and it toppled to the floor with a loud clank.

"Nice job, idiot." Hutch was turned around watching her. "Oh yeah, I said it that time."

If Devon wasn't so tired she might have had a good comeback to that. She might have bothered to be upset but the only response her body had left was to laugh. All she could do was laugh. Laugh loud and hard and without reason. Reason had slipped out the kitchen under the locked door while they were making pancakes. Tears sprung to her eyes as if the force of her laughter pushed them out.

Hutch started laughing, too. He doubled over, steadying himself on his knee while still clutching the cake cutter. His laugh slowed to a slow drip, steady but further apart.

"You know, there are two kinds of people in this world," she said. "The ones that carry credit cards, and the ones that carry cake cutters."

Hutch held up the metal cutter for inspection. "You doubting my cake-cutting skills?"

"Yeah, I'm absolutely doubting your cake-cutting skills." She took a step closer, the triangle blade of the metal caught the light outside. Hutch was smiling at her. He reached his hand out for her and she took it. Hutch pulled her close and let her hands fall on his shoulders. They stood there, her face at his neck and his breath hitting her forehead. Hutch's hands wrapped around her waist. Devon tried not to exhale. Her over-analytical mind told her to pull away, not to give in just yet. But, his hands around her, his eyes looking down at her, she couldn't move. It felt too good right here.

Slowly he shifted from one foot to the other, Devon leaned with him, and then they were swaying together as if music were playing. Hutch hummed a tune and Devon leaned her head onto his shoulder, relaxing into his grasp. With the outside yellow light cutting lines through the dim kitchen, they could have been at a school dance or in a dark club. Hutch slid a hand along her arm and held her hand aloft in his like they were dancing the Waltz. He hummed louder.

"Are you singing 'At Last?'" she asked.

"No," Hutch said, and kept dancing. "I'm humming it. But I can sing it."

"Let's hear it," she said.

Suddenly Hutch spun Devon under his arm, her hand reaching up and over her head. "And life is like a song," Hutch sang. His cheeks scrunched up and his head bobbed with each note. "Oh yeah, yeah, At last . . . can't beat Etta James, huh?"

"Did you grow up in a juke box or something?"

"I just like old music. I don't know; there's more feeling in it. Maybe it's listening to it on records at my grandfather's. Love songs sound better on vinyl."

"Is that a thing?"

"Yeah, it's a thing." Devon could feel Hutch smile as he spoke.

He leaned back, looking at her now. "I think there should be another thing. This. Us dancing. It needs to happen again. Want to make a deal?"

"What kind of deal?" Devon felt herself blush.

"Senior year. No matter who we're with, whatever happens until then, go to prom with me. I don't want to leave Keaton and not have another night with you. This way at least we'll have one guaranteed."

"You sure you want to commit to a long-term deal like that? I mean, we do have four more years here together."

"I know we do," he said with a smile. He leaned down and kissed her. And kept kissing her. Devon stood on her toes again to kiss him back, her hands wrapped around his neck. Out the window behind Hutch, Devon noticed the sky was shifting from black to a glowing gray.

"The sun's coming up soon," she said.

"I'm going to get us out of here," he said.

Hutch went back to work on the door, and this time Devon stood behind watching. He wedged the metal in between the door and the frame. It fit. Wiggling his cutter side to side he pushed it deeper in place. It clinked against something. "The lock." Hutch's face contorted as he twisted and dug the metal knife further. With a push they both heard the lock click back into the door. They looked at each other, frozen.

"Was that. . . ?"

Hutch gritted his teeth and pushed the handle of the door. It opened. The cool air of the night blew into the kitchen. They could see a streak of pink spreading through the gray sky.

"We're out," Devon said.

"Told you I'd get us out." Hutch held the door open for her.

Devon stepped outside absorbing everything. The gravel driveway seemed new, almost exotic. The air was cool and fresh, waking her up. She turned back to Hutch. "You did," she said. "We're free."

He nodded, but still hung in the doorway. "I hope you don't hate me. It was a stupid idea that backfired. But I'm glad it did."

"I don't hate you. I think this was the first real fun I've had since getting here."

"Do you ever have those moments where you feel like you're in the middle of making a really good memory? One that you're going to remember when you get old? I think we just lived one of those moments."

"You really think when you're like fifty and have a wife and two kids and the house and fancy career, you'll really remember this one little night?"

He didn't so much as blink. "I'm going to remember this night until I die. Maybe even after that."

"Me, too." Devon's feet were moving before she could think about it. Her lips were against his before she could talk herself out of it. She pulled him back into the kitchen and closed the door behind them. Hutch spun her around against the door and kissed her. His hand in the small of her back pulled her up to him, helped keep her from letting her body melt into the floor. Finally she pulled herself away and looked up into his brown eyes. Those thick eyebrows and big ears.

"Good night, Hutch," she whispered.

Hutch kissed her palm again, folding her fingers around his imaginary kiss. "Good night, Devon."

Present Day
October 16

THE BLACK LIMO, THE Town Car, and the silver Mercedes took up most of the parking spaces in Reed's driveway as Raven's Volvo pulled in.

"Blending right in," Raven said.

"Who are all these people?" Devon asked as she got out of the car.

"The peanut gallery, as Reed calls them. Bill, Mitzi, some

lawyer or three. It's a shitstorm around here these days. Come on, there's a better view from the guest house." Raven's flip-flops shuffled on the gravel as she walked down the hill. Devon followed her, kicking off her shoes as they headed straight down the stairs into the office hub. Bodhi was at the desk watching the monitors.

"Oh hey," he said.

Cleo was reading a magazine on the nearby couch. "Hey, Dev. You here for the weekend, too?" She stood up and wrapped her arms around Bodhi at his chair.

"Just for a quick visit," Devon said. "Reed wanted to see me."

"Good luck," Cleo said. She nodded toward the monitors where Bill Hutchins was arguing with two lawyers. "Turn it up, babe. She should hear this."

Bodhi spun a volume knob.

"She tricked him into a relationship. He was under stress. Why is this so hard to understand?" Bill was yelling and throwing his hands into the air.

"Bill, you have to understand. That does not mitigate the physical evidence against him. The girl is pregnant. She's dropping out of school." The lawyers were also throwing up their hands in the air: a chorus of overdramatic exasperation.

"Is this happening right now up at the house?" Devon asked.

"Yep. Reed wanted records of everything said around here. You never know where this thing is going to go." Raven lay on the sofa and closed her eyes. She suddenly perked up and checked her cell phone. "Reed's waiting for you at the Mount."

"The Mount?" Devon asked.

"The highest point of the vineyard. It's where Athena and Hutch are buried. Just walk out the front door, turn right, and follow the trail up hill. I'll take you back to school when you're done."

Everyone was watching Devon. She nodded and then walked out. What was she walking into?

The trail was well-worn and led directly to the rows of grapes below the guest house. She spied a familiar cowboy hat silhouette at the top of the hill.

Reed took off his hat to greet her when she arrived at his spot.

Two simple stone headstones lay side by side at his feet. The valley of grapevines extending to the ocean was the view below.

"It's a great view, isn't it?" Reed said. "This way they can enjoy it, too."

Devon noticed Hutch's gravestone.

JASON REED HUTCHINS
(1996–2012)
THE ROAD LESS TRAVELED.

She felt her eyes sting upon reading the inscription. The Frost poem. Devon took a seat on the stone bench next to Reed. He looked at the hillside below.

"There's going to be a fight over this land. And Eric and this baby with Maya is just the beginning. Francis Keaton put the school here for a reason, and I intend to protect it from the likes of Edward Dover. But, I need your help."

"Does this have something to do with the *Tres Abbitas*?"

Reed ran the brim of his hat along his fingers. "Keaton, Dover, and Hutchins. The three trees. This was our mountain."

"What happened?" Devon thought back to the newspaper picture. Reed and Edward smiling as Francis broke ground on the school.

"Power, money. It has a way of poisoning men."

"But weren't you all friends?" Devon searched Reed's face. He was looking at Athena's gravestone.

ATHENA SCOTT HUTCHINS
(1926–1968)
BELOVED WIFE & MOTHER

Reed turned to Devon, a sad smile on his face. She could tell there was pain behind that smile.

"There's a reason Hutch picked you. He lost himself with Isla and wanted to keep his feet on the ground this time. I told him to find the person he trusted. The person who no matter what, no matter how much he changed, would always recognize the real Jason Hutchins underneath everything else. He said that was you. You were the only one that really got him." Devon looked at her open palm, then slowly, like Hutch had done, closed her fingers around his imaginary kiss. "Whether you want to be or not, you're a part of this now."

Devon looked at Grandpa Reed. His weathered, wrinkled skin around his eyes. She saw Hutch's warmth in his face and knew that Reed knew how she felt about Hutch. And that was okay. Reed wouldn't be around much longer to guide her way. She would do whatever needed to be done.

ACKNOWLEDGMENTS

This book would not exist without the trust, guidance, and extreme patience of the great and powerful ~~Oz~~ Daniel Ehrenhaft: Soho Teen guru, editor extraordinaire, taskmaster, fellow boarding school delinquent, and an all-around very cool dude. Thank you for your faith in me.

Many thanks to the rest of the gang at Soho Press: Queen Bee and kickass author, Bronwen Hruska; publicity maven Meredith Barnes; and the amazing help from Simona Blat; Paul Oliver; Rudy Martinez; Janine Agro; Juliet Grames; Mark Doten; Katie Hoffman; and Rachel Kowal. There are not enough Nutter Butters in the world to thank all of you properly.

The wonderful and inspired Keaton School logo is all due to the creative ingenuity and generosity of Sita Raiter and the gang at Yeti Creative Boutique in Vietnam.

To Julie Kane-Ritsch, Jeff Portnoy, and everyone else at the Gotham Group; thank you for your enthusiasm for this project and all of its iterations.

Octavia Spencer, Jennifer Niven, McCormick Templeman, and Sara Shepard: thank you ladies for your votes of confidence. I feel incredibly blessed to be in your orbit.

Lexa Hillyear, Lauren Oliver, and Stephen Barbara: your wisdom helped me turn the possibility of writing a YA series into a reality. Thank you.

Joel "Kodachrome" Dovev: thank you for your Hutchian inspiration, Nutter Butter pancake experiment, and your limitless love and support.

Julia Cohen and Jason Martin, a.k.a my Brooklyn family: thank you for the brainstorming, edits, dinners, and rosé—not necessarily in that order.

Lots of love to my family for your support, polite suggestions, related articles, and endless cheerleading. And Dad, thanks for comparing me to Hemingway as only you could.

Many thanks to Cate School and The Thatcher School for your help in my research.

To my high school friends from California and England: the secret missions, the crushes, the pranks, the heartbreak, the school spirit, the work crews, the roommate drama, the food fights, the bus rides, the senior pages, everything that was wrong and everything that was right about boarding school ... I thank you for all of it.

ABOUT THE AUTHOR

Margaux Froley grew up in Santa Barbara, California, and attended not one, but two boarding schools during her high school years in California and Oxford, England. She studied film at University of Southern California, and has worked for such television networks as: TLC, CMT, Travel, MTV, and the CW.

She currently lives in Los Angeles and still loves Nutter Butters.

Escape Theory is her first novel.

You can visit her at www.margauxfroley.com.